HE COULDN'T BELIEVE IT.

From that distance, with that intensity, the phaser blast should have knocked her unconscious. The only indication that Demora Sulu seemed to register from having been shot was to go even more berserk.

Her fingernails raked across Harriman's forehead. He screamed as they drew blood, and Demora's howl of triumph was earsplitting. If he'd heard a recording of it, there was no way he would have thought any human at all could ever produce such a sound, much less an eminently civilized, charming, and witty human such as Demora.

And even as the thought flashed through his mind, even as he saw that Demora's frothing mouth was poised directly over his throat, he realized that he was still clutching his phaser in his right hand. He angled it around, jammed it directly against her bare skin, and fired.

Look for STAR TREK Fiction from Pocket Books

Star Trek: The Original Series

Star Trek: The Next Generation

Star Trek: Deep Space Nine

Star Trek: Voyager

STAR TREK®

THE CAPTAIN'S DAUGHTER

PETER DAVID

POCKET BOOKS

New York   London   Toronto   Sydney   Tokyo   Singapore

This book is a work of fiction. Names, characters, places and incidents are products of the author's imagination or are used fictitiously. Any resemblance to actual events or locales or persons, living or dead, is entirely coincidental.

An *Original* Publication of POCKET BOOKS

POCKET BOOKS, a division of Simon & Schuster Inc.
1230 Avenue of the Americas, New York, NY 10020

STAR TREK is a Registered Trademark of
Paramount Pictures.

A VIACOM COMPANY

This book is published by Pocket Books, a division of
Simon & Schuster Inc., under exclusive license from
Paramount Pictures.

ISBN: 0-671-52047-4

First Pocket Books printing December 1995

10 9 8 7 6 5 4 3 2 1

POCKET and colophon are registered trademarks of
Simon & Schuster Inc.

Printed in the U.S.A.

SECTION ONE

DEATH

Chapter One

IF DEMORA SULU had known her funeral would be in a week, she would have had the chocolate mousse.

She fixed an icy glare on the woman in front of her. It was hard to sustain the glare, because the bowl of mousse kept moving directly into her line of sight. The reason the mousse was mobile was because the woman was holding the dish, bringing it close to Demora's face, drawing it back, even having it engage in a little happy high-calorie jig.

"Get it away, Maggie," Demora warned her.

Maggie didn't seem to have heard. In a cheerful voice, she said, "Look at me, here I go, a happy carefree chocolate mousse . . . oh no! Somebody's watching me!" She brought it so close to Demora that half a centimeter nearer would have lodged it squarely against Demora's nose. "Could it be . . . you?"

Oblivious of the concentrated silliness going on in the center of the room, various off-duty crew members of the *Enterprise* 1701-B went about their business. The food dispensers set into the walls of the crew mess hummed

3

steadily. There was the customary dazzling assortment from all over the galaxy. No one wanted for anything.

Except for Demora, who "wanted for" the chocolate mousse.

"Maggie, you're going to be wearing that," said Demora.

Lieutenant Maggie Thompson, science officer, didn't seem particularly intimidated by the threat. Her face was round, her thick dark hair rather curly, her brown eyes sparkling in amusement. She wrinkled her freckled nose at Demora. How Maggie maintained freckling while spending so much time in space had been an utter mystery to Demora, a mystery that Maggie had been disinclined to explain.

Demora was quite the opposite: serious when Maggie was being playful, yet possessed of a mordant wit that caught people completely off-guard because she had a calm air about her that some mistook for passivity. Her shoulder-length hair was black and straight, her dark brown eyes gracefully almond-shaped.

Her most interesting feature was her voice. There was a musical quality to it, a gentle lilt so distinctive that, even when Demora was speaking casually, she sounded as if she were singing. Except when an emergency was presented. In fact, that's how one could tell when matters had suddenly turned serious: Demora would speak in flat, inflectionless—albeit confident—tones. When she sounded like that, that was the time to, if not panic, at least proceed with extreme caution.

"You want it," Maggie told her. "You know you want it. It's delicious," and she indicated her own empty bowl. "Trust me."

"You can't be serious."

"I am serious, and this is seriously good mousse, and I would be nothing less than a total creep of a so-called friend if I willingly allowed you to pass this up. Just one taste." She dipped a spoon into it and waved it in front of Demora.

"I'm warning you, Maggie . . . I know karate . . . kung fu . . ."

"And several other dangerous words. I don't know which

is a worse offense, Demora . . . threatening a superior officer, or using old jokes on her."

Demora actually looked surprised at that. "That's an old joke?" she said.

"Centuries."

"Oh." And there was a look of such unmistakable, undiluted disappointment that slowly Thompson lowered the spoon and stared at Demora in confusion.

"What's wrong?"

Demora forced a smile, which was unusual since normally smiles came so easily to her. "Nothing. It's silly."

"Silly how?"

"Well," and Demora shrugged, "that joke. About 'dangerous words.' My father said it, ages ago. And I thought it was so funny, and I just laughed and laughed . . . I couldn't stop laughing, in fact. And I had always just, well . . . I'd just assumed he'd made it up. I don't know why that's important to me, or why it should bother me. But it does. Isn't that weird?"

"Not really," replied Maggie. "I remember . . . God, I haven't thought about this in years. I remember when I was real little, my father would sing me this song at nighttime. It was called 'Bushel and a Peck.'"

"What and a what?"

"It's old-style units of measurement. I didn't know that when I was little, mind you. I thought they were just sort of nonsense words. The song went, 'I love you, a bushel and a peck, a bushel and . . .'"

Maggie Thompson had many fine qualities, but on-key vocalizing was not among them. She was reminded of this when several crewmates started looking in her direction. Quickly she stopped singing, but continued, "In any event, I just—in my childish way—kind of figured that he'd made the song up just for me. And I was shocked to find out that it was actually from an old musical show called *Guys and Dolls.*"

"It was about men playing with dolls?"

"It was about gamblers, I think."

"Gamblers?" Demora made a face. "Singing gamblers?"

"Well, the same era also had shows about singing cats and singing barbers who killed people and turned them into meat pies. What can I tell you; it was an odd and perverse time. In any event, the point is . . . I understand how you feel. No reason to feel sad or even disappointed and yet you still do."

"I guess so."

"Your father and you close?"

Demora shrugged. "Oh . . . sure," she said in a less than convincing tone.

"Why do you say it like that?"

"I'd rather not discuss it."

"But maybe if—"

"I *said* I'd rather not discuss it," and it was clear from her tone and expression that there was no "rather not" involved. It was simply not up for further debate.

Maggie looked a bit chagrined. "Sorry."

"It's okay," said Demora. "I didn't mean to snap at you. And you really have been great to me, and a good friend."

"I know. And I just hate to see you upset, and think that I was responsible. You know what you need to feel better?" She shoved the chocolate mousse in Demora's direction.

Demora slid it back. *"What* is your *problem* today?"

"My problem is I already ate it, and I know I'm going to put on weight from it, and you said chocolate makes you put on weight, and misery loves company. *Okay?"*

"Ohhh, *fine!"* She slid the dish of chocolate mousse over toward her side of the table, grabbed a spoon . . . and stared at it. Then she looked up at Maggie and said, "I am a chocoholic. I admit it freely. That's something else I get from my father. If I give in to it, then I will be uncontrollable in all my subsequent urges, devour all chocolate in sight, and blow up faster than a ship with a warp-core breach. I want you to understand that you are dooming me to weeks, even months of uncontrolled weight gain until I manage to recapture my sanity. You, my alleged friend, are doing this to me."

Maggie sighed, reached over, and slid the dish back toward herself. "I hate you."

"I hate you too. That's what friends are for."

The ship's intercom promptly whistled. "All bridge personnel, report in."

"So much for that," she said, stood, and crossed over to the comm unit. She tapped the Receive button. "Thompson here, and Sulu is with me. Go ahead."

"We're receiving a distress-beacon call, Lieutenant," came the voice of Commander Tracy Dane, ship's first officer. "Your presence is requested."

"On our way," said Thompson. She clicked off, turned, and made a small finger-waggling gesture for Demora to follow her. With a sigh Demora rose, and together they walked quickly out of the officers' mess.

The chocolate mousse was left behind, unwanted and unloved, until Ensign Li noticed it abandoned some minutes later and took pity on it by devouring it in under thirty seconds.

Demora took her seat at helm, and smiled gamely at Lieutenant j.g. Magnus. Magnus, for his part, was a somewhat officious individual. Extremely competent, and extremely aware of his competence . . . and, for that matter, never hesitant to let others know that he was certain he was on a fast track for command some day. He always sat ramrod straight, and spoke in a crisp, clipped tone.

As it was, it was difficult for Demora to warm up to him. Previously that chair had been occupied by Ensign Tommy Singer. Demora and Singer had come up through the Academy together. They had many similar interests, had fallen into instant rapport . . . and had even, on occasion, fallen into bed. They had a nonexclusive relationship, but the relationship they did have was comfortable and pleasurable for both. In short, they meshed in a variety of ways.

And when they had both been assigned, by luck of the draw, to the *Enterprise,* they had been pleased beyond belief. After all, perhaps part of what had prevented their relationship from going any further was the mutual, back-of-their-head concern over where their assignments would take them. With them working side by side with Starfleet's blessing, well . . . who knew?

Who knew?

Who knew that on the maiden voyage of the *Enterprise* 1701-B, Demora would find herself cradling the corpse of Tommy Singer in her arms, dead from flying shards that had killed him instantly while the valiant starship fought for its life in the grip of gravimetric pressures.

Lord, what a hideous launch that had been. Oh, sure, ships bearing the name *Enterprise* had had shaky launches before. Most notably was the time that the refitted *Enterprise* was five minutes out of drydock and she suddenly found herself trapped in a wormhole.

But that had been a cakewalk compared to the fiasco of the *Enterprise* 1701-B launch. It had not helped that the media coverage had been less than generous. Reporters had been right there, on the spot, seeing what Captain John Harriman was going through in his endeavor to rescue the two trapped transports. They didn't focus on the dozens of lives his efforts did manage to save. That was a piddling detail, quickly omitted from all subsequent stories in favor of discussing the lives that had been lost despite Harriman's labors.

And one life in particular, mentioned in report after report.

Starfleet had gone over the log of Harriman's actions with a particle microscope. It was as if they were hoping to find something he had done wrong, so that the media's howlings for a scapegoat could be fulfilled. But Harriman was finally judged to be blameless.

The tragic initial launch of the *Enterprise*-B had consumed gigabytes of coverage on the galactic web. The calmer, sedate, and utterly routine relaunch had barely garnered any notice.

With all of that, the loss of Tommy Singer had seemed almost incidental to many. A sidebar at most.

But not to Demora Sulu.

The death of Kirk had hit her as hard as anyone else . . . harder, considering how often and glowingly her father had spoken of him. So much so that . . .

She shook it off. She didn't want to start thinking about that. That way lay madness.

A pair of fingers snapped in front of her face and she

looked around, startled. Magnus was looking at her sourly, which was how he looked at everyone. For that matter, it was how he looked at the world.

"Got something on your mind, Sulu?" he asked.

"No," she said quickly.

Dane was in the command chair, studying the preliminary reports. Dane was tall and muscular, with a triangular face and hair of prematurely gray and white that made her look far older than her thirty-three years. When Harriman strode in, Dane said crisply, "Captain on the bridge," rose promptly from the chair, and snapped off a quick salute.

Harriman shot her a look of resigned annoyance. Dane came from a family with a history of service dating back to the Civil War, fighting in the Union Army. Although Starfleet wasn't military per se despite its trappings, nevertheless Dane routinely acted as if she were operating on rules of procedure from centuries ago. It had been so thoroughly drilled into her that it was second nature; she didn't even know she was doing it, and couldn't help herself.

At first it had bugged the hell out of Harriman. However, there was no debating the fact that Dane was a superb officer. So he decided to tolerate her little quirks, particularly since they served to keep her sharp. "Report, Commander?" he said.

"Distress beacon, Captain," she said. "Originating . . ."

"From a heading of three-two-four mark three," Demora volunteered when Dane hesitated slightly.

Harriman nodded to Demora, acknowledging the information, and turned to Dane. "Any known vessels in that sector?"

"No registered vessel has filed any flight plans with Starfleet within the last six months that would coincide with those coordinates," Dane told him.

Harriman nodded slowly. "Which means nothing, of course, except that it's not a Starfleet vessel. Which pins it down to one of several thousand independent operators."

From the communications board, Lieutenant Z'on spoke up, his gravelly voice reproduced electronically through the rig attached to his crinkled blue throat. "I've managed to

9

cut through some of the local interference, sir," Z'on said. "Getting a clearer reading on the distress signal now."

"On audio, Lieutenant," said Harriman. He leaned thoughtfully on the edge of the command chair as a female voice issued through the bridge speaker. He frowned, the words a steady stream of incomprehensible syllables.

Demora looked up immediately, blinking in surprise.

Harriman turned to Z'on, frowning. "What is that? Sounds like . . ."

"Chinese," Demora said, turning in her chair. "Actually, one of the more obscure dialects."

"I'll run it through autotranslate," said Z'on.

"Don't trouble yourself, sir," said Demora. "I'm slightly rusty, but . . . it's a general call for distress. It just keeps repeating, 'We are in distress. Please help. We are in need of aid from any vessels in the area. We are in distress,' and so on."

"No specifics?"

"None. Just what I said, over and over."

"Pinpointed the origin," Z'on said. "Askalon Five."

"Askalon Five," Dane said without hesitation, "Class-m world, but uninhabited, and not particularly hospitable. Traces of a long-dead civilization were discovered in preliminary planet scans; awaiting further research from an archaeological team. The system's star is in a transitional stage, the gradual cooling having a less-than-positive impact on the planet's surface environment."

"Does the cooling sun offer any danger to the ship?"

"Remote."

"Remote meaning . . . ?"

Dane smiled thinly. "If we remain in orbit around Askalon Five for several hundred thousand years, there might be some jeopardy posed."

For a long and surprising moment Harriman said nothing; it was a period of silence that actually drew several curious glances from his crew. But then Harriman chuckled softly, low in his throat. "I believe we'll have to take that risk. Helm, lay in a course for Askalon Five."

"Course plotted and laid in, sir," said Magnus.

Harriman, out of habit, rapped his knuckles once on the

arm of his chair before giving the command evocative of another captain of a ship called *Enterprise*. In the style of the great Captain Christopher Pike, he said, "Engage."

In his quarters, Captain Harriman stared out at the passing starfield and reflected that a ready room might be a really great idea. Some sort of special quarters for the captain, just off the bridge. That way if he wanted or needed some private time—some time to think or plan or just get away from the crushing burden of being in charge—he could avail himself of it without having to leave the bridge entirely, and go all the way back to his quarters.

He didn't like to leave the bridge.

Unfortunately, these days, he wasn't especially anxious to remain there, either. . . .

"Captain?" came a slightly concerned voice from outside, jostling him out of his momentary reverie, and he realized that his door was chiming.

"Come," he called.

The door slid open and Ensign Sulu walked in. She looked slightly tentative.

"Yes, Ensign?"

"Sir . . . permission to join the rescue party to Askalon Five, presuming there is one."

From behind the desk he looked up at her. "Why wouldn't there be one, Ensign? There's a beacon calling for help. We're on our way to help. Once we're there, you don't actually think we're going to just stare at the place, do you?"

"No, sir."

"Odd choice of words, then."

"Yes, sir. I'm sorry."

"Landing party is hardly a 'party,' Ensign, despite the term. This would be your first one."

"Yes, sir." Trying to sound relaxed, she offered, "I could wear white."

He stared at her. "That would be an attempt at humor, I take it."

Her mouth moved slightly, no words immediately forming. Finally she got out, "Yes, sir." Then, rallying, she said, "I wanted to bring it up to you now, sir, rather than just keep my fingers crossed, or discuss it with you on the bridge in front of everyone."

"Out of consideration for your feelings, Ensign, or mine?"

"I . . ." She shrugged. "I didn't think it appropriate, sir."

"Well, you were right." He paused, and then his own shrug mirrored her own. "Very well. You'll be assigned to the landing party."

"Thank you, sir," said Demora. "You see, I figured I would be an asset because the distress message was in Chinese . . ."

"Yes, I know that."

"Plus if there really are ruins down there, ancient civilizations are a hobby of mine. . . . I have quite a few hobbies, in fact. Actually, for a brief while there I considered a career ch—"

"Ensign," said Harriman forcefully but gently, "there's an old expression: Once you've won your case, get out of the courtroom."

She blinked. "Pardon, sir?"

"You came in here to request permission to go. I've granted permission. Don't stand there telling me all the reasons I should make a decision that I already made in your favor. The only thing that's going to do is make me want to change my mind. You don't want me to do that, do you."

"No, sir," said Demora. Reflexively, she started to open her mouth to say something else, but then she thought better of it, closed it, and got out.

It was only after she had left his quarters that Harriman allowed himself to smile, ever so slightly. But then the smile faded.

He tapped a button on his desktop console. "Personal log, supplemental," he said. He had made a terse and fairly standard log entry earlier in the day. But his conversation with Ensign Sulu had stirred a distant sadness within him.

And he had no one to talk to.

He couldn't talk to his junior officers; that wouldn't be appropriate. The ship's engineer was older than he, as was the doctor . . . but he didn't feel secure enough to seek out their counsel. He was, after all, the captain. He couldn't start seeking out substitute father figures. He was the one to whom everyone was supposed to be looking. It made him feel very, very isolated.

So he did the only thing he could: He talked to himself.

"Was I ever that young?" he mused aloud. "Well, now, that's the problem, isn't it. It seems like only yesterday I was that young. Here I am, in charge of a starship—*the* starship—and yet in many ways I still feel that tentative, uncertain little ensign inside me. Looking to advance, looking to try new things, but not wanting to cause problems, not wanting to stir things up.

"Dammit, I was tentative up on the bridge. Not by much. Just the slightest bit. But the crew could tell, I know they could tell. I was asking too many questions about safety. I was being too damned careful!" He slapped his open palm on the desktop. "The moment I determined that there was a call for help, there shouldn't have been any further discussion! Someone needs our help, we help, and that's it, and that's all!

"Every time . . . every time I step out on that bridge, I see Kirk sitting there. Staring at me, watching every move I make. Judging what's going on. And I'm always coming up short. Always. Every decision I make, any order of any consequence, I mentally double-check with Kirk to make sure that it's the right move. And he never tells me. He *never* tells me. Just . . . just sits there. Sits and watches.

"They think I don't know. They think I haven't heard the nickname floating around for this ship. 'The Flying Dutchman.' Behind closed doors, behind the backs of their hands, they say I'm the captain of the death ship. The ship that killed the living legend.

"And it's my fault. It is. They cleared me, all right. Cleared my involvement, cleared my name. All so we could keep the dirty little secret, the one that we all know. I should never have let the ship be taken out before she was ready. I was so grateful and excited for the opportunity, I let them steamroll right over any misgivings I had. Key weapons, key defense mechanisms, not on-line until Tuesday. So why the bloody hell didn't I just insist we *wait until Tuesday!* Oh,

13

but no. Couldn't allow that to happen. Some high muck-a-muck arranged for all the press conferences, then found out we were going to be delayed a week and didn't want to risk looking like a fool. 'Take the ship out, Harriman. Everything will be fine, Harriman. A quick spin around the solar system, what could go wrong, Harriman. Obey orders, Harriman. Do what you're told, when you're told, and there's a good boy Harriman. *Damn them!* Damn them and their sanctimoniousness. Thanks to them, I wound up taking this ship into a rescue mission that we simply weren't equipped to handle, and now I get to be known as the captain whose first mission destroyed the indestructible Kirk. The man who survived a thousand dangers, until he found the one thing he couldn't overcome: the command of Captain John Harriman."

He was silent then, staring at the computer terminal. Then he said, "Computer . . . delete all of today's entries in personal log."

"Deleted," said the computer.

Harriman tapped the desktop for a moment, and then said, "New entry. Captain's personal log: All is well."

It was a noteworthy log entry for two reasons. First, it was commendably brief. And second, it was identical, word for word, to the last two weeks' worth of log entries. All of which had come about in much the same way.

One week before he would be slugged by Commander Pavel Chekov, Captain John Harriman shut off his computer and headed up to the bridge.

Chapter Two

ASKALON V lived up to its billing of not being someplace anyone would wish to be voluntarily.

A haze of a deep purple hue hung over the sky. The air was filled with a steady breeze that was deceptively gentle. However, after only about thirty seconds the members of the landing party realized that a deep, tingling chill to the bone was creeping through them.

The ground was soft, almost claylike beneath their boots. Consequently walking was something of a chore. So there they were, with the ground defying them, the wind starting to freeze up their joints, and the dark sky adding to the general air of gloom. All in all, not the sort of atmosphere that lent itself to high spirits or jaunty feelings of exploration.

Harriman himself was leading the landing party. It was a practice that had been common enough back in Kirk's time, certainly. Federation policies had begun to shift, however, when other captains followed Kirk's example. In following this practice they displayed bravery and ingenuity; what they did not display, however, was Kirk's almost supernatural luck.

This was not to say that captains were dropping like flies; far from it. There had been, however, several hideously close calls . . . not to mention two cases of lost limbs, and one unfortunate and wasteful demise when a captain had unknowingly trod on a small patch of land that seemed utterly routine. He had no way of knowing—indeed, probably never even had time to realize—that it was an alien equivalent of quicksand, except ten times faster and a hundred times more corrosive. There had barely been enough left of him for DNA identification.

Certainly no one would have been "happier" if it had been the second-in-command, or a security guard, or someone of lower rank who had met such a ghastly death. One life was not intrinsically worth more than another. But what it boiled down to was the cold, hard realities of space, and of training for that hostile and unforgiving environment. In that respect, captains simply had to be considered in a different class.

Plus the Daystrom Institute had produced a fascinating, if somewhat controversial, study. Thousands of landing-party assignments had been fed into a vast database, processed through positronic circuitry as perfected in the M9 computer. The computer made its own selections, which were then turned over to a Starfleet blue ribbon panel for comparison. The panel's decision, which sent something of a chill through the Fleet, was that the computer's picks made more sense. They couldn't be swayed by cronyism or other, even subliminal, human considerations.

The most conspicuous inequity was in the selection of captains spearheading away teams. The computer dismissed the need for the ship's chief commanding officer in ninety-five percent of those cases, describing them as nonessential personnel.

Consequently there was already word of changes filtering down through Starfleet regulations. The right of a captain to lead a landing party, previously sacrosanct, was now up for discussion and review.

This was a hard pill to take for many captains. First and foremost, they were explorers. They had joined Starfleet to explore strange new worlds, seek out new life and new civilizations, and everything else described in the literature. Being stuck on the bridge while everyone subordinate to you was given the opportunity to do so firsthand seemed a less than stellar reward for years of dedicated service.

What it all boiled down to was that Harriman should have been—indeed, was—aware that his presence as leader of the landing party was questionable, particularly given the current atmosphere within Starfleet.

Harriman decided, however, that he didn't care. He was going to do what he wished to do, and if others didn't like it, then they could go to hell. He did not like the feeling of always second-guessing himself, and he was going to put a stop to it. The selection of the landing-party lineup seemed as good a time as any.

Given all that, Harriman still couldn't help but wish that he had chosen to lead a landing party into a tropical, lush paradise, instead of this relative hellhole they were staggering around in.

Well, maybe next time.

Demora Sulu huffed a bit as she made her way across the uncooperative terrain. From just behind her and to the right, Lieutenant Thompson muttered, "What were you *thinking?*"

"Pardon?" said Demora.

"You *wanted* to come along on this detail?" said Maggie as Demora slowed down, allowing her to catch up. "Good lord, why?"

"May I remind you it was your suggestion?" Demora pointed out to her. "*You* told me that the signal being in Chinese was an interesting coincidence. *You* said that I should approach the captain about it."

"Nooo, I said *if* you were interested, *then* you should. I didn't really think you'd volunteer. Good lord, Demora, of all places to want to attach memories of your first landing party, and it's *this* place?"

"It's exciting," said Demora with genuine enthusiasm. The ground started to incline and she braced herself as best she could before pushing herself up it. Maggie followed nimbly.

"God protect us from newbies," Maggie Thompson commented, but she couldn't quite keep the smile off her face. "I'll tell you one thing, Sulu: Your enthusiasm is easily the best thing about this pile of . . . *whoaaa!*"

The outcry came as a result of the ground going out from under Thompson's feet. Demora turned just in time to see Thompson fall to her belly and skid back down the short but steep hill. She left a deep groove behind her in the claylike surface.

"Lieutenant!" called Demora. "You okay?"

Slowly Thompson pulled herself to her feet. Her uniform was covered with the clay. It was also in her face, and she spit out a large glob of it that had gotten into her mouth during her abortive outcry.

"Oh . . . fine," said Thompson, making no attempt to hide her aggravation. She brushed off the filth as best she could, but her best wasn't even close to adequate. "See, Demora? If you hadn't come along, see what you'd have missed?"

Demora waited patiently as Thompson found another, slightly more hospitable way up.

From behind them, they heard Harriman's voice. "Lieutenant! How close are we to the origin of the distress call?"

Harriman, along with security officer Kris Hernandez and medtech Adrian Tobler, was bringing up the rear. He walked with easy steps, apparently not the least bit perturbed by the terrain. Both Thompson and Sulu were slightly envious. The captain was disgustingly surefooted.

"Just ahead, sir. Over that rise, as near as I can determine," she said as she checked her tricorder.

Harriman paused and regarded her. "Took a tumble, Lieutenant?"

"I'm fine, sir."

He nodded and started for the same embankment where Thompson had run into trouble. Demora started to say something in warning, but Thompson rested a restraining hand on Demora's forearm. The message was clear: *Shut up.*

Then Harriman suddenly seemed to pick up speed. He took several long, sweeping strides, and then vaulted up the side of the embankment as if gravity were of only passing interest to him. He landed at the top in a crouch, next to his junior officers.

"Nice bit of exercise you get around here, wouldn't you say?"

"I would indeed, sir," agreed Thompson reluctantly.

"Any signs of life-forms?"

There had been none when they'd first gotten there. But it had been difficult to be absolutely certain, because the atmosphere was heavily enough charged that it might be interfering with the ship's sensors. Now, on the ground, Thompson checked her tricorder once more. "Nothing so far, Captain. Still a remote chance, but . . ."

"But not likely." He nodded. "That's what I was afraid of. Still, we're obliged to check it out thoroughly. Let's go."

Demora, for her part, didn't like the smell of the place. Her enthusiasm as they made their way across the surface remained undiminished. But the air had a certain staleness to it that made her lungs burn after a time. She did the best she could with it through slow, steady, controlled breathing. But it was still something of a hardship.

And then, utterly unbidden, thoughts of her father came to her.

He had told her so many times about the occasions when he had been standing on an alien world. He had made it sound somewhat romantic, just as he seemed to take a romantic view of most aspects of life. He regaled her with incredible stories about far-off spheres. About worlds with time portals, or run by supercomputers, or populated by white rabbits and samurai (although the latter even the gullible Demora had thought sounded somewhat far-fetched).

He had made the universe sound like an incredible place. So why hadn't . . . ?

Demora quickly shut down that avenue of thinking.

There was no point to it, no way of resolving it. That way lay any number of concerns and problems that simply had no business being addressed. And she wasn't about to start now.

"Sulu!"

It was Harriman's voice, from farther up ahead than she had realized. "Taking your time, aren't you?" he called to her.

"Sorry, sir," she said, chiding herself. She had to stay focused, rather than let unresolved concerns about her father cloud her thinking. The consequences of muddied concentrating, after all, could be extremely disastrous.

She had to stay on her toes.

Then she felt something tug at her ankle. She looked down in surprise and gasped.

Her last fully aware thought was an echo of Maggie's words: *See what you'd have missed?*

Thompson had no idea how long the distress beacon had been there, or who had placed it.

Harriman stood several feet away as Thompson closely inspected the device. It stood approximately three feet tall, on a tripod. It looked weather-beaten and a bit corroded, but it was still resolutely sending out a signal recorded by a person or persons unknown.

"Any idea of its pedigree, Lieutenant?" asked Harriman.

Slowly she said, "Well, that's what's odd about it, Captain. It has a general look that says late twenty-second-century Earth . . . but there's markings on it I've never seen before." She tapped the metal exterior. "Not only that, but if you look closely, you'll see variations."

Harriman studied the markings. "You're right," he said. "Several different styles. It's as if it's printed in several different languages, suggesting some sort of . . . joint venture. Any of them Chinese? Sulu, is—?"

He stopped and looked around.

There was no sign of her.

"Sulu!" he called again.

Still no answer.

Hernandez and Tobler glanced about them. Lieutenant

Thompson straightened up, and now she looked around as well. "Sulu!" she shouted. But the only thing that came back to her was the sound of her own voice.

She started to reach for her communicator, but Harriman had already flipped his open. "Harriman to Sulu, report." He paused a few moments and then repeated himself. There was no response from the other end.

If Harriman was concerned, he restrained it well. "Tobler . . . Hernandez," he said matter-of-factly, "backtrack, would you please? See if you can locate our wandering helmswoman."

"Aye, sir," they echoed each other and headed back.

"Permission to aid in the search, sir," said Thompson.

"I already have two people looking for a third, Lieutenant," Harriman said briskly. "That will be sufficient, I'm sure. Now, let's get these markings translated. They might tell us . . ."

Then his voice trailed off as he saw something. There had been some cloud cover, but the clouds—swept by the winds of the planet's surface—had parted to reveal a city.

Or the remains of one, in any event. High towers stretched along the horizon, but many of them were battered and broken, the jagged edges quite visible. It was impossible to tell from that distance what they were made from—stone or steel, or something else.

But even from that far away, Harriman knew that the city was dead. There were no lights burning anywhere. Death and decay, in Harriman's imaginings, were draped over it like great shrouds.

" 'Behold my works, ye mighty, and despair,' " he said softly.

Thompson looked up from the distress probe with polite confusion. "Pardon, sir?"

"An old poem, Lieutenant," said Harriman, unable to tear his gaze away from the far-off ruins. "A man traveling in the desert discovers the broken remains of a statue. And there's an inscription that reads, 'I am Ozymandias, king of kings. Behold my works, ye mighty, and despair.' The point of the poem was the transitory nature of man's accomplishments. Here was this great and powerful 'king of kings,' who apparently had ruled a vast empire . . . and there was nothing left of him or anything that he had done except a ruined statue. The rest of it had been lost to time."

"We all get lost to time, sir," said Thompson matter-of-factly. She had flipped open her communicator. "Z'on? You got it?"

"Got it," came Z'on's voice. "Analyzing now."

Thompson turned to Harriman. "I fed the images of the markings into the tricorder, and from there up to Lieutenant Z'on."

"Good work, Lieutenant." Harriman looked in the direction that Hernandez and Tobler had gone. He frowned a moment in concern and then spoke into his communicator once more. "Harriman to Hernandez." What Harriman found a bit daunting is that he had absolutely no idea what he would do if Hernandez failed to answer. That would mean that he had more than a lost crewman on his hands; he had a genuine situation. Couldn't *anything* go routinely for him at any time?

Fortunately enough he was spared having to concern himself. Hernandez's voice came through immediately in that customary, laconic tone of his. "Hernandez here."

"Any sign of Ensign Sulu?"

"We found her tracks, sir. Following them now. But they seem to just go in a circle. We're trying to find another possible trail."

"Keep me apprised," said Harriman as he closed his communicator. Thompson looked away from him quickly, obviously trying to mask her own concern and maintain as much as possible her professional demeanor.

Thompson's own communicator beeped and she flipped it open. "Thompson," she said crisply.

"Got a translation for you," Z'on's voice came back with no preamble. "Two problems: It's somewhat rough, and it's somewhat useless."

"What does it say?"

"It says, 'If found, please return.'"

Thompson and Harriman exchanged looks. "That's *it?*" she said incredulously.

"Yes, ma'am," Z'on said. "None of the symbols were

anything vaguely Terran. I managed to cross-reference it off similar, already translated symbols from digs on Minox Nine and Alpha Prime Twelve. It corresponds to the known written language of an ancient, apparently long-dead race called . . ."

He paused. Thompson frowned. "Called what?"

"The Blumbergs."

Harriman stepped over. "Say again?" He couldn't quite believe he'd heard it correctly.

"The Blumbergs, sir," said Z'on with an air of resignation.

"The *Blumbergs?*" Despite the dreary atmosphere, despite the concern over the missing Ensign Sulu, it was all Harriman could do not to laugh. "What kind of a name for an alien race is that?!"

"Apparently, sir, the kind of name given them by the man who first discovered traces of their existence and has written all the major papers and studies regarding them. That man, as one might guess, being Dr. Matthew . . ."

". . . Blumberg," both Thompson and Harriman said in unison.

"Correct."

"All right. Thank you, Lieutenant. Thompson out." She snapped off the communicator and looked to Harriman, who shrugged expansively. "I don't know," said Thompson after due consideration. "Kind of a different name for a race, when you get down to it."

"Oh, absolutely, Lieutenant. The Klingons, the Romulans, the Blumbergs. All of them names to strike terror into the hearts of millions." He sighed, looked around once more. "This is a waste of time," he said finally. "There's no sign of habitation here, or any sign that there ever *was* habitation. No sign of a crashed ship, no sign of natives, no sign of anyone attending to this distress beacon. Whoever left it here is long gone. Let's find Ensign Sulu and get the hell out of h—"

There was a low growl behind them.

Harriman knew, even without turning around, that the life scans of the planet had been wrong. There was indeed some sort of indigenous life on Askalon V. And from the sound of it, it was big . . . it was most likely covered with very thick fur . . . it probably had teeth the size of steak knives . . . it was very hungry . . . and it was long past its dinnertime.

Both Thompson and Harriman, as was standard for landing parties, had their phasers strapped to their belts. The growl seemed to be coming, best guess, from about twenty feet away. For a predator about to spring, that distance was nothing at all. It could cover it in one leap, and Harriman's first inclination was to turn and shoot as quickly as possible. But if he moved fast and rushed the shot—and in so moving, spurred the creature to spring instantly—he or Thompson (or both) could be down beneath its claws before there was time for another action to be taken.

The creature growled again. By this time both Harriman and Thompson had their hands resting on their weapons. Their gazes were locked on each other and Harriman mouthed the word *Slowly* to Thompson. She gave a nod so slight that her head didn't even move, but the acknowledgment was there all the same.

Slowly, ever so slowly, they turned to face the creature who threatened their lives.

Their jaws dropped in mutual astonishment.

It was Demora. Not only was she barely recognizable as herself, she would barely be recognized as human.

She was crouched on a boulder overlooking them. Her uniform was gone; she was stark naked, her hair so wildly askew that her eyes were barely visible beneath it all. But when the hair did blow aside enough to reveal her eyes, there was nothing in them but a feral, animal gleam.

Her lips were drawn back and her teeth were bared. Spittle was hanging from the corners of her mouth. Her fingers were spread in a palsied, clawlike manner. Her entire body was trembling, like a barely restrained missile wanting to tear itself loose from its moorings.

They froze there for a moment, the three of them, like some bizarre tableau from an alternate universe where humans were stalked, not by animals, but by animalistic humans. The only sounds were the whistling of the wind and the distant rumbling of the seething sky.

Thompson could barely get a word out. "D . . . Demora?" she stammered.

The word broke the spell, and Demora leaped.

Incredibly, impossibly, as if she'd been possessed by a puma, Demora covered the entire distance in one leap. She crashed into Thompson, knocking her back, sending her head slamming into the distress beacon. Thompson went down, the beacon crashing atop her. With the howl of a wild beast, Demora leaped upon Maggie, and at that moment she looked completely capable of ripping Thompson apart with her teeth.

Harriman brought his phaser up and fired.

The blast hit Demora squarely in the small of her back, knocking her clear of Thompson. Thompson didn't get up, and Harriman saw a trail of blood from her forehead.

He started toward Thompson, taking for granted that Demora was out cold. The first and only warning he had of his error was the full-throated roar that ripped from Demora's throat, and then Demora plowed into him, bearing him to the ground.

He couldn't believe it. From that distance, with that intensity, the phaser blast should have knocked her unconscious. The only indication that Demora seemed to register from having been shot was to go even more berserk.

Her fingernails raked across Harriman's forehead. He screamed as they drew blood, and Demora's howl of triumph was earsplitting. If he'd heard a recording of it, there was no way he would have thought any human at all could ever produce such a sound, much less an eminently civilized, charming, and witty human such as Demora Sulu.

And even as the thought flashed through his mind, even as he saw that Demora's frothing mouth was poised directly over his throat, he realized that he was still clutching his phaser in his right hand. He angled it around, jammed it directly against her bare skin, and fired.

The blast knocked her clear of him. The pressure momentarily gone, Harriman tried to get to his feet. He grunted in pain, his leg twisted back around, and then, oh God, she was getting back up. A little bit less steady, but no less angry, no less dangerous.

Blood poured into his eyes from the cuts on his forehead and he heard her roar once more, sensed rather than saw her charge. Blinded by his own blood, he desperately thumbed the power level on his phaser, jacked it up, and fired in the direction of the sound coming toward him.

The whine of the phaser combined with the shriek of its target, and Harriman couldn't see what the result was. He scrambled back across the ground, trying to put some distance, however meager, between himself and his frenzied helmswoman. He drew an arm quickly across his eyes to clear them of blood and then brought his phaser up, double-handing the grip to keep it level.

That was when he saw Demora.

She lay on the ground, sprawled on her back. Her head lay still and lifeless, her eyes staring at nothing. Her torso was dark with burns from the close-range phaser blasts. Her legs lay twisted.

Harriman's breath was ragged in his chest. He couldn't believe it. He simply couldn't believe it. What had happened? *What the hell had just happened?*

He heard movement from just above the ridge, whirled with his phaser, and came within a hair of firing blindly before he realized it was Tobler and Hernandez.

They skidded to a halt, appalled at the scene before them. The captain, his face smeared with blood as if he'd been in a war. Thompson, down and unconscious. And Demora . . . dear God, what had happened to Demora.

Tobler's communicator was already in his hand, however. "Tobler to *Enterprise!* Medical emergency. Beam us all directly to sickbay!"

Harriman nodded in acknowledgment of the order, and said nothing else as they vanished from the surface of Askalon V.

Chapter Three

THERE WERE MANY "firsts" in Dr. Metcalfe's career in which he could take genuine pleasure. The first operation he performed . . . the first life he saved . . . the first child he delivered . . .

But now he had to pronounce the first death aboard the *Enterprise*.

Oh, certainly, the ship was associated with calamitous death and destruction. But Metcalfe hadn't been there for any of it. He, along with the rest of the medical personnel, had not come aboard until after the debacle of the ship's launch. Technically many had died, but it hadn't happened under Metcalfe's watch. Indeed, he felt a small degree of guilt (nothing major—he was too old a hand at this—but small nonetheless) over not having been there at the time of the ship's first crisis. Perhaps in some way he might have managed to save some lives.

But there was no great point in contemplating the past. Only the future at this point was of any interest to him. Unfortunately, it was a future that did not include the young woman laid out on the table in front of him.

Metcalfe was an older gentleman, with a salt-and-pepper beard and a gleaming bald head. He was studying the readouts that his instruments were making, speaking softly and for the record that was automatically entering his words into his medical log. Standing nearby was a stone-faced Captain Harriman, his arms folded resolutely across his chest. His forehead had been cleaned and a thin layer of plasticskin had been applied against it to seal the wound.

"Deceased died from catastrophic cellular disruption caused by a series of phaser blasts in increasing grades of intensity," Metcalfe said tonelessly. "One in the small of the back . . . shot from behind," and he glanced at Harriman with eyebrows raised in apparent reproof. Harriman met his gaze levelly and said nothing. Metcalfe continued, "One in the side positioned squarely between the third and four ribs . . . and the third, the most intense blast, in the solar plexus. Blood flow was halted in——"

Harriman couldn't stand there and listen anymore. He turned and strode out of the lab area of the sickbay, into the main area. Thompson was lying there, still unconscious, but breathing steadily. Her injuries had likewise been attended to and her condition had been stabilized. Tobler was looking over readings and noticed Harriman looking on.

"She's going to be fine, Captain," Tobler offered tentatively.

Harriman nodded once, briefly, and then started for the door. He stopped and turned as Tobler said to him, "Captain?"

"Yes?" His arms were still folded resolutely across his chest. Clear body language telling anyone who might be looking on to keep their distance.

Nonetheless Tobler said rather gamely, "Sir, maybe I'm out of line, but . . . I just want you to know, you saved Lieutenant Thompson's life."

Harriman said nothing for a moment. Then he asked flatly, "Is that it, Tobler?"

"Yes, sir. I guess it is."

The sickbay doors slid shut behind Harriman's retreating figure.

* * *

Commander Dane entered Harriman's quarters, taking immediate note of the fact that it was rather dim. She could barely make him out. "Captain?" she said with just a trace of uncertainty.

"Yes," came Harriman's voice from the darkness.

Dane straightened her shoulders a bit, mentally remonstrating herself for slouching. "We're still in orbit around Askalon Five. Awaiting your orders on how to proceed." He said nothing at first, and Dane continued, "I have another landing party selected, if you wish to continue exploring the planet surface."

"That's easy enough, I suppose," Harriman said after a moment. "A crewman dies, at the hands of her captain. So bring in another crewman to fill the slot. That's all they are, after all. Slots to be filled. Life goes on, doesn't it, Dane."

"Yes, sir. It does."

"Except for Demora Sulu. Life isn't exactly going on for her, is it."

Dane paused a moment. "I'll take that to be rhetorical, sir."

Harriman laughed softly, and it was not a pleasant sound. "God, you are a cold one, aren't you, Dane. They offered me a Vulcan first officer, you know. It was down to you and him. I went with you. Vulcans . . . fine people. Brilliant minds. I admire the hell out of them. But, provincially, I felt more comfortable with a human at my side. And you know what? You give me the creeps sometimes."

She looked down.

"I'm sorry," he said softly after a moment. "I've spent the past hour tearing at myself. Now I'm starting on you. It's not fair and it's not appropriate."

"It's understandable, sir. Losing a crewman under any circumstance is difficult."

"I didn't lose her, Dane. That makes it sound like she was misplaced and might turn up if I check under the seat cushions. I killed her."

"You had no choice."

"That doesn't exactly mollify it, does it."

"No, sir. It doesn't."

He said nothing for a moment and once again Dane prompted, "The planet, sir? Askalon Five. How shall we proceed?"

"You want to know if I'm interested in risking more of my people in the exploration of a world that turned one of them into a homicidal berserker . . . all in the hope of rescuing nonexistent people in distress."

"I wouldn't have phrased it in quite that way, but yes, sir. That's basically the question before us."

"No, I am not interested in doing that. Slap a quarantine on Askalon Five, inform other ships to keep away, and have done with it."

"With all respect, sir, the ruins down there shouldn't be made off-limits to—"

"Which is more important to you, Dane? Ruined buildings? Or ruined lives?"

She opened her mouth with an immediate answer, but then thought better of it and instead simply said, "Yes, sir. I'll order course set for Starbase Nine. We can transfer the . . . Ensign Sulu . . . to them, and proceed from there to the Donatti system."

"Take us home."

She blinked. "Pardon?"

"The statement seems self-explanatory, Commander. Set course for Earth."

"Sir . . . we're due in the Donatti system. You're scheduled for a reception with the—"

"Set course . . . for Earth."

"As you wish, sir. I feel constrained to point out that Starfleet's orders as to our expected arrival date in—"

And Harriman rose from his chair, his body trembling with barely contained fury. His jaw set, his voice a low growl, he said, "I don't give a *damn* about what Starfleet's orders are. I don't care if they came via subspace, or appeared on the main monitor screen in flaming letters two feet high! Demora Sulu was the daughter of Hikaru Sulu, and I killed her, and I will show her the respect that both her parentage and the circumstances of her death dictate! I don't care if the only way we have of setting course for Earth is having you go outside and push! If that's the case, then the only question I have for you is, How long can you hold your breath?!"

"Actually, sir, holding one's breath in a vacuum would hasten the . . ." Then she saw his expression and cleared her throat. "I'll give the orders, sir."

"You do that."

She walked out, leaving Harriman behind with his grief.

At Starfleet Academy, they had tried to mentally steel trainees on the command track for that inevitable day when people under their command went down and didn't come back up. The decisions that had to be made which might sometimes result in the death of crewmen.

But there were some things that somehow didn't quite make it into the curriculum. Things such as how you deal with it when a living legend dies on the maiden voyage of your greatest command.

And how you deal with informing one of the oldest, most dedicated associates of that selfsame living legend that you killed his daughter.

Chapter Four

CAPTAIN HIKARU SULU woke up trembling and covered with sweat.

"Demora," he murmured.

He sat in the darkened quarters for a moment, and then said, "Lights." They came on in prompt response.

He felt an absurd sense of relief. He was, naturally, still within the confines of the *Excelsior*. No reason he wouldn't be; that was, after all, where he'd gone to sleep at the end of his shift.

But for a moment it had all seemed so real.

Demora had been dead.

The dream could not have been any more clear, or any more frightening. She had been lying there, unmoving, on the surface of a dark and frightening world. Phaser burns covered her broken body. And Sulu had been there, shouting her name, unable to make himself heard over the steady roar of the wind. It had seemed to blow the name back into his face.

He had tried to reach her, to get to her somehow so that

he could help her. But he'd been unable to move. Indeed, he had seemed intangible, incapable of physically interacting with the world in any way. So he'd stood there, an impotent and frustrated ghost, shaking fists that no one could see and shouting names with a voice no one could hear. He was so close to her, so close, and yet unable to help her.

"Demora," he said again. He checked the time and discovered that he had awoken an hour before he was supposed to. He tried lying back down, but it did him no good. He simply lay there and stared at the ceiling until he couldn't stand it anymore and roused himself out of bed.

As he showered and dressed, he thought of Demora. He also thought of the dream about her. He'd read any number of cases wherein a relative—mother, father, sibling—had a sort of psychic "flash" at a time of a loved one's crisis. It didn't matter how much distance separated the two. There was somehow, in some way, a connection that no one really professed to be able to understand. It happened without rhyme or reason. Many people who reported such instances made no claim to psychic ability. They'd had no similar experiences before, and could go (and probably happily would go) the rest of their lives without having such a thing recur.

Some scientists tended to dismiss such notions out of hand. There were some, though, who gave it credence and greater study. It was their position that the human mind was capable of far more than it was generally given credit for.

Demora, he thought again, and he did not like one bit the tremendous discomfiture he was feeling every time Demora's name crossed his mind now.

He had hardly been in touch with her since her assignment to the *Enterprise*. Something had happened between the two of them, and he wasn't entirely sure of what it was. Ever since she had gotten into Starfleet Academy there had been a change in her. She was still polite to him. That much was unfailing. But it had come across as very . . . formal, somehow. The warmth wasn't quite there the way it used to be. Or at least so he thought.

"Velcome to reality," Chekov had said to him. Chekov and Sulu had spoken of it, right around the time that Sulu had been given command of the *Excelsior*.

"What are you talking about?" Sulu had asked.

"Eesn't it obvious? A child always rejects her father. All part of growing up, Meester Sulu."

Sulu had smiled in amusement. "The wifeless, childless Pavel Chekov is the world expert on what children do and don't do, eh?"

"Of course I am the expert," Chekov had said sagely. "Only an expert in children vould be intelligent enough not to have any."

"Well, that's tough to argue with, I suppose. Although that is an alarming attitude for my daughter's godparent to have."

Chekov had shrugged and then gestured expansively. "Vat can I say?"

Sulu had been unwilling to accept Chekov's easy answer, in any event. Sulu had never "rejected" either of his parents, and he had done just fine. . . .

Demora . . .

His mind had drifted, and was once more pulled back to his feeling of unease. If he tried to contact her on the *Enterprise* out of the blue, what would he say? "Honey, I dreamed you were dead; how are you doing?" That wouldn't sound particularly good.

Besides which, they were probably nowhere near enough to the *Enterprise* to have a real-time conversation anyway. He'd probably have to settle for a letter. Yes. That was definitely the way to go. A letter.

He sat down at his workstation and said, "Activate messaging service."

"Service activated," the computer informed him.

"To Demora Sulu. Ensign, helmswoman"—the latter he added somewhat unnecessarily, but with distinct pride— "*U.S.S. Enterprise*. Demora . . ."

He stopped a moment, unsure of what to say, and came to

the surprising realization that he'd never composed a letter to her that was merely for the purpose of chatting.

Oh, he'd sent communications to her, of course. Many a time, in fact. But there was always a specific reason for it that was based in conveying information: promotions, extended stays, unexpected events that could have an effect on her. That sort of thing. For all his hobbies, for all his interests, simple "Hi, how are you" gabbing over subspace was not something in which he indulged.

Which was why he was struggling now. The "information" to be conveyed was that he'd had a bad dream about her. But he couldn't call her and tell her that, because either he'd make himself look foolish or else he'd worry her needlessly. Needlessly because he didn't *really* think anything was going to happen to her. He was just trying to quell his admittedly irrational concerns.

Left to her own devices, Demora might very well get around to contacting him on her own. Then again, she had acquired Sulu's knack for being unable to turn out anything except the most perfunctory of missives. Unless something genuinely major happened to her, it might be ages before he heard from her. The only way to speed up the process was to write to her himself.

And maybe it was about time he did that.

"Waiting," prompted the computer, just in case Sulu had forgotten he'd left the function on.

Sulu looked into the screen, trying to appear relaxed, since it was a video message and his image was naturally going to be recorded. "Honey . . . I'm just writing to say hi," he started, using the term "writing" in its traditional sense—as so many still did—even though he was, of course, not really writing anything. "I was thinking about you . . . thinking about all the things you're experiencing and . . ."

Might as well be blindingly obvious about it.

". . . I'd like to hear from you. Things that seem trivial to you will very likely be interesting to me. Think of it as me being selfish, wanting to see early days aboard the *Enterprise* through your eyes so that I can relive my own early career just a little. As I said, selfish. I hope you can forgive me the indulgence. Of course, since I outrank you, I can order you to forgive me." He flashed a smile and hoped that the joke seemed remotely funny. Ah, well . . . if it didn't, well, to paraphrase Leonard McCoy, he was a captain, not a comedian.

"I hope all is well, and that you'll inform me soon of how things are going. Very truly yours . . . your father." The closing line seemed a bit hokey, considering that she would have to be both deaf and blind not to know who was sending her the letter. But it was traditional, and besides, there was something about the way the words "your father" rolled off his tongue.

"Computer, end transmission and send."

"Sending."

Sulu nodded with satisfaction. It was on its way. Now it would just be a matter of time before he received a response from Demora. It would be one of her usual pleasant, straightforward letters, perhaps with a touch of mild surprise that her father had initiated the contact. But why shouldn't he have done so? He was her father, after all. They weren't estranged. Sure, there was that distant way she acted sometimes, but hell, she had a lot on her mind. Starfleet Academy, as Sulu well knew, was enough to change anyone's behavior patterns. Why should Demora be any exception?

She'd respond, the sheer normality of her reply helping to ground him once more. And that would be that.

He headed for the door of his quarters, only to discover Lieutenant Commander Janice Rand, the communications officer, standing outside his door about to push the door chime.

"Janice," he said, somewhat in surprise. "Is something wrong?" It was a natural question to ask. As far back as the two of them went, nevertheless it was unusual for Rand to simply drop by, particularly at such an early hour.

She looked down. "Captain . . ."

"Captain?" He made no effort to hide his amusement. "Getting somewhat formal on me, aren't you, Jan—"

Then his voice trailed off because he knew, he *knew*.

He backed up, his legs suddenly feeling weak, and when he bumped into a chair it took no effort at all to release the muscles in them so that he dropped heavily into it.

"Demora," he said.

Rand blinked in surprise. But her wonder vanished immediately as the gravity of the situation reasserted itself. "Yes" was all she could bring herself to say.

There was a long moment of silence. Then, sounding about a thousand years older, he said, "How?"

She paused a moment.

"How?" he asked again. "In combat? An accident? Ambush? What?" It was amazing—truthfully, he himself was amazed—how calm and even he was keeping his voice. Actually, it took no effort. He was simply numb.

She looked down, and could barely get out the words: "Friendly fire."

It was a term that had survived centuries. Terms that have such remarkably self-contradictory perversity often do.

All the color drained from his face. "What?" he said, the word thudding from him. "One of the crew shot her?"

"Captain . . . maybe you should just read the report. . . ."

He looked at her oddly. "The report . . . would have been marked 'Personal.' You read something directed to me that was indicated to be personal."

She looked down guiltily. "Yes, sir. It was from the *Enterprise* . . . but from the chief medical officer. I . . . put two and two together. I am aware that my actions could be considered cause for severe penalties . . . even court-martial, if you choose to pursue it . . ."

"Oh, be quiet, Janice," he said, but there was no heat in his voice. Indeed, just for a moment, he sounded like the Sulu of old. The one who, back when she was a yeoman and he was a helmsman, she would bring sandwiches to while he messed around with whatever his latest hobby might be. Back when they were both young, and the galaxy was an infinity of possibilities.

And in the spirit of those long-gone days, the ranks fell away for a moment. She stomped her foot in irritation. "Well, dammit, Sulu, what did you expect me to do? I mean, this message comes in, and I can pretty much guess what it says. And I'm supposed to just forward it down to you without comment?"

He walked to her and rested a hand on her shoulder. "If you wanted me to read the report, you'd simply have sent it down to me. Obviously you wanted to cushion the . . . the blow." And now it was an effort to keep his voice level, the initial numbness having worn off. "I can handle it. Tell me."

"It's . . . I don't pretend to understand it, sir. It . . ." She gathered her strength and then it all came out in a rush. "The report is that she began attacking other crewmen while on a landing party. Assaulted the science officer, nearly killed the captain. He was compelled to shoot and ki . . . to use terminal force against her."

He stared at her as if she'd grown antenna. "The . . . captain shot her? Are you serious?"

"Yes, sir. The report was very specific."

Sulu looked as if he'd been sucker-punched. "And . . . and what caused it? Caused her to attack her own people?"

"They don't know. They haven't been able to determine any . . ."

"There must be an answer," Sulu said, his efforts to rein in his frustration stretched to their limits. "It's insane. Demora wouldn't just . . . something must have caused it. Some virus, some animal that bit her . . . something. What sort of subsequent investigations is Harriman performing?"

"Reading between the lines: None. The CMO made mention that the planet's been placed under quarantine. No one in or out."

"That's a reasonable precaution," he admitted slowly. "But my daughter's life ended there. I see no reason that the investigation should end as well. Are we close enough to *Enterprise* for a direct subspace link?"

"No, sir."

He nodded. "That's . . . probably fortunate. I don't think I'd . . . trust myself to speak with Harriman right now. I need time to . . . deal with this, so that I can act in an appropriate manner."

"Meaning a manner more appropriate to the decorum of a Starfleet captain than to a grieving father."

Rand took a step toward him and said softly, "I know how you feel."

"I know. No one knows better than me how close you and Demora . . ."

"It's not just that. I mean, that's part of it, sure. But . . ." She looked down. "There's something I never told you."

He looked at her, waiting. He didn't feel like he had the strength to say anything.

With a sigh that sounded heavy with exhaustion, Rand said, "It was years ago. Years and years. Didn't you wonder why I took a leave of absence from Starfleet for a time?"

"Your record cited personal reasons. I never felt it was my business to ask."

"Yes, well . . . that was the personal reason. Her name was Annie. She lived until the ripe old age of two, and then she got sick and died. Because for all our medical knowledge, sometimes people—even young people, even very young people—still die. And after she was gone, I was at loose ends for a time before I was able to bring myself to return to Starfleet. End of my life as a mother."

He put a hand on hers. "Janice . . . I'm so sorry. . . ."

"This is not the time for you to be comforting me. I just . . . I wanted you to know how much I feel for you."

"Do you still think about her?"

Rand smiled thinly. "Only on days ending in the letter *y*."

Sulu stared straight ahead. Rand reached over and touched his back. Every muscle under his jacket was knotted. It was like touching rock. There seemed to be nothing more to say, so she headed for the door.

"Rand . . ."

She stopped, turned, and looked at him questioningly.

"The father," Sulu asked. "Do you mind my asking . . . who it was."

She sighed. "It doesn't matter," she said. "He's dead now, too."

"Did you ever tell him?"

"I didn't want to risk sidetracking his career. You see . . . I suspected that he was headed for a great destiny, and I didn't want to do anything to distract him from it."

"And did he fulfill his great destiny, Janice?"

With a sad look she said, "We all do, Sulu. We all do." And she walked out of his quarters.

Sulu sat there for quite some time. He waited for the tears to come . . . but none did. There was a slight stinging in his eyes, but overall it was like the sensation of a sneeze that's puttering around one's nose but doesn't quite escape.

He was still numb. That was it. Still overcome by the shock.

Demora was dead. His little girl, whom he had known for so brief a time, was gone. Never to laugh with him or at him again, or to puncture any of his pretensions with her musical laugh or her mischievous wit.

Never again to look into Demora's face, or into her eyes, and see *her* staring back at him.

Her . . . Demora's mother.

The lunatic. The madwoman. The exotic nut, straight out of those old adventure stories that Sulu had read when he was so young, a lifetime ago . . .

You know the old Russian saying . . . be care—

Sulu shook it off. He didn't want to think about those times now. Didn't want to dredge up the old memories of that period in his life. Of that insane time, with *her,* and the mysterious enemies, dangerous cities with threats hiding within every shadow, a roller-coaster ride which, for all that he had experienced in his very full life, remained for him the pinnacle of loopy, non-sequitur bizarreness . . .

And the tears still weren't coming.

He wanted that release. Wanted to get the anger and rage

and hurt out of his system, but it wouldn't go. What the hell was the matter with him? Had he become so closed up, so out of touch with his emotions, that he couldn't even properly grieve his daughter?

Or was it that with this loss, coming so hard on the heels of the demise of James Kirk, had simply overloaded him. Robbed him of his ability to deal with any more grief.

He thought of Demora, and he thought of Ling . . . and couldn't deal with thinking of either of them.

He informed the bridge that he would be indisposed for a short time and would be late in arrival. And then he lay back on his bed and, even though he had just awoken from a full night's sleep . . . he closed his eyes.

The words echoed once more . . . *You know the old Russian saying . . . be careful vat you vish for . . .*

. . . and then, mercifully, the darkness claimed him before the memories could return.

Word spread quickly through the *Excelsior,* as such things are wont to do. Rand never did find out the origin of the news; she sure knew they hadn't heard it from her. Regardless, within hours of Rand's talk with Sulu, it seemed that every crew member from the newest ensign to the oldest hand knew of Sulu's loss. And, of course, Sulu knew that they knew. It was clear from the deference paid above and beyond that which he normally received in his day-to-day life as captain of the *Excelsior.* Crewmen would greet him in low, respectful tones, and a number of them had trouble making eye contact. It wasn't just the death of Demora, although that was certainly odd enough. It was the bizarre circumstances surrounding it.

Sulu walked out on the bridge. The bridge was never filled with bustling, idle chatter even under normal circumstances. But this time it was silent as . . .

As the grave, thought Sulu.

Sulu's first officer—a Maternian named Anik—was newly assigned to the *Excelsior.* Anik was tall and thin, almost ethereal-looking, with skin so thin that one could see blood flowing against the surface. Normally, when Sulu was off the bridge, Anik would have been seated in the command chair. But today she felt a certain reluctance. As if it would somehow be disrespectful, although she couldn't exactly articulate why.

He stepped out of the turbolift, and he could feel the difference in the atmosphere. Everyone was looking at him and, by the same token, trying to look away.

Opting to take the initiative, Anik stepped forward and said, in her accented English, "Captain, the crew wishes to extend to you its condolences for the loss of your daughter."

He stood there for a moment, his hands draped behind his back. His voice sounded especially gravelly as he said, "I appreciate that. I appreciate the support from all of you. Some further news of interest to all of you, I'm sure: We'll all be going home. Our current heading brings us close enough to Earth so that the readjustment in our schedule is minor. So crew members who have friends or family on Earth will have the opportunity to visit."

"That being the case, sir," said Anik, "I would anticipate a considerable portion of the crew asking about the appropriateness or desirability of attending the funeral services."

Sulu gave it a moment's thought with furrowed brow, and then shook his head. "If any of them happened to know Demora personally, then attending is, of course, their prerogative. But if anyone feels obliged purely out of deference to me . . . by all means, they should not. What they should do is go and spend some time with the people they love. I certainly think Demora would have far preferred that."

"Yes, sir," said Anik, and there were nods of understanding from around the bridge as well.

Sulu had been standing with his hands resting lightly on the back of his command chair. Now he moved around to the front and lowered himself into it.

It was all in his imagination, he was sure, but all at once

he felt his age . . . and older. He could swear his knees audibly creaked, and there was a pulling sensation in his thigh. His body mass seemed to have tripled, and it was all he could do to keep his head up.

"Captain?"

He suddenly realized that Anik was standing directly in front of him. Why was she doing that? Why had she walked around to be in front of him that way?

"Yes, Commander?"

Anik tilted her head slightly in that curious manner of hers. "We're . . . awaiting your orders, sir."

"Oh. Of course." He let out an unsteady sigh. "Set course for Earth."

"Course plotted and laid in, sir."

"Take us home, then."

He stared at the screen, not really registering the shift in the star patterns that indicated the great ship was coming around. Instead he was watching in wonderment as the screen seemed to waver and then blank out. Moments later another image appeared on it.

It was a town. A town that Sulu had not seen for many, many years.

By any definition, it was primitive . . . which was its entire charm.

It was the last place that Sulu wanted to think of. For a moment he thought he was losing his mind, because, of course, it couldn't possibly be that the town was there on the screen.

He realized at that point just how badly he had slept, as if tossing and turning in premonition of things to come. He should just get off the bridge, get the hell off.

But he didn't want to just up and bolt. Go hide in his room like some upset child. He was the captain of the *Excelsior*. He could deal with this.

To hell with it. He was not afraid of his memories. He was not afraid of thinking about the things he had done. It was many years since he hadn't dwelt on that wild, insane, deliriously dangerous week . . . and yet, in odd contradiction, it had never really been far from his thoughts.

And he had no regrets. No regrets over what had happened a little over twenty years ago. (Twenty years ago! Could it have been that long? An eyeblink it had been, certainly.)

No regrets. None at all.

Well . . .

. . . maybe except for his deciding to listen to Chekov . . .

SECTION TWO

FIRST DATE

Chapter Five

"YOU KNOW the old Russian saying . . . be careful vat you vish for . . . you may get it," said Chekov.

Around them the streets of Demora bustled with activity. The air was thick with smells of cooking meat, and from all around them in the bazaar there were merchants hawking wares at the top of their lungs.

As Chekov and Sulu made their way down the main boulevard, outrageous beggars, with eye patches or thick beards, would try to bum money off them, offering to do odd jobs, offering their children in trade . . . the absurdity of the attempts to get funds escalating with each passing moment.

"I will be your eternal slave, sir! I will lick your boots until such time that it will give you pleasure to kick me in the teeth!" said one particularly aggressive fellow.

"That sounds like a serious offer," Chekov deadpanned, and looked to Sulu for confirmation.

Sulu sighed and shook his head.

Sternly, Chekov said, "Ve vill consider it and get back to you."

"Thank you, sir! Oh, thank you!" He bowed and scraped, shuffling off in the other direction.

Sulu looked at Chekov with undisguised incredulity. "'We'll think about it and get back to you'?"

Chekov shrugged. "He seemed sincere."

Sulu shook his head and quickened his stride, gliding smoothly between the crowds in that effortless way he had. Chekov, a bit more bull-in-China-shop, had to elbow his way through, wondering how in the world Sulu made it look so easy.

"Slow down, Sulu!" said Chekov as he managed to get alongside the quickly moving officer. "You're not soaking up the ambience!"

"Ambience?" Sulu shook his head. "Chekov . . . how can you be interested in any of this? How can you make yourself a part of it? It's all . . . it's all nonsense!"

"Life is nonsense. Anyvun who believes othervise is kidding themselves. Here. Over here," and, taking Sulu firmly by the arm, he indicated a small café.

With a sigh, Sulu accompanied him, and moments later they were seated at a small table, watching the crowds of tourists hustling past.

"This is ridiculous," Sulu said again for what felt like the hundredth time since yesterday when they'd first arrived.

"But you vished for something like this, just as I said before," Chekov reminded him. "You said you vanted something exotic. Something adwenturous. Vell—?" He gestured around them to take in the scope of the city.

"But Chekov," said Sulu, leaning forward and sliding aside his cup of coffee. "Don't you see? It's all . . . manufactured."

He was correct, of course.

It hadn't happened overnight. The transformation of Demora from barren desert to tourist attraction had taken quite a few years. It had been a logical outgrowth of technology, however. After all, terraforming techniques were being used on far-off worlds to transform them into Earth-like environments. So it was only logical to use those same techniques to change sections of Earth as well . . .

48

while maintaining some of the ambience of the surroundings.

A group of private investors purchased one section of the Sahara and proceeded to transform it into an inhabitable area. Permanent sunblock satellites hovered several thousand feet above Demora, high enough to appear as nothing more than dots in the sky, but effectively moderating and screening out the intensity of the sun. Buried dearridizers made the air more breathable and added a bit of moisture . . . not so much that one completely lost the desert flavor, but sufficient that guests were not made to feel incredibly uncomfortable. The object, after all, was to show the folks a good time. Give them a feel for the mysterious, romantic, and adventurous cities such as the fabled Casablanca.

Unlike a simple amusement park, however, Demora was a genuine city unto itself, populated by a variety of people.

Some were employees of the owners. They were provided free room and board, spending their private time and off hours in plush subterranean apartment complexes. They were "actors," in a sense. Hired to provide color and excitement for the tourists, portraying a variety of mysterious, shady, and ultimately entertaining denizens of Demora's underbelly.

Then there were genuine entrepreneurs. Most of them operated booths, stores, and shops in Demora. The management skimmed ten percent off the top, and also provided housing consisting of apartments of varying quality within the confines of Demora itself. It was a fun and colorful place for artists, craftsmen, or even would-be future moguls to operate. It was the closest thing available to stepping back in time and setting up shop. The shopkeepers even had their own alliance and union, voting on local affairs and considerations. A school had opened up to accommodate the small number of children living there as well.

There was some concern over kids who were born and raised in the city. It hadn't happened yet, but it was inevitable, and there was some debate over the ethical considerations involved. Imagine spending one's developmental years in the isolated and unique environs of Demora and then, for whatever reason, leaving to go out into the "real" world. The culture shock would be staggering, and several hotly debated town meetings had done nothing to resolve the situation.

Then there were the tourists, of course. Most of them were there on some sort of package deal, which included a stay in one of the elaborate luxury hotels that studded Demora. Interaction with the city's population was 100 percent.

Some tourists even tried to get into the swing of things by obtaining costumes for themselves, roaming the streets as beggars, musicians, petty conjurers, whatever caught their fancy. One young couple went there on their honeymoon, on a very tight budget. They staked out a street corner, and the young wife—in a scanty, gauze outfit—proceeded to put on belly-dancing displays while her husband cheerfully accompanied on drums. At the end of each show they'd pass a hat for credit chits. By the time they left, they were in better financial shape than they'd been in upon their arrival.

There were even Demora employees who were "disguised" as run-of-the-mill tourists. They would seem normal at first, but if you spent any time at all with them, it quickly became apparent that they had some sort of mysterious dark side to them. Invariably they would lower their eyes in the midst of conversation, take on a cautioned, even frightened air, and mutter something along the lines of, "This is not a good time for us to talk. We'll rendezvous later. Watch your back." Then they'd vanish into the ever-present shadows of Demora, usually never to be seen again.

The result of the mixed-bag population was that one could never quite take for granted whom one was interacting with. Might be a employee, a fellow tourist, an independent operator . . . whomever. It added to the excitement; to the feeling that no one was necessarily what they seemed, and that anything could happen.

The city was walled, ostensibly to protect it from passing desert raiders. (The raiders attacked on cue Saturday at 1900 hours precisely. There were seats that could be purchased at some key points along the wall, as well as monitors for those who were feeling slightly less adventurous or slightly more economically minded.) Entrance to the city was through the main gate, where a nominal admission fee was charged. Nothing major, though; the organizers of Demora (unsurprisingly, headed up by one Mr. Demor) wanted to keep the entrance cost down. The better to put people at ease, so that the significant spending of credits could occur inside. After all, if visitors left half their budget at the front gate, they'd cling with greater urgency to the remainder. If admission, on the other hand, was only a small fraction of whatever credits visitors had available to them, they'd be feeling pretty flush upon entering the city . . . almost guaranteeing that they would wind up spending the entirety of their funds before their stay was over.

Many things had changed about humanity over the course of centuries. The fundamental knack, however, of separating the fool and his money was a constant.

At the moment, Sulu was feeling like something of a fool.

"You said you vanted excitement," said Chekov. "I don't understand."

"No," sighed Sulu. "I guess you wouldn't." He rose from the table and said, "I'll see you back at the hotel, Chekov."

"At the hotel! But vy? The day is young!"

But Sulu didn't respond. Instead he simply walked away without so much as a backward glance.

Sulu sat on the veranda, watching the sun drift toward the horizon. It was a cloudless evening, as always. The temperature in the desert actually tended to get pretty cool. He was wearing loose clothing, the sleeves fluttering in the breeze. A drink was perched on the table next to him, but it was barely touched . . . the ice long melted, watering it down.

He heard the door to the room swing open on squeaky hinges. It had taken him a while to grow accustomed to a door whose handle you had to turn to enter. Indeed, when they'd first arrived at the room, Sulu had unthinkingly walked right into the door in calm anticipation of it sliding open. This had gotten him a bruised nose and a snort of derisive laughter from Chekov.

"Hello," said Sulu without turning.

He heard the door close again, and there was a soft grunt

followed by the rustling of packages being set heavily onto a table. Then Chekov stepped over to his side.

"Lovely," said Chekov, looking out at the sunset. The sun was a red obelisk hanging in the sky. Then he said, "So . . . you vant to tell me vat's on your mind?"

"Not especially," Sulu replied. He got up from the chair and walked over to survey Chekov's acquisitions. A shirt or two, a garish statue, a small prayer mat, and a couple of other odds and ends. "You've been busy."

"Sulu," said Chekov patiently, "vat is bothering you? I thought you vould love it here."

"Love it here?" Sulu looked at him skeptically. "Chekov . . . this place is a joke. Why couldn't we have done something normal!"

"That's not vat you vanted, remember? I suggested that." Chekov paced the room with wide strides, gesticulating for emphasis. " 'Vere is the adwenture in that, Chekov? Vere is the excitement? How can some quiet staring at mountains or natural vonders on Earth compare to vat vee have seen.' Remember saying all that?"

"I remember saying it with more correct placement of 'v' and 'w,' " Sulu said half-seriously, getting a derisive snort from Chekov in response. He dropped down onto one of the twin beds. It was amazingly comfortable . . . more so than his bed on the *Enterprise* had been, in fact. He looked around the room, with the rattan furniture, the tiled walls, and the large ceiling fan turning leisurely overhead. "But I didn't exactly have this place in mind."

"Vat *did* you have in mind? Ve both wisited our respective families. Ve deserve to do something fun while the *Enterprise* is being refitted. Earth is our home, Meester Sulu. Ve should enjoy it vile ve can."

"I don't know about that."

Chekov stared at Sulu uncomprehendingly. "Pardon?"

"Don't you see, Pav? That's part of the problem. I have this sense of . . . of disassociation. People like you, and other officers . . . you come back to Earth, and you feel like you've come home. But me . . . when I set foot on Earth, all I can do is think about leaving."

"I see," he said slowly.

"Do you?" asked Sulu. "It's a hell of a way to be, Chekov. To find that I consider a starship to be more of a home than the world I was born on."

"But vy do you feel that vay?"

"Because Earth is boring, Pav! The things we've seen and done . . . and then I come back here, and I do what? I sit and talk with my family and try to tell them about what I've experienced. They can barely grasp it, Chekov. How do you tell them about beings like Trelane, or Charlie Evans? How do I tell them that the world they knew vanished out of existence, and was replaced with a timeline where Hitler won World War Two? My mother asked me what a typical day for me was like. Well, let's see, Mother. There was the typical day a madwoman switched minds with my commanding officer. Or the typical day we were face-to-face with a planet eater. 'Oh, my, Hikaru, that sounds strenuous! Don't you ever get shore leave?' Well, certainly I do, Mother. And it can be relaxing, except when a samurai jumps out of nowhere and tries to cut me in half."

"Vat's your point?" said Chekov with a rather dry tone.

"The point? The point, Chekov, is that with all the new life-forms and new civilizations I've encountered . . . I come back to the planet of my birth, only to find that the people I love most in the world are alien to me. My shared experiences are all with people other than them . . . and those experiences have changed me. When you come back 'home' there's a certain expectation that you revert, mentally, to the way you used to be. But I can't. I've been through too much. We've just come back from our five-year mission, and all I can think about is getting back out there as soon as the *Enterprise* refit is finished. When I first embarked on my career with Starfleet, the hardest decision I had to make was leaving my family, knowing it would be years until I saw them again . . . *if* I saw them again. That was so difficult for me, I can't express it. It used to be that the greatest pride I took in myself was my family and lineage. Yet now, I sit with them and I get . . . bored. There's no other word for it. Bored."

"Bored because you vant . . . vat?"

"Because I want excitement. I want that feeling of being

on the edge." Sulu swung his legs down off the bed and strode back to the veranda. The sun was very low now in the sky, the sand gleaming red. And the stars . . . the stars were already becoming visible. He stared up longingly at them, studying the constellations, the positions, even making rapid-fire calculations of how long it would take to travel from one to the other. And he did it for no other reason than love of doing so.

"When I sit at the helm of the *Enterprise,* any second . . . *any second* . . . something could happen. I'm on my toes every second of every minute on my watch. Waiting to see what the next thing we encounter will be; knowing that, sooner or later, something will happen. Something always does. How can I say all that to my family?"

"You said it all to me."

"Yes, but you understand."

"Never assume." He frowned. "If you miss it so much . . . vy are you still here? It vill be another six months until the refit is finished, even with Mr. Scott overseeing it. You could have taken assignment on another ship, instead of agreeing to teach at the Academy like I did. I, personally, didn't mind the prospect of staying on Earth for a little vile. But you . . . ?"

"Because," Sulu sighed, "it's the *Enterprise.* It's working under Captain Kirk. It's . . . everything. A position on another ship would simply feel like a step down, almost by definition."

"Even a captaincy?"

Sulu shrugged. "Well, I wouldn't see myself turning *that* down. Then again," he added thoughtfully, "it would depend, wouldn't it. Helmsman of a starship versus captain of a ten-man science vessel? Maybe I wouldn't be so quick to agree to that captaincy after all."

"So let's see if I understand this," Chekov said slowly. "You feel Earth has no challenge for you."

"That's essentially correct."

"You feel like an outsider . . . alien . . . out of touch, with little to no connection to your homeworld."

"More or less."

"You vant to get back into space on the *Enterprise,* and until then you're just marking time."

"Basically."

"All right," said Chekov. "I understand now." And then he sighed heavily and shook his head. "You realize you are in major trouble now."

Sulu frowned. "How so?"

"Vell, you remember the old Russian saying I mentioned earlier?"

In spite of himself, Sulu smiled. Chekov always made comments such as these with such an utter deadpan that it was impossible to tell whether he was joking or not. "I'd always thought it was from an Aesop's fable myself, but all right," said Sulu. "Just for laughs, we'll say it's the latest in a long line of 'Russian inwentions.'"

"Good. Because, you see, there's another famous saying—a curse, actually—vich I am afraid you have brought down on yourself."

"Let me guess," said Sulu, as the last of the sunlight vanished, leaving the desert in cool, stark relief. "'May you live in interesting times.'"

Chekov clapped his hands in appreciation. "You read my mind."

"You are aware, of course, that that isn't a Russian saying."

To Sulu's surprise, Chekov retorted indignantly, "Of course I know that! You think I am a fool? I know wery vell that it isn't a Russian saying."

"Well, that's good," said Sulu.

"It's Polish."

Sulu rolled his eyes and returned his attention to the sky. The sun had set completely, and the stars in their full bloom called to them.

His heart answered in silence.

Chapter Six

Sulu HAD BEEN DISCUSSING cutting their stay short, but he had patiently allowed Chekov to talk him out of it. In a way, he was envious. He wanted the younger man's enthusiasm to be infectious. Unfortunately he couldn't begin to muster the same excitement as Chekov.

They had split up today, promising to meet for lunch at a predetermined restaurant at the corner of Humphrey and Rick's. Sulu watched, arms folded and shaking his head in amusement, as a "police officer" made inquiries of tourists over a bit of unpleasantness that had occurred at a café. With grave and serious demeanor he had turned to Sulu and asked if he knew anything of it. Sulu apologetically replied in the negative.

He walked away then, still trying to figure out what in the world Chekov saw in the place. It was so manufactured, so artificial. Compared to the natural wonders that space had to offer, Demora was a joke. It was a pleasant getaway for those with an utterly pedestrian life. Not for someone who had basked in the glow of a thousand different suns, and had trod worlds so remote they had no names.

It was ten in the morning, and Sulu was bored already. He moved through the streets, feeling apart from everyone on them. An old-style car motored past, the driver gesturing imperiously for people to get out of the way. Sulu gave way, shaking his head and trying to wonder how others so managed to lose themselves in the nonsense of . . .

He never saw her coming.

She slammed squarely into him, rocking him back slightly on his heels. Nevertheless his concern was immediately for her as he said, "Whoa! Are you all right?"

At first she didn't seem to focus on him. She was clearly of Chinese extraction, with long black hair and a slightly confused look about her. Her face was quite triangular, and her features were very delicate.

And her eyes . . . her eyes were green. That was unusual, to put it mildly. Green as emerald, with a sparkle in them like a diamond.

She was glancing over her shoulder. The shoulder was bare, for the loose white shirt she was wearing had slipped down slightly. And Sulu spotted a small, diamond-shaped birthmark on her shoulder. She saw where he was looking and quickly adjusted her shirt, and then started to move past him.

"Are you all right?" he said, noting her distracted air. He moved in synch with her. "Is something the mat—"

"Excuse me," she said quickly. She placed her hand squarely on his back and pushed around him.

Sulu watched her go as she disappeared around a corner. "Now, *that* was odd," he murmured to himself, and then shrugged.

But then he noticed something very curious. Three men, moving quickly, went around the same corner that the woman had vanished around moments before. It appeared as if they were following her.

Sulu looked around to see if anyone else had noticed, but no one seemed to. He started after them, picking up speed and rounding the corner just in time to see the three men standing several yards away, looking around in frustration.

The trio was a mixed bag of types. One of them was

Asian, with hair shaved close to his skull. The second was Caucasian, large and muscular, with shoulder-length blond hair that gave him a decidedly Nordic look. The third was black, slim and wiry, bald but with a thick, curly beard.

There was no sign of the woman.

Then the three men spotted him, and glanced quickly at each other. Clearly they recognized him as the man that the mysterious woman had been talking to.

As one, they started to approach Sulu, the look in their eyes uniform in intent and hostility . . .

And then he realized.

He began to laugh to himself.

Oh, he had fallen for it. Fallen for it with the proverbial hook, line and sinker.

It was a setup. Another Demora setup.

No, more than that. This had Chekov's fingerprints all over it. The Russian had made all those oblique comments about living in interesting times, saying that Sulu should be careful what he wished for.

It was now all painfully clear. Chekov had arranged this. Gotten together with some Demora employees and cobbled together some half-witted "adventure."

Did he really think that Sulu would fall for it? Did he truly believe that Sulu was that stupid?

It didn't seem likely. What seemed *more* likely was that Chekov expected him to see through it, but hoped that Sulu would be willing to play along.

Sulu could have, should have, pulled the plug on it right then and there. But his long friendship with Chekov stopped him from doing so. Here Chekov had gone to all this work to arrange this . . . this whatever-it-was. Was Sulu now going to blow it off with a quick dismissal of the players involved? Would that be what a friend would do?

It wasn't any different than somebody arranging a surprise party that the "victim" accidentally found out about. The accepted, expected reaction was to act surprised.

Far be it from Sulu to flaunt proper protocol, especially in the face of Chekov's efforts on his behalf.

The Asian man was in the forefront. Perhaps he was the

leader; it was difficult to tell. "Excuse me, sir," he said in a gravelly voice. "That young woman earlier . . ."

"Yes?"

"Are you . . . acquainted with her, by any chance?"

Sulu paused a moment, weighing the variety of responses. What the hell. Might as well play it to the hilt.

He stepped in close to the other man and said in a low voice that was as dangerous as he could make it, "So you're the ones she mentioned."

The other two were moving in now. The black man now spoke in a silky voice, "Is there a problem here, Taine?"

The one he'd addressed as Taine didn't look back at his companion. Instead he kept his attention focused on Sulu. To Sulu, it felt as if the air around him had become filled with a sort of dark energy.

"There may be," said Taine evenly. "I'm not certain if we have a joker here . . . or simply a fool."

The black man gestured with a nod of his head in Sulu's direction. "He know her?"

"I'm not sure. For some odd reason, he may simply be trying to be a hero. Tell me, hero . . . what's her name?"

"Her code name is Jade Eyes. That's all you need to know."

At this, the three men laughed. And then, shaking their heads, they started to move off.

And Sulu called out, "You'll never get the device."

It was a reasonable thing for him to say. In adventures such as this, there was *always* a device. Either that or a rare statue or religious artifact. It didn't matter, of course. This whole thing was a setup by Chekov, and they would undoubtedly play along with whatever he came up with.

It worked like a charm. The trio froze in their tracks. The one called Taine turned to him, and this time there was genuine suspicion in his eyes. Passersby walked past them, oblivious of what was transpiring.

"The device," said Taine slowly, but then he added derisively, " 'Jade Eyes' told you of it, did she?"

"Her code name is Jade Eyes. As for me, I call her Diamond . . . after her birthmark."

And this was enough to cause the blood momentarily to drain from Taine's face. In a voice darkly sinister, he said, "All right. Now . . . we talk."

He briskly nodded to the Nordic-looking one. "Thor," he said, "escort the gentleman to somewhere quiet."

Thor. Oh, that was too much. Chekov had really gone over the edge on this one. Naturally he was named after a Norse god. Thor. That was rich.

Thor stepped forward, clamping a hand on Sulu's forearm.

Sulu moved quickly and, with a brisk twist of his arm, yanked it free. Thor stood there, looking momentarily confused.

"Stay away from us," said Sulu. "We're backed by an organization so huge, you can't even begin to grasp it."

Thor's face darkened and he swung a huge fist. Sulu effortlessly ducked under it. And then, before Sulu ever saw it coming, the fist swung back again and slammed him on the side of the head.

Sulu went down, head momentarily spinning. Clearly these guys were taking it seriously. They played their part well. Well, naturally that would be the case. Chekov would see to that. Perhaps Chekov even entertained the notion that Sulu might actually be taken in by it all if it seemed real enough.

But . . . all right. If that's how they were going to be, then Sulu saw no reason to be any gentler with them than they were with him. Whatever Chekov was paying them, Sulu would make damned sure they earned it.

Thor reached down for him and Sulu saw his opportunity. He lashed out with a fist, catching Thor just behind the right knee. Thor's leg crumbled under him. Sulu slammed a fist up into Thor's gut, knocking him flat on his back.

"Rogers!" Taine shouted, summoning the black man to join him, and the two of them converged on Sulu. Thor, the wind momentarily knocked out of him, was trying to pull himself up.

Observers slowed down to watch the scuffle. On their faces were momentary looks of confusion.

Sulu slipped in between the charging forms of Taine and

Rogers. Rogers started to turn and Sulu whipped his foot around in a spin kick. It connected solidly and Rogers' head snapped to the side. He went down, the world spinning around him.

Now the observers laughed and applauded. It was now obvious to them what they were witnessing: Street theater, of the type so typical in Demora.

Sulu spun to face Taine. Taine had adopted a defensive posture, his lips drawn back in a contemptuous sneer.

They circled each other for a moment, feinting, each trying to ascertain the other's weaknesses. Taine moved with far too much confidence for Sulu's liking.

Sulu lashed out with a foot and Taine caught his ankle with ease. He sent Sulu tumbling to his back and then leaped, slamming down with both his feet directly toward Sulu's head. Sulu barely rolled out of the way in time, and Taine sent a fierce kick into Sulu's side that felt as if someone had jammed a fireplace poker into him.

Several feet away was a merchant selling carpets. Sulu scrambled to his feet as Taine came after him, snapping, "I don't know who you are . . . but you're going to be sorry you mixed into—"

Sulu grabbed one of the carpets and swung it around. It sailed through the air and enveloped Taine's head. For just a moment, he was blinded. Pushing off the balls of his feet, Sulu slammed a fist into the bump under the carpet that represented Taine's head. Taine staggered, grasping at air. Sulu easily dodged in between his outstretched hands and struck again. This time Taine went down, still entangled in the carpet.

"Hah!" Sulu said, and turned just in time to see a massive fist winging toward his face. Then he saw nothing else as the world went dark around him.

Chekov sat at the café table, drumming his fingers in annoyance on the tabletop. A waiter drifted over and said politely, "Do you have any idea when your friend will be joining you, sir?"

"He should have been here by now," Chekov said with mild impatience. "Do you know the time, by any chance?"

"Twelve-thirty, sir," said the waiter. "Can I get you anything?"

"That vould be nice. Do you have any wodka?"

The waiter looked at him oddly. "Pardon, sir . . . did you say 'wotka'?"

"No. Not wotka. *Wod*ka."

Clearly embarrassed, the waiter shifted uncomfortably from one foot to the other. "Sir, I'm . . . not sure we have any of that."

"You don't have any wodka?" Chekov was appalled.

"No, sir, I'm . . . afraid I never heard of it."

"Never *heard* of wodka?"

"Never, sir. Although it does sound rather exotic. Perhaps I could interest you in something to drink instead."

Chekov stared at him as if he'd lost his mind. "Something to drink? Instead of . . ." Then he paused and, very slowly, said, "You make mixed drinks, yes?"

"Absolutely, sir. Best in Demora."

"Good." Chekov searched his mind for the appropriate old-style drink that would typically be served in these environs. Finally he said, "Bring me screwdriver. You can do this?"

"Absolutely, sir."

But before he could walk off, Chekov raised a finger as an afterthought, keeping him in his place. "If you don't mind . . . no orange juice."

"What? No orange juice?"

"That is vat I said, yes."

"But sir," said the waiter patiently, "if there's no orange juice in it, then all that will be left is . . ."

Then his voice trailed off and a slow smile crossed his face. "Wotka," he said understandingly.

"Ah-ah," said Chekov, waggling his finger. "Not wotka. *Wod*ka. Be careful how you speak. It must be very hard for people to understand you vit that accent."

"I'll be more cautious in the future, sir."

"See that you are," Chekov said sternly.

The waiter went off to get the drink, slowly shaking his head in amusement. Chekov was no less tickled by the entire exchange, until he came to realize that more time had passed and there was still no Sulu in evidence.

Where the devil had the helmsman gotten off to?

"Perhaps," Chekov said out loud to no one in particular, "he found some charming young woman to occupy his time. That vould be wery nice. Wery nice indeed."

Sulu's first thought upon coming to was that Chekov had gone just a bit too far, even for arranging an adventure.

His face ached a bit and he wanted to reach up and rub his throbbing forehead. He was unable to do so, however, because he realized very quickly that his hands were tied together behind him.

He sat in a chair, his hands anchored behind him as noted, his legs tied to the chair legs. Seated directly across from him, straddling the chair, was Rogers. His eyes narrowed as Sulu came around.

The room itself was nothing special: dark, probably because the windows were boarded over. A ceiling fan hung low but wasn't turning. There was a skylight above, caked with dust so that only a small bit of sunlight was able to filter through.

Out of the corner of his eye, Sulu caught brief movement nearby the edge of the room. Some sort of small vermin; a mouse, most likely. It darted out of sight behind a narrow black case that was propped up against the wall.

"Well well well," said Rogers in a purring, singsong voice. "Look who woke up. The hero."

Sulu said nothing; merely glared at him with intensity. Or at least with what he hoped passed for intensity.

"You won't get anything out of me," said Sulu.

Rogers smiled thinly and slid a razor-thin knife from the sleeve of his jacket. Placing the flat end gently against Sulu's throat, he murmured, "Oh, I expect we will. It'll probably be red, and warm, and go trickling down your throat and ruin that fine shirt of yours. Shame to see such an excellent shirt go to waste."

The door at the far end of the room opened and Taine walked in, Thor bringing up the rear. Thor closed the door behind them and remained there, massive arms folded.

"Thought you'd be coming around about now," said Taine. "You are most fortunate that Thor went lightly on you. I've seen him hit men with sufficient strength to make their bodies lonesome for their heads."

"As opposed to making them merely lonesome for intelligent conversation."

The comment didn't appear to register. "You *do* realize the level of trouble that you're in," said Taine. "We've done some quick checking on you. It appears, my dear fellows, that we have one Lieutenant Commander Sulu of Starfleet among us." He leaned forward, his face a question. "So tell me, Lieutenant Commander . . . what interest does Starfleet have in Ling Sui, eh? Oh, I forgot. Jade Eyes. What interest does Starfleet have in Jade Eyes?"

"None of your business," Sulu said, even as he filed away the name that Taine had just spoken. *Ling Sui.* A mildly musical name. An exotic name, even, for an exotic woman. No less a woman would do, of course. One couldn't have an adventure with a heroine who was a hausfrau from upstate New York or some other similarly unlikely location.

"Oh, I disagree, my dear L.C. Sulu. It's very much my business. So . . ." He leaned in closer to Sulu. "Are you here as part of Starfleet covert intelligence?"

"You expect me to tell you? You expect me to just spill to you whatever happens to be on my mind?" Sulu laughed disdainfully. "You really underestimate us, don't you."

Taine regarded him for a moment, stroking his chin thoughtfully. "L.C.," he said at last, "you are either incredibly brave or incredibly ignorant. If it is the former, then my problem is simple. I merely torture you until you break. And you will break, sir. Every man, no matter how brave, has his breaking point. We will find yours. You may turn out to be stronger than you think, or weaker than you think. It all depends on self-image, I suppose.

"If, however, it is the latter case—if you are incredibly ignorant—then the problem becomes that there is nothing you can tell me. I will not be prepared to believe that, however, until you are dead. By that point, of course, it will be too late. That would be a most unfortunate outcome for all concerned, but . . . what can one do? One has to work with the tools available to him, does he not?"

Sulu looked at him with a contemptuous glare. The smug look of confidence in Sulu's face was in no way an act. He had every certainty that he was in total control of the situation.

Taine shook his head sadly. "Very well. Have it your way, then. Rogers," and he snapped his fingers briskly.

Rogers nodded once in understanding and stepped out of the room.

"What will it be?" said Sulu defiantly. "Electric current? Mental scans? Mind probes?"

"Please, L.C. Have you no respect for your surroundings? For the ambience? No," said Taine, "we want to have respect for traditions here."

Sulu felt the source of warmth before he actually saw it. Rogers walked in briskly, using thick mitts to carry a glowing brazier. Rogers paused and tilted the brazier slightly for Sulu to see that it contained coals, gleaming a dull red.

"If I'd known we were having barbecue, I'd have brought a steak to toss on the grill," Sulu said wryly.

"Your wit is most appreciated, L.C. Sulu, if not your timing," replied Taine. He passed his hand over the coals and nodded once approvingly at the heat. "Another several minutes, I think, to make sure that they are as hot as possible. Do you have your tools, Rogers?"

Rogers nodded and walked toward the case Sulu had noticed earlier. He flipped the latches, opened it, and began to extract rods. The rods had points of different widths, and Rogers examined each of them as if he were trying to choose the appropriate golf club for a difficult shot.

"Rogers is particularly expert at these sorts of things," said Taine.

Sulu stifled a laugh. He wanted to play along as much as possible, but this was really pushing it. *Ambience?* These guys were going to use primitive torture techniques because they were concerned about ambience? How ridiculous could one get?

"So . . . tell me your plan," said Sulu.

Taine looked at him askance. "I beg your pardon? Are you under the impression that *we* are here to answer *your* questions?"

"Oh, but that's usually how these things work, isn't it," Sulu said confidently. "I, the hero, am tied up and helpless. You, the smug and stupid villains, believing that I'm finished, proceed to tell me my entire insidious plan."

The three captors looked at each other, then back at Sulu. Rogers laughed out loud at that point, and Thor glowered. Taine, for his part, merely stared at Sulu with undisguised pity.

"You've seen too many old movies," Taine said sadly. "You really *are* a fool. Ah well. No concern of mine, really."

Sulu paused a moment, the wheels turning. "Ohhh, *I* see. You're going to walk out of here, secure that Rogers will extract information from me . . . and then, with the odds more even, I'll manage to break free from this chair and overwhelm him."

"No," said Taine, leaning back against a wall, his arms folded across his chest. "We're not going anywhere. We have people watching the exits from the city. Ling Sui can't get away. Nor can you, although your situation is a bit more dire than hers at the moment."

"Then in that case," said Sulu, "there's only one answer left in this little dance: a daring last-minute rescue."

Thor was beginning to look rather impatient. Rogers had his rods heating to a blazing red against the coals. Taine seemed genuinely confused.

"Lieutenant Commander," he said, "you seem to be under the impression that this is a game. That it's an artifice of some sort. Is that truly your belief?"

"He's just trying to make us think he's an idiot," Rogers commented dismissively.

"Well, he's succeeding admirably. L.C. Sulu . . . you are genuinely in trouble here. There will be no last-minute rescue. There will be no extended discourse from us, giving you the key pieces of information you require. We are going to do you bodily harm until you tell us what we want to know, or we will kill you . . . or both. Any other outcome is purely in your imagination."

Sulu smiled grimly. He had to give them credit: They were damned effective. Particularly Taine, the Asian. He was going all out to give the proceedings an air of genuine menace. If Sulu hadn't been so certain of his true status, he might actually have begun to get worried.

"Quieting down," noted Taine. "Going for stoicism? Inscrutability, perhaps? Well, we'll attend to that. Rogers?"

"Ready," said Rogers, standing over the heated brazier. With his thick gloves, he removed one of the rods. Sulu noted with mild interest that the tip was glowing red. Smoke was pouring from it.

"At your convenience, Rogers," said Taine, gesturing toward the bound Starfleet officer.

Rogers approached slowly, savoring the moment. Sulu watched confidently, waiting for the last-minute rescue. Knowing that salvation would be imminent. Any second now there would be the whine of phaser blasts, or the crashing in through the skylight.

(Rogers drew closer.)

Something to stave off doom because, in situations like this, the hero never *really* got maimed. Was never *really* put through some grueling, hideous . . .

(The broiling point of the rod was closer still. . . .)

. . . ordeal, such as having heated metal stroked across the skin, searing it, blackening it, causing it to peel back and away while the hero screamed for mercy . . .

(He could feel the heat, the intensity, and he saw the total lack of pity in Rogers' eyes.)

And just for a moment, Sulu's confidence slipped.

He started to pull, yanking at his bonds, but they were too tight. All he managed to do was cut off circulation to his hands.

His abrupt signs of struggle brought Rogers to a momentary halt, before he chuckled and started to advance.

"Feeling a bit nervous?" asked Taine silkily. "Suddenly realizing you're overdue for a rescue?"

That was, indeed, precisely what Sulu was realizing. He pulled more furiously at his bonds, but they simply drew tighter as the rod drew closer.

"Now," said Taine, "tell us what you know."

The air seemed to shimmer from the heat directly in Sulu's eyes.

Taine repeated, caressing each word, "Tell us . . . what . . . you know."

Sulu licked his lips briefly and then said, *"Heading* is a mathematical expression describing a direction with relationship to the center of the galaxy. A heading is composed of two numbers, measuring an azimuth value and an elevation value in degrees. A heading of zero zero zero, mark zero, describes a direction toward the geometric center of the galaxy."

Rogers and Taine exchanged confused glances.

Sulu didn't slow down. "In terms of navigation on a planet's surface, this is analogous to describing a direction in degrees from north, in which case a course of five degrees—"

"What are you doing?"

"—would be slightly to the right of a direction directly toward the planet's north pole. A heading differs from a bearing in that it has no relationship to the current attitude or orientation of the spacecraft."

There was a pause, and Taine and Rogers thought Sulu was finished.

He was just catching his breath.

"Now *bearing,* by contrast, describes a direction in space with relationship to a space vehicle. A bearing measures the angular difference between the current forward direction of the spacecra—"

"Shut up!" Thor roared from across the room. It was the first thing he'd said since Sulu had had the misfortune to encounter him. Sulu had begun to assume he was mute.

"What is the purpose of this, L.C.?" asked a befuddled Taine.

"You said I should tell you what I know," said Sulu. "Would you like me to move on to fencing techniques? Fun facts about botany? Old Earth firearms, perhaps."

Taine regarded him for a long moment.

"Oh, to hell with this," he said finally. He turned to Rogers. "Kill him. Slow, fast, I don't care. Just kill him."

Chapter Seven

ROGERS NODDED, perfectly happy about the instruction. He turned toward Sulu, swung back the rod, and brought it around in a baseball-bat-type arc.

Sulu managed to push off, sending the chair tilting backward, and he slammed to the ground as the heated rod swished over his head, barely missing him.

"Don't dance with him," said Taine in genuine irritation.

Rogers grimaced with annoyance as he strode forward. Sulu was still helpless, tied to the chair, and Rogers gripped the rod with both hands and prepared to bring it slamming down squarely into Sulu's chest.

And it was at that precise moment that the skylight smashed inward.

Sulu's captors looked upward in confusion just in time to see a small, round device plunge from overhead. It struck the ground and exploded, and in that instant everything went completely black.

Sulu had no idea what was going on. Actually, that wasn't true strictly speaking. His faith in his situation had been confirmed. It was, in fact, a last-minute rescue. They'd really had him going there for a minute, but now he knew beyond doubt that this was all an elaborate hoax staged by Chekov.

What he didn't know was who was staging the rescue, or how it was being done.

He heard yelling from the trio of captors, but they were as blind as he. He heard people slamming into each other, the sounds of tripping or falling bodies.

And then there were hands pulling at his bonds. A quick, sharp tug and then they came free. "Who's there?" he whispered.

"Be quiet and you'll live," hissed back a female voice. He recognized it instantly. It was Ling Sui.

There was a tugging at the ropes binding his right leg. By the time he had pulled it loose she'd already cut through the one on his left. She pulled at his arm and said, "Come on!"

"She's in here!" came an angry voice, clearly belonging to Taine. "Find her!"

"Here!" came her fierce whisper to Sulu, and she was shoving something onto his face. Instantly the room glowed with a dim red light and he was able to see.

Clearly she had made use of a blackout bomb, plunging the room into total blackout by disrupting all the visible wavelengths in the room. But the special goggles enabled the wearers to discern their surroundings.

He saw the three men staggering about in the darkness. Rogers was waving one of the heated rods, and the metal brushed against Thor's right arm. Thor spun with a yelp of indignation and swept his arm around, tagging Rogers squarely on the head. Rogers went down, the metal rod clattering to the floor.

"Let's go," grunted Ling. She wrapped fingers around his forearm. It was like having one's arm in a vise; her grip was that strong. Then abruptly Sulu was yanked into the air. He felt a surge of power that seemed to be coming from the vicinity of her feet. And then the next thing he knew they were up and through the skylight.

They landed on the roof and Sulu looked around quickly, trying to get his bearings. Although he and Chekov had been in the city for several days, they hadn't even begun to cover all the sections. It was, after all, situated on twenty-three square miles of land. Other roofs spread out around them like a vast field of black tar, buildings clustered closely together.

Ling Sui was, naturally, dressed entirely in black. Actually, not entirely. She was wearing a thin green choker with a small locket on it. Her brow was covered with a thin line of sweat, but otherwise she looked unhurried and unperturbed. There was, however, an intensity about her. A sense that she was completely and utterly in charge of the situation. She yanked off her goggles, and stretched out a hand for Sulu's. He handed them over and she shoved them into a small knapsack attached to her belt.

"Where are we?" he asked.

"Thieves Quarter," she replied.

"Of course." He looked down at her feet. "Nice antigrav boots."

"The power cells are low. Come on."

Even though the boots could be somewhat clumsy when the antigrav field wasn't in use, they didn't seem to slow her down as she ran across the flat roof. Either that, Sulu realized, or else she was even more fleet of foot when she wasn't wearing them.

Sulu ran quickly after her, no slouch in the speed department himself. She afforded him a quick, approving glance and then together they leaped over the gap separating the rooftop they were on from the next.

Sulu paused to catch his breath, but Ling didn't slow. "Come on," she urged once more. He started to follow her . . .

. . . and a disruptor blast sliced just above his head.

The smell of burnt ions hung in the air as Sulu and Ling went flat on their bellies. From street level they heard the angered shouts of voices which Sulu knew instantly belonged to their pursuers.

"Stay low!" she said and started to run. Sulu followed her, thinking to himself, *So much for ambience.*

The air crackled again, this time mere inches to Sulu's right. They were managing to close on the targets. Sulu and Ling got to a roof edge and barely ducked back in time as a disruptor blast ripped up from the street. Sulu didn't even have time to see who was wielding the weapon; it was all he could do to get out of the way.

Ling turned to him. "You have to trust me," she said tightly.

"You can't be serious."

"Deadly serious."

"Well, when you put it that way," he said, trying to sound casual.

She pulled him to her. "Hold on as tightly as you can," she said.

He did so. Her body was small and compact, but remarkably muscled for what was there. He tried not to smile as he gripped her. "When do we start the deadly part?" he asked.

There was a door that opened onto the roof behind them. It burst open and Taine was standing there. He yanked out a disruptor and screeched in inarticulate rage.

"Now," she replied, and kicked the antigrav boots into overdrive. The boots roared to life and drove them forward, arcing over the rooftops like a pair of missiles. Taine fired and missed. From the street below, more blasts ripped upward, but none of them managed to nail the fast-moving forms of Sulu and Ling.

The rooftops hurled past them at dizzying speed. It was an odd sensation for Sulu. Compared to moving at warp speed, this was a crawl. And yet he felt as if he'd never traveled quite as fast in his life. The outraged invective pouring from the mouths of their pursuers was left far behind.

Then something shuddered beneath them. Sulu had only a moment to realize that it was the gravity boots beginning to give out.

"Warned you" was all Ling said as their momentum carried them forward a short distance before they arced downward, the street coming toward them at dizzying speed.

This is going to hurt, thought Sulu as he saw they were angling straight toward a building.

His helmsman instincts kicked in, and he threw his weight to one side, hauling Ling with him. They banked sharply to the left, missing the building by centimeters. They hurtled down an alleyway, almost hitting the building on the opposing side. Sulu kicked out like a diver, striking the wall squarely with his feet and propelling them back in the other direction and then down.

They crashed into laundry.

It was hanging suspended between the two buildings, large blankets and comforters flapping in the breeze. *How convenient* crossed Sulu's mind before the dangling laundry encompassed them. It momentarily blinded them, but it also helped save them from serious harm as they hit the ground and skidded the length of the alley. They slowed to a halt inches away from the alley's dead end. For a moment neither of them said anything as they just lay there, recovering their breath.

"Just for the record," he finally managed to get out, "I'm Hikaru Sulu."

From somewhere within the folds of the blanket, she replied, "Ling Sui. Charmed."

He pulled the blanket off their heads and looked into her face. He was surprised—and yet, not entirely so—to see that there was laughter in her eyes.

"You realize," he said, "that we're simply going to *have* to get married."

She tilted her head slightly, regarding him with bemusement. "How do you figure that?"

"Because it would be worth it just so we could tell our children how we met."

She laughed incredulously. "You are really quite a unique individual. You seem to take all of this," and she gestured vaguely, "this . . . strangeness . . . very much in stride."

It helps that I've seen through the deception, he thought, but he simply said, "In my line of work . . . one is not easily rattled."

"Indeed. Let's discuss lines of work . . . someplace where we won't be shot at."

They got to their feet, dusted themselves off, but at the same time never quite took their eyes off each other. She continued to stare at him as if not quite believing that he was there.

Sulu, for his part, was amazed. Obviously this was not something that Chekov had simply thrown together. This woman and the others . . . they were pros. Pros up and down the line. It would have been so easy for him to be sucked into the exquisite unreality of it all.

Fortunately enough, he was far too smart for that.

Chapter Eight

CHEKOV WAS BEGINNING to get worried.

It was now getting on evening, and Sulu had been a no-show. Perhaps there had been some sort of screwup. Some sort of miscommunication that had resulted in Sulu waiting for him at another restaurant. Chekov wished that they had their *Enterprise* communicators with them. Then it would simply be a matter of flipping his open and asking Sulu where the devil he was.

But they didn't have their communicators, so clearly that wasn't an option.

He stepped out onto the veranda and drummed apprehensively on the railing. He saw tourists going about their business, the various inhabitants into their usual routines. For the first time the artificiality of it all crept through to him. None of it mattered. None of it was real. What was real was the fact that his friend was absent, and he had absolutely no idea why.

Well, enough was enough. It was time to contact the authorities. Chekov had been reluctant to, for fear of looking like a total fool if he sounded an alert and it only turned out that Sulu was out somewhere having a good time. But he saw no choice at this point.

At that moment, the comm screen inset into the wall (one of the few allowances made in the room for modern conveniences) bleeped at him. Chekov quickly went to it and toggled the On Line switch.

Sulu's smiling face appeared on the screen.

"I vas vondering!" said Chekov in exasperation.

"Oh . . . I just bet you were," Sulu replied.

It seemed an odd response for a man who had vanished for the better part of a day.

"I'm on to you, Chekov," Sulu continued. "Admit it."

Chekov blinked. *On* to him? On to what? Did he mean that he knew Chekov had been concerned about his absence? Well, of course, that was self-evident. "I admit it freely," Chekov said, trying not to look as confused as he felt.

"I knew it," said Sulu triumphantly. He leaned forward and said conspiratorially, "I have to admit, I'm impressed. I knew you wanted to sell me on this place . . . but I never thought you'd go to all this trouble."

"No trouble at all," Chekov said reasonably.

"And *she* is quite remarkable."

Again, Chekov blinked. *"She* is?"

"You don't have to sound so surprised," said Sulu. "I should have had faith in your judgment."

"That's always a good thing to have," Chekov nodded, still feeling as if he were in the midst of another conversation entirely. One thing was clear: Sulu had found female companionship. It was, of course, a possibility that they had both discussed before arrival, and each had mutually agreed to give the other as much room as required to do justice to that situation. "Uhm, Sulu . . . where are you now?"

"Her place," said Sulu. He lowered his voice still further. "She's registered here under an assumed name. I could have guessed that, I suppose."

"I suppose," agreed Chekov. "Do you vish to stay vith her for a bit?"

Sulu looked slightly guilty. "It . . . *would* be pleasant. If that's all right with you."

"Pffff," Chekov made a dismissive noise. "Vatever you vish. You are . . . sure you're all right?"

"Well, there were some close calls in there. But that's part of what makes it all so interesting. After all, isn't that what the captain once said? 'Risk is our business.' I'll be in touch. And Chekov . . . thanks again."

"You're velcome," he said grandly. "No thanks necessary."

The picture blinked out, leaving Chekov grinning. Indeed, no thanks *had* been necessary. Sulu, that lucky dog, had found a fetching companion. He hardly needed Chekov's blessing or permission to pursue her.

He, Chekov, should be so lucky.

Ling Sui sat on a rattan chair, regarding Sulu in amazement as he looked around the room. It was small and dark, because Ling had the shades drawn.

"We'll be safe here," she said, never taking her eyes off him. Then she gestured for him to come over, which he did. One of her long legs was crossed casually over the other. She pointed downward. "Kneel," she said.

He eyed her with level gaze.

"Stand," he replied.

She smiled in amusement. "All right," she said, and rose, propping herself up on one knee. "Turn around, at least." From the folds of her garments she had pulled a small device that looked somewhat like a small electronic tuning fork.

He did so, wondering what was going on. He felt her brush the edge of the tuning fork along the back of his shirt. It gave off a faint humming noise. Then, when she reached a point just around the area of his right shoulder blade, the noise jumped slightly. Apparently it had located whatever it was she was looking for. "Hold still, please," she said. "Okay. Got it."

"Got what?" he asked, turning to face her. "The secret formula? The hush-hush plans?"

"Something like that."

"On some sort of microminiature data chip."

"Good guess."

"May I ask what it was doing on my back?"

She seemed to be weighing the option of bald-facedly lying to him before dismissing the idea. "I put it there," she said matter-of-factly. "When I bumped into you in the street. I knew they were after me, and in the event they caught up with me, I didn't want to be in possession of it. You should have been in no danger at all. And I knew I could always use this," and she held up the tuning-fork device again, "to track you down and retrieve it. I didn't expect you to try and come riding to my rescue."

"I saw those goons chasing you," said Sulu at his most gallant. "I'm not the type to just stand aside and let a woman be harassed."

"I know that *now*," she informed him. She tossed her head slightly to keep her long hair out of her face. She'd done it once or twice since they'd first gotten to the room. Obviously it was a bit of a nervous habit, although he had no idea what she had to be nervous about. She was an absolutely brilliant actress, virtually radiating charisma. She had down cold the part of the daring mysterious heroine. She was exciting and vibrant . . . everything that one could wish for in a mystery woman. Sulu felt himself falling in love with her already . . . except it probably wasn't really a matter of being in love with her, but rather with what she represented. Adventure. Intrigue. When involved with a female like this, any second could herald a new escapade. Just like involvement with another female . . . one named *Enterprise*.

"I know you, don't I," she said after a long moment. "The name was familiar. Hikaru Sulu. From Starfleet, correct?"

He wasn't surprised, of course. Chekov would have given her all the information she needed. Still, he was interested in the rationalization. "That's right. May I ask how—?"

"Oh, there are some people whose careers I've been following somewhat closely. A bit of a hobby of mine. Comes from my own abortive attempt at a career in Starfleet."

"You?" he said with raised eyebrow. "What happened?"

"It . . . wasn't for me. I'm not terribly good at following orders. Too much of an independent thinker." She paused and then added, with amusement, "No offense meant."

"None taken." He allowed himself to preen slightly. "If you have any questions about Starfleet . . . about the *Enterprise* . . . I'd be happy to . . ."

"Well, actually, I do."

He stood with folded arms, waiting.

With an expression of intense curiosity, she leaned forward and asked, "What's Captain Kirk really like?"

Sulu felt like a deflated balloon. *You told her to say that, didn't you, Chekov. I'll get you for that one, my friend.*

"Yes, well," and he cleared his throat. "He's . . . well, what can you say about someone in whom you'd trust your life implicitly? What higher compliment can you give someone than that? If I ever get command of a starship, and I'm half the commander that James Kirk is . . . I'll be satisfied."

She studied him appraisingly. "I don't believe that," she said flatly, challenge in her eyes. "That would be 'settling.' I can't see you as being the type of man who would settle for anything."

"And you? What type of woman are you?"

"Do you really want to know?" she asked challengingly.

He thought about it a moment, and then shook his head. "No. What sort of mystery woman would you be if I knew too much about you? All that matters is where we go from here, and what you owe me."

Her gaze was steel. "You risked your life, and it was a stupid thing to do. And I had to risk my life to bail you out. If you hadn't decided to be heroic, neither of us would have been in that fix. So what, precisely, do I owe you?"

He stepped forward, "invading" her personal space. She didn't flinch, didn't back up so much as a millimeter. Her green eyes glittered, reminding Sulu of nothing so much as a cat.

"Fifty percent," he said. "We're partners now."

It was hard for him to read precisely what was going through her mind: Anger? Astonishment? Amusement? A tension, caused by . . . what?

"What did you say?" she asked in slow, measured tones.

Slowly he brought his lips to her right ear and whispered, "I said . . . we're partners now."

She pirouetted away from him with a grace that indicated she had dancer's legs. With undisguised amazement she said, "May I ask how you figure that?"

"Simple. As of this point, this little operation of yours continues purely at my whim. I could shut the whole thing down with one well-placed call. But I'm not going to do that . . . provided I'm a partner."

"Who do you think you are, Sulu? You're Starfleet, not a law-enforcement official."

"True enough," replied Sulu. "But I have reason to believe that the property you're dealing in has interplanetary, even galactic, ramifications. That makes it Starfleet business."

"And what reason do you have to believe that?"

"I'm suspicious by nature. That's good enough."

Her mouth was so thin as to be almost invisible. And yet those eyes, those gorgeous green eyes, seemed more intrigued than angry.

"Fifty percent, Ling Sui," he said. "That's a considerable bargain. An alliance with a Starfleet officer. Certainly that would be fairly handy in your line of business . . . that is, whatever business you might be involved with at any given time."

"It would," she admitted. She gave the matter some consideration, playing her "part" to the hilt. "Twenty percent," she said finally.

"You wish to insult me now, is that it? Fifty percent."

"Thirty."

"Sixty."

She blinked in surprise. "It's not quite supposed to work that way, Sulu. I go higher, you go lower, and we meet somewhere in between. If I, for example, offer forty, you should counter with . . ."

"Seventy," he said with absolute deadpan.

She let out a long sigh. "All right. Fifty."

He scratched the underside of his chin thoughtfully. "Oh, all right," he said finally. "You talked me into fifty."

"Which is where you started."

"Is it?" he said, looking at her with feigned innocence.

She shook her head. "Of course, I still have to deal with one problem. Namely: I have no reason to trust you."

"I risked my life to help a woman I didn't even know. Just imagine what I can do when I actually have personal involvement."

She eyed him thoughtfully. "Ahh. And just how 'personal' did you envision our association getting?"

"My dear woman," he said, drawing himself up. "I am, in every respect, a gentleman."

"Is that so?" she asked. She ran a finger lazily along the line of his jaw, and he felt a sensation as if she were running a live wire across his skin. "Pity. But then, I knew you had to have a drawback *some*where."

Chapter Nine

THE SHADOWS were growing long in the southwest corner of the Thieves Quarter. There were not too many people on the streets, what with most folks hustling to dinner appointments. Besides which, the Thieves Quarter was not the most crowded of areas even during the busiest times. It was, after all, where only the most adventurous of folks chose to go. Anything and everything could happen in the Thieves Quarter, and even though it was all a show, it was most definitely not for the faint of heart.

Sulu and Ling Sui stuck to the shadows, which was easy since they were fairly copious. Ling Sui craned her neck, peering around a corner and then ducking back.

"Any sign of your contact man?" asked Sulu.

"Not yet."

"Is he dependable?"

"I've worked with him before. His name is Kelles. His strength is, he's good. His weakness is, he knows he's good."

"And he's your buyer?"

"Of course not. He's representing them."

"Do you trust him?"

She glanced at him. "My, you're full of questions. Will I work with him? Yes. We'll be making the exchange right here. I give him the information, and the credit transfer will be made immediately thereafter.

"But will I trust him? No, of course not. I don't trust anyone."

"Not even me?" asked Sulu with a mock look of hurt on his face.

But Ling Sui did not smile. "Trust you?" she said flatly. "You? A Starfleet officer out to turn a profit? Allying himself with some strange woman dealing in some sort of nefarious who-knows-what? Sulu . . . let's be honest with one another, all right? I tend to react to people on a gut level. And on that level, I find you handsome . . . brave . . . perhaps someone who even fancies himself a bit of a lady's man . . . with a charming sense of chivalry and an overdeveloped sense of being a swashbuckler. If these were calmer times I would be very taken with the idea of seeing you socially. And if I happened to discover you in my bed, I doubt I would kick you out."

"That's . . . honest," said Sulu, surprised that his voice suddenly sounded a bit hoarse.

"But *trust?*" she continued. "No, trust you, I don't. I would be crazy to. I won't turn my back on you, nor take my eyes off you. And I fully expect you to treat me in the same manner; and if you don't, you're a fool."

"I see," he said evenly. "Now shall I be honest with you?"

"Don't bother," she informed him. "Since I don't trust you, then obviously it doesn't matter what you say since I have no reason to assume you're being honest with me. Q.E.D. Besides," and she inclined her chin slightly, "unless I'm mistaken, here comes Kelles."

It was not at all what Sulu was expecting. The vehicles that he'd seen in the city had mostly been period vehicles. Not this. This was a very impressive antigrav craft: a three-man shuttle, the type designed for inner-city use in that it didn't travel more than a few feet off the ground. After all, not everyone was licensed to maneuver the higher flying shuttles. Anarchy in the skyways would be the result; it had in years past when technology had briefly outstripped humanity's ability to regulate it. The legendary two-thousand-car pileup in San Diego remained a testimony to those dangers.

The shuttle's burnished exterior was sleek, almost looking like the head and beak of a bird of prey. Sulu recognized this particular model: Despite its street-level uses, it was called a Peregrine, after the falcon. The heavy-duty front windows were smoked, insuring privacy.

The Peregrine slid to a halt mere feet away from Sulu and Ling Sui. It hovered there a moment, then settled to the ground. The side door swung open with a sigh of air, and a tall, heavyset black man stepped out. He wore a battered brown hat pulled down low over his face, a white shirt with brown vest, and loose-fitting slacks. His black boots were thick with dust and looked as if they hadn't been polished for months.

"Kelles!" hissed Ling Sui.

Kelles looked toward Sulu and Ling in almost leisurely fashion. "You're early," he said. His voice was very low, and yet it seemed to carry.

"What kind of vehicle is that?" she demanded. "You're the one who always told me to be subtle. You're getting sloppy in your old age."

"Sloppy?" said Kelles, looking offended. "It's reverse psychology, girl. Drive something conspicuous; that way the enemy doesn't notice you because they figure you wouldn't be that stupid."

Ling looked dubious.

Kelles, in the meantime, was looking Sulu up and down. "Who's your friend?" he asked, the question addressed to her, the attention paid to him.

"Doesn't matter."

"It does to me," said Kelles. There was a quiet danger in his voice.

Sulu wondered how this new arrival fit into the grand scheme of things. There seemed to be only one truly logical answer. This fellow, Kelles, was going to be the means through which the whole charade finally ended. Ling would give him whatever it was she has allegedly stolen. He would pay her off. Maybe there would even be one final close call or two. And then it would be over. Ling would say something appropriately mysterious, vanish into the back alleys of the Thieves Quarter, and that would be that.

It was hard for Sulu to believe that it had all happened in one day. He had to admit that when Chekov organized something, he really pulled out all the stops.

"He's my new partner. Look, let's discuss this later," said Ling impatiently. "For all we know, you were followed."

Kelles gave her an incredulous stare. "No one followed me, Ling. That, I promise you. Now, where is it?"

She had a bag strapped around her waist. She started to reach for it.

And for no reason that Sulu immediately understood, his own words suddenly floated through his head. Words describing what it was like to helm the *Enterprise,* that sense of perpetual anticipation . . .

At any second, anything could happen . . .

Kelles's head exploded.

Sulu wasn't prepared for it, of course. After all, everything seemed to be going perfectly normally. It was only seconds later that the whine of the disruptor that had gunned down Kelles made itself heard. It was an angry sound, like hornets massing.

For a moment, just for a moment, it seemed to Sulu that he could perceive everything simultaneously. He saw his own jacket, with the blood from Kelles staining the front. He saw Kelles's body in motion, still in the process of falling to the ground. He saw Ling Sui's horrified expression, the blood draining from her face. He even saw the shooter, on a rooftop overhead, bringing his disruptor to bear. He saw the door still open to the Peregrine.

His course was laid in. All he had to do was keep her moving.

Before Kelles's body hit the ground, Sulu grabbed Ling by the wrist and yanked her toward the Peregrine. Another disruptor blast roared over his head. Close shot off the bow. It was a clean miss, though. *Ignore it. Stay on course.*

He practically threw her into the shuttle, leaping in behind her. The shuttle rocked slightly beneath his feet. He took in the controls at a glance. He'd never operated this particular model of shuttle in his life. It didn't matter. One look and he instantly knew how to operate it.

He leaped into the driver's seat, his fingers flying over the controls. "Belt in!" he shouted as the shuttle roared to life. The vehicle started to lurch forward . . .

. . . and someone shoved his way in through the still-open door.

Sulu's head snapped around in alarm. It was a man that Sulu hadn't seen before; he was roughly the size of a small mountain. He hadn't quite gotten his footing yet because of the vehicle's movement.

Ling Sui braced herself, gripping one of the two remaining seats firmly. She swung her legs forward, slamming them into the chest of the newcomer. He staggered, his arms pinwheeling, and Ling released her hold on the seat. She leaped through the air, spinning like a black-clad top, and slammed a spin kick to the side of the newcomer's head. He grunted once, which was the only sound he made during the entire encounter, and then fell backward out of the shuttle. The ground beneath the vehicle was moving faster and faster, and he tumbled out and away.

The entire encounter had taken no more than a couple of seconds. Sulu, who had instant mastery over the steering and operation of the Peregrine's engines, had taken a moment or two more to locate something as simple as the mechanism for closing the shuttle's door. But he found it now, activated it, and the door swung shut with a hiss.

The Peregrine shuddered as something struck in a concentrated blast. Sulu recognized it immediately for what it was: a disruptor, being shot directly at the vehicle. Fortunately enough for them, handheld disruptors—while devastating against human bodies—were less so against heavy-duty inanimate objects such as shuttles.

Pedestrians scrambled to get out of the way as the Peregrine roared down the main street. Sulu quickly glanced at the exterior monitors, surveying the area around them. Then he afforded a quick glance at Ling Sui. She was staring resolutely straight ahead, finishing the process of belting herself in to her chair. Her face was slightly flushed, but otherwise she had composed herself very quickly.

For Sulu, it wasn't quite that simple.

He had leaped to a conclusion the moment that Kelles's head had exploded onto him. But it was not one that he had fully assimilated until just this moment as he scrutinized Ling Sui.

"That man was dead. Really dead."

"I know," said Ling Sui tightly. "Damn him, I warned him. *Warned* him." In anger she slapped the control board in front of her. "He got too damned self-confident. Even so, he deserved better than that."

"Really dead."

She looked at him with mild confusion. "Not to sound insensitive, but you must have encountered the occasional corpse before."

"But I thought this was all a—"

But then he stopped talking as he noticed something on the monitors. "Oh, no," he said.

"What?" She leaned over to see what had elicited his worried comment.

There were pursuers. Four of them, clinging fiercely to high-speed stratopods. They were small, one-man, high-speed vehicles, oblong in shape. Sulu had had one in his youth. He'd been fairly adept at steering it, and knew how maneuverable they were. Far more maneuverable than a Peregrine inner-city shuttlecraft.

For a moment he thought that perhaps they were the authorities. That being the case, Sulu would immediately bring the Peregrine to a halt, get out and explain the situation. . . .

Although that was somewhat problematic. Explain the situation and say what, precisely? That his female companion was involved in some sort of shady dealing? That he was involved as well, except he'd thought it was an elaborate setup?

It quickly became moot, however, because Sulu suddenly recognized one of their pursuers as the gunman from the rooftop who had, only moments ago, redecorated the front of Sulu's jacket.

All around them, people were scrambling to get out of the way. Some weren't fast enough, knocked aside by the stratopods. The drivers of those small vehicles clearly weren't concerned about whatever damage they might do. If matters continued in the current way, civilians were going to be injured, even killed. This was an intolerable situation.

In the depths of space, Sulu had instrumentation to tell him where he was and where he was heading. That, however, really served as little more than backup to his own innate ability to determine such things. With the briefest of glances at star groupings, Sulu could easily locate himself and the *Enterprise* in relation to all the many systems that he carried around in his head.

So determining where he was now in relation to the rest of the city was, comparatively, child's play.

A map of the city sprang into his mind, and he immediately "saw" where he was relative to the rest of the environs. He also quickly determined his only option.

"Hold on!" shouted Sulu.

Ling Sui did so, gripping firmly the sides of her chair even though she was belted in.

Sulu cut hard left. The Peregrine angled sharply, its rear swinging around and slamming against the corner of a building before the shuttle continued on its way. The stratopod drivers course-corrected instantly and maintained pursuit, but without managing to close the distance.

"Where are we going?" demanded Ling Sui.

Sulu replied with an inclination of his head. Ling Sui looked ahead of them and gasped.

Large entrance gates to the city of Demora loomed squarely in front of them. They were several stories tall and made of synthetic wood. They were more than adequate to repel the attacks from fake desert raiders.

Whether they could, however, withstand a direct hit from a fast-moving shuttle was another question. Ling Sui was somewhat appalled to discover that they were going to get the answer firsthand.

"Are you *crazy?!*" she demanded.

"We've got no choice," he shot back. "I'm not putting innocent people at risk."

"What about *us?*"

"We're already at risk! Brace yourself!"

One moment the gate seemed to be at a great distance, and the next they were on top of it. Sulu had a brief glimpse of people trying to wave him off, and then they were clearing the hell out of the way.

Sulu resisted the reflex to slow down and instead sped up even more. The Peregrine smashed through the gate, synthetic wood shattering under the impact with an earsplitting crack. The shuttle roared forward and out into the desert.

The stratopods, not slowing, kept in tight pursuit.

Chapter Ten

SULU SHOVED THE PEREGRINE to its maximum speed, hoping that, whatever that might be, it would be faster than their pursuers. Ling Sui had lapsed into silence. She was, however, gripping the armrests so tightly that her knuckles were dead white. She stared resolutely out the smoked front windshield, watching the ground race past them at dizzying speed.

"Don't worry," said Sulu confidently. "This is a lot smaller and a lot slower than a starship. If I could helm that, I can certainly handle this."

"I think you should know," she said slowly, "that I have a fear of moving at high velocity."

"No reason to be concerned about going fast," he told her.

"I know, I know. It's the abrupt stops that should concern me."

"Exactly."

It was odd. With all the insane events in the past hours (again, it was hard to believe that it had all happened so quickly) he had remained confident. It was a confidence built on an incorrect belief on his part . . . a belief that he had nothing to worry about, because all the jeopardy was manufactured.

Yet now that he knew, beyond any doubt, that the danger was real—that his life and that of his companion were at risk—he felt no less confident. Because he was at the helm. He had his steady hand managing his fate, and he had utter belief in his ability to be master of his own destiny.

He had the conn, and when that was the case he knew he could certainly steer the ship to safety.

There was a heavy impact against the side of the shuttle, and the vessel rocked slightly under it. Sulu glanced at his monitors and, sure enough, the stratopods were closing. He could see the four pilots crouched, strapped in, controlling their trajectory with one hand and gripping disruptor guns in the other.

The city of Demora had already been left far behind. In front of them stretched endless vistas of the desert—unchanged, unspoiled. The Peregrine hugged the curve of the land as it swooped and dove, shooting up one sand dune, hurtling down another. The stabilizers kept the shuttle relatively even, but the sensation of forward motion was steady and, in Ling's case, apparently somewhat daunting. Despite the peril they were in, Sulu found it a bit amusing that this capable, resourceful, and intelligent woman had a bit of a weakness. It made her seem more accessible somehow.

The stratopods were closing and the riders fired again and again. The collective barrage was starting to take its toll. The last couple of hits caused the Peregrine to buck under Sulu's steady hand, and the helmsman came to the realization that simply moving wasn't going to be enough. He was going to have to attack somehow.

The thought of possible loss of life wasn't of major concern to him. Certainly he had launched enough photon torpedos, targeted enough phasers, so that the prospect of having to kill an opponent was not a daunting one. It was a necessary evil, but if it was a question of who was going to survive, then as far as Sulu was concerned it was no question at all.

The only problem was that the Peregrine had no weapons. Nor was Sulu himself armed. Nor was . . .

He looked at Ling. "Do you have a weapon on you?"

"I wish."

Okay. So much for that.

She looked at the monitor. "Here they come."

They were coming in a two-by-two formation, moving faster than Sulu would have thought possible. His first instinct was to activate deflectors. His second was to open fire. He had to remind himself that neither option was viable.

"All right," he said. "I suppose we're going to have to get innovative."

There was something in his voice that prompted her to glance at him. She saw where his hand was hovering. "Excuse me . . . that's the door," she said, trying not to sound patronizing.

"I'm aware of that," he said. There was one good thing about maneuvering through the desert; there were even fewer obstacles than steering through space. He watched the monitor steadily, gauging the speed of their approach. Closer they were coming, and closer, and still his right hand remained poised unflinchingly over the door button. One could have balanced a glass filled with wine on the back of his hand, and there wouldn't have been so much as a ripple in the surface of the drink.

They were drawing up right alongside the speeding shuttle. With any luck, that would prove to be a tactical error.

"Just keep steady," he said under his breath to the pursuers, although naturally they couldn't hear him. "Three . . . two . . . one . . ."

He activated the door.

Obediently it swung upward, slamming into the stratopod driver who had, at that very moment, pulled alongside the Peregrine. It slammed him to the side and he lost control of his vehicle, the gyros smashed by the impact of the door. On the monitor Sulu had a brief glimpse of his face, twisting in a soundless shriek, and he recognized him as the man who'd been on the roof. The stratopod spiraled and then hit the ground, shattering and turning from a vehicle into a twisted mesh of metal. By the time it stopped rolling, the shuttle was long gone and Sulu was already concentrating on the other three.

He had already slammed the door shut again, reasoning that there was no way they were going to fall for such a stratagem again.

They were straddling the shuttle, pacing him on either side (although the fellow on the right, as Sulu had surmised, was keeping back from the door).

"Hold on," Sulu told Ling again. This time she didn't utter any word of protest, made no snide comment. Instead she simply nodded, and a smile had crept across her face. She seemed in the process of reassessing him.

The Peregrine lurched wildly from side to side as Sulu tried to send the shuttle slamming into the pursuers. He clipped one, but the operator recovered with more adroitness than the one whom Sulu had already managed to dispose of.

Sulu wished desperately that the Peregrine could go at a higher altitude, but it simply wasn't designed to maneuver that way. It had to be within a few feet of ground for the antigrav to function properly.

There was the shriek of weapons fire again, and this time the wall right nearby Sulu's head dented. He snapped his head back reflexively and cast the wall a worried look.

"All right," he said. "This is going to be tricky. I hope you don't get dizzy easily."

"What do you mean by th—?"

She didn't have time to finish the question, nor was it necessary. Sulu quickly demonstrated precisely what he meant.

He sent the Peregrine into a spin. The shuttle whirled, sailing to the left and moving like a buzz saw. It slammed into one of the stratopods, crushing the pod and driver instantly. The stratopod overturned and smashed into another one of the drivers. The driver howled in fury and overturned, colliding with the rear of the still-twirling shuttle. The stratopod erupted in flame, hitting the ground and leaving a skid mark thirty yards long.

Sulu felt the jolt, glanced at the controls. He'd lost some

power to the engines from that last impact. He fought to pull the shuttle out of the spin. Ling Sui, for her part, gripped the sides of her chair firmly. Her jaw was set, giving her a very determined air, although Sulu suspected that most of the determination centered around not wanting to vomit.

The last of their pursuers had clearly decided to give them considerable distance. He was hovering meters away, keeping a safe distance from the wildly pivoting shuttle.

Sulu fought desperately with the controls, trying to bring the shuttle on line. The vehicle was within a hairsbreadth of flipping completely over, tearing up a large stretch of the desert sands. Sulu battled and pulled the vehicle back into line. It bucked slightly and then roared forward.

Another disruptor blast, and another, rocked the Peregrine. It was all Sulu could do to hold it on course. He checked the engine readings and didn't like what he saw at all. Then he looked at the monitor at their lone remaining pursuer, and he liked it even less.

For now he could clearly make out what he hadn't before; the man who was after them was Taine, his face twisted into an infuriated snarl. He brought his disruptor gun up and squeezed off a shot.

And then, suddenly, the shuttle shuddered under more disruptor fire and the monitors blinked out. Taine, resourceful fellow that he was, had managed to knock the exterior cameras out of commission. Except for visibility through the front windshield, they were flying blind.

Sulu surveyed their options and didn't find too terribly many. The hull of the Peregrine whined in protest. The vehicle was designed for travel, not combat, and Sulu had already pushed it to the limits of its structural capacity. Maybe even beyond the limits.

His mouth started to form words, but Ling beat him to it. "Let me guess: 'Hold on,'" she said.

"Exactly," he replied. He watched as Ling Sui braced herself once more. She looked at him with an expression that held utter confidence. It was fortunate she had it in him, because his own confidence was starting to waver ever so slightly.

"Here we go," he murmured, and slowed the shuttle's forward motion by half.

The stratopod shot right past it, Taine's head whipping around as he realized his target was no longer beside him. Sulu, banking on his reactions, counted on him to slow down out of reflex.

Which was precisely what he did.

And as he did that, Sulu immediately gunned the shuttle. As a result, the Peregrine leaped forward, roaring past the stratopod.

Leaving the next move as the trickiest. Sulu, one step ahead of his opponent, deduced that Taine—suddenly finding himself left behind—would immediately try to speed up once more. In anticipation of the move, Sulu slammed the shuttle to a complete halt . . . but at a ninety-degree angle relative to its previous position. Basically, he had just turned the Peregrine into a roadblock.

It all happened so quickly that Ling Sui didn't even have time to question what was going on. The result of Sulu's maneuver was exactly what he figured it would be: a loud *thunk* and a shudder as the accelerating stratopod collided broadside with the shuttle. In front of them, a twisted and empty stratopod fell away.

There was deathly silence for a moment . . . a moment to contemplate how fortunate they were that the monitor was down, so that they didn't have to stare at the sight of the stratopod's former occupant smeared all over the exterior of the shuttle.

"You . . . you did it," Ling Sui managed to say.

Then the windshield cracked, accompanied by the now-familiar whine of a disruptor.

It was the only warning that Sulu had. Hopefully it would be enough as Sulu sent the vehicle flying forward.

"He's on the roof! The bastard's on the roof!" shouted Ling Sui.

She was right. Sulu heard a thudding from overhead, the sound of a body tumbling. But it hadn't necessarily fallen off.

And then it happened. Repeated blasts from overhead, the ceiling denting in and then ripping open. Sulu tried to steer the shuttle violently enough to throw off their dedicated pursuer, but there were spiders who were less tenacious than this.

All that was visible was Taine's hand clutching the disruptor as he shoved it into the cabin of the Peregrine. He fired blindly as Sulu leaped away from the controls barely in time. The blast struck the control board, sparks flying from it, the board starting to melt into rivulets from the impact and the impending fire.

"Take over!" shouted Sulu as he lunged for the intruder's arm.

Ling looked helplessly at the ruined control board. The shuttle's forward motion had not diminished; if anything, it was picking up speed. "Take over *what?*" she shouted in exasperation.

Sulu wasn't exactly in a position to reply at that moment. He had barely dodged another blast, and now he had grabbed the wrist of their assailant and was struggling desperately, trying to pry the disruptor loose from his hand.

The hole in the ceiling ripped wide, and Taine tumbled down and through into the cabin. He was still clutching the disruptor with single-minded determination.

For all the battering he had taken, Taine did not seem to have been slowed down in the least. He nearly lifted Sulu off his feet as he slammed him up against a far wall.

Ling desperately tried to reroute control functions back through the main board, but there was nothing she could do. The shuttle was completely out of control, lurching wildly. Smoke was starting to pour from the ruined panels, blinding her. Then she heard Sulu's alarmed voice shout *"Get down!"* and she did so as a disruptor bolt ripped just above her head and blew apart the already-stressed windshield. Wind blew in, accelerating the spread of smoke through the cabin.

Sulu was still struggling hand to hand with Taine.

"You *idiot!*" snarled Taine. "I don't know what kind of game you think this is . . . but you're going to lose it!"

Sulu didn't bother to respond. What was there to say? He *had* thought it was a game. He pushed away from his mind the realization that he had been incredibly lucky thus far.

Here he hadn't been taking the threat of Taine and his thugs seriously, and he could easily have been dead before realizing that he was in any true danger.

He struggled for leverage, found it, and drove a knee into Taine's gut. Taine grunted, didn't quite double over, but the wind was knocked out of him. He did not, however, lose his grip on his disruptor.

Ling Sui was trying to get close to help, but she was moving warily, keeping an eye on the barrel of the disruptor. It fired again and she barely managed to get out of the way.

One of the lower struts of the shuttle struck a dune, flipping the shuttle around. It sent Sulu and Taine tumbling, crashing into Ling Sui, and all three of them went down in a tumble of arms and legs.

For a moment they were frozen there, the three of them, and Taine and Ling Sui were snarling into each other's faces. Then Ling Sui head-butted him. He rolled back, clutching at his face, and Sulu yanked her to her feet.

In Ling Sui's hand was the disruptor. She swung it around and aimed it squarely at Taine.

"No!" shouted Sulu, yanking her hand wide, the disruptor blast exploding against the far wall.

She looked at him in shock. Sulu didn't bother to exchange words with her, because with the Peregrine hurtling wildly out of control, now was not the time to discuss the relative morals of the situation.

Taine lunged at them. Sulu sidestepped, gripping the disruptor firmly, and slammed the butt into Taine's head. It opened up a vicious gash in Taine's head, blood flowing from it and blinding him. Sulu shoved him aside, spun, and fired short, fast, and concentrated blasts at the top and bottom of the door. The door swung open, hanging loosely by strips of metal, and Sulu had a brief glimpse of the ground whizzing past.

Snagging Ling's wrist, he started for the door, apparently ready to hurl himself to his death. For the briefest of moments Ling hesitated, and she looked into Sulu's eyes.

And for the first time since the whole mad adventure had

begun, something seemed to "lock" between them. As if in seeing each other, they actually *saw* each other for the first time.

She gave the slightest nod of her head, and moved with him. Sulu charged forward and slammed into the door, ripping it free from its moorings. For a moment Sulu and the door teetered on the edge, and in that moment he swung Ling Sui around so that she grabbed on to his back. And then the door fell clear of the hurtling shuttle, Sulu lying flat on his belly and Ling Sui holding on for dear life.

The door hit the desert sands and continued moving at the same clip as the shuttle. It was like being a child and riding on a sled, which would have brought back fond memories for Sulu if he'd grown up somewhere other than San Francisco. Sulu, however, was nothing if not a fast learner.

His fingers held fast to the underside of the door, the sand ripping his knuckles. He gritted his teeth, oddly reluctant to give in to his impulse to cry out. Ling Sui's body, curiously enough considering the circumstances, was relaxed against him. Maybe she had utter confidence in him. Maybe she had just shut down her mind so as not to deal with the still-imminent possibility of their mutual demise.

The door fishtailed around, slowing, and then suddenly it flipped completely over. And now Sulu did yell, an alarmed yelp, and he lost his hold on the door. They tumbled off, but fortunately they had slowed enough so that they were able to roll to a stop with only a few more bumps and bruises on them.

"You all right?" Sulu shouted.

"Yes. You?"

"I'm fine!" he shouted.

"Good!" She raised her voice. "Why are you shouting!?"

It was because his head was still ringing and his hearing was thrown off, but there was no need to go into details. Instead Sulu, his sleeves ripped, already feeling aches in his joints that would only get worse as time passed, looked after the hurtling shuttle.

It was moving so quickly that it was already a speck on

the evening horizon, vanishing behind a series of dunes. Then suddenly there was a burst of light, followed moments later by the sound of the explosion.

Sulu and Ling Sui watched for a long time as flame danced across the miles-off dunes, smoke curling lazily into the air.

"Is he dead, you think?" asked Ling Sui after a while.

"We're not," Sulu pointed out.

"Yes, but we're the good guys."

"Are we?" Sulu propped himself up on one elbow and looked around, surveying their situation. The sun had almost set, which was actually the most positive thing they had going for them. Because the fact was that they were out in the middle of the Sahara with no supplies, no conveyances, and no way of covering the distance back to the city except on foot.

"What do you mean, 'Are we'?"

"We'll discuss it later."

"Sulu . . ."

"Later," he said firmly. "Come on."

"Come on where, exactly?" She looked around. "I can't see Demora from here. And we flew so far, so fast, I have absolutely no idea where the hell we are. Which way do we go?"

He paused a long moment, then looked up to the sky. The long red fingers of the setting sun were almost totally withdrawing, replaced by the twinkling of the stars.

"Wait," he said.

"Wait for what?"

He put up a finger and repeated patiently, "Wait."

She opened her mouth, but then closed it again, deciding to wait and see what this most curious of gentlemen was up to.

The sun vanished, the coolness of the nighttime desert settling in. Sulu continued to stare upward, as if communing with the stars. Ling found herself watching him with rapt fascination.

When he spoke it was so abruptly in the silence of the desert that it made her jump slightly.

"That way," he said, pointing.

She squinted, trying to imagine what in the world he might be pointing at. There was no sign of the city from this distance. "How do you know?"

He smiled confidently and held up his palm. "You might as well ask me how I know this is my hand. I look to the stars, and the stars guide me. People can be deceitful. People can tell you one thing and do another. But the stars don't lie."

She didn't say anything, merely shrugged.

Without another word, Sulu set out, with Ling Sui falling into step behind him.

Chapter Eleven

THEY TRAVELED QUICKLY, and in silence, for the first hour. There was the unspoken understanding that it was important to try and cover as much distance as possible. Traveling during the day would not be a terribly pleasant experience with the desert sun beating down on them. Night was the time to cross the sands.

Sulu glanced at her every so often to make sure that she was keeping up. She seemed to have no trouble. At one point she stopped, removed her boots, and then continued walking. She actually moved faster barefoot. So much faster, in fact, that she passed him and Sulu quickly became aware that she could probably outdistance him with little trouble. She realized it at about the same time, apparently, and slowed down so that Sulu could keep up. She glanced at him as they drew side by side, and there was a degree of impishness on her face as they trudged up one sand dune and down another.

"You're very quick," he said finally, the first words spoken in over an hour.

She stopped and raised the soles of her feet for inspection.

They looked hard as shoe leather. "I do a lot of walking," she said.

"So do I. Every morning. Although not barefoot, and not in conditions like this."

"I've crossed a desert or two in my time," she said.

"And what else have you done in your time?"

They got to the crest of a sand dune and Sulu slipped a bit going down it, but righted himself before he could fall over. "Well?" he said.

She looked at him curiously. "Well what?"

"Well what else have you done in your time? What's your time been spent doing?"

"This and that."

"And whatever it is you were ready to sell to Kelles . . . does that come under the category of 'this' or 'that'?"

She stopped walking and stared at him defiantly. "Don't be coy, Sulu. It doesn't suit you. You want to ask a question, ask it."

"All right. What is it you were trying to sell, and from whom did you steal it?"

Her gaze was level and she was quiet for a time. Then she said briskly, "None of your business."

He threw his hands up in exasperation. "Well *that's* helpful."

"The fact that you have to ask the question means that the answer is pointless."

"And the answer is—?"

"You won't believe me."

"Don't tell me what I will and won't believe." He stopped walking and waited. "Well?"

She kept walking. "I'm not going to tell you."

"I'm not moving until you do."

"Fine. Don't move then. To hell with you." She kept on going.

Sulu stayed exactly where he was, and was annoyed to find that he was admiring the sway of her hips and the way that her shoulder blades stood out against the back of her tight black shirt. Her hair swung pendulum-like as she strode away.

She got about a hundred feet, then came to a stop and

sighed audibly. Then she turned around and walked back to Sulu, standing there with arms folded and reluctant amusement on her face.

"I don't know where I'm going."

"You mean short-term or long-term?"

She raised an eyebrow in a manner that eerily reminded Sulu of a certain Vulcan. "The latter depends somewhat on the former."

"True enough."

She sighed. "Okay. Come on."

He paused a moment to make sure that he understood her intent, and then he walked alongside her. As they continued their steady pace, Ling Sui licked her lips once—the only indication she gave that she was at all thirsty. "I'm freelance."

"Freelance? Freelance what?"

"Freelance whatever it takes. Freelance inventor, pilot, researcher, explorer . . . adventurer, for want of a better term. The technology I had to sell was invented by my current client."

"Your current client being—?"

"My current client being none of your damned business," she told him, although she didn't sound particularly angry when she said it.

"All right. Fair enough." They started up another sand dune. "Go on."

"My client had an assistant, name of Taine. I'm sure you remember him; he was trying to kill you a short while ago."

"He's somewhat fresh in my recollections, yes."

"Taine stole all the material related to my client's discovery. All the research, the findings . . . all of it. This is something one can accomplish when one is in a position of trust, as Taine was . . . although he's not anymore, as I'm sure you can surmise. This drove home to my client his vulnerability, not to mention the transitory nature of the exclusivity of discoveries. So he hired me to retrieve it: retrieve years and years' worth of computations, calculations, test results . . . more than my client could possibly have endeavored to reproduce simply from memory. Retrieve it . . . and line up a powerful buyer for it."

"If it was stolen, why didn't he just report it to the authorities?"

She looked at him in amusement. "You can't report matters to the authorities when there are questions connected that you'd rather not answer. Not all areas of research are 'approved,' Sulu."

"Was he involved with something dangerous?"

"By dangerous you mean would people become sick or die from it? No, not at all. Sometimes, though, things are forbidden. Once upon a time, it was heresy to suggest that the Earth revolved around the sun. But just because something is forbidden doesn't mean you don't have to investigate it anyway. Sometimes you do what you have to, even if the authorities would frown on it. Do you agree?"

Briefly Sulu's thoughts flew to the numerous times that James T. Kirk had stretched General Order 1 almost into unrecognizability. And yet somehow things had always managed to work out for the best, Kirk's instinct unerringly guiding them through the rocky shoals of Starfleet regs. Nor was Kirk unique; Mr. Spock (and who was more respectful of the logic of rules than a Vulcan?) had risked death to fly in the face of General Order 7.

But Sulu had never been in that position. He wondered what would happen if someday he was in a command situation and was asked to choose between orders and his sense of what was right and wrong. Indeed, it was only a matter of time before that did happen. He hoped he would do the right thing . . . or even be able to figure out precisely what the right thing was.

Yes . . . he knew he would figure it out. Because whatever it was, it would be the honorable thing. Right and wrong, rules and regulations—these things could be discussed and analyzed to death and even beyond. But honor was immutable. Honor was known. A question of honor was answered with as much clarity as the North Star.

"Yes . . . I agree," he said.

She looked surprised. "Hmmf. A Starfleet officer agreeing with that philosophy. Again you surprise me, Sulu. So . . . in any event, that's why I was brought into this. Because I wouldn't sit in judgment, and I wouldn't start quoting regulations or get involved in politics. I'd come in, do the job, and get out." She paused. "Except I didn't exactly do the job, it seems. I managed to steal the technology back from Taine, set up the meeting place for the sale to occur. And then the whole thing went straight to hell. Not your fault, though. Mine. Only mine."

"It was my fault, too. I . . ."

He paused, and she stopped walking and turned to look at him. "What's up with you, anyway?" she said in that slightly musical voice of hers. "There's something going on here, something you're not telling me. What is it? I've been as honest with you as I can. . . ."

"You'll laugh."

"Maybe," she agreed. "If it's stupid enough."

He stopped, sat down on a dune and pulled off his boots. Upending them, he watched sand pour out as he looked around their surroundings. "Is the entire Sahara like this?" he asked.

"Oh, no." She gestured. "This erg, for example . . ."

"Erg?"

"Sand dune. It's only, what? Ten meters high? There's ergs go as high as two hundred meters." At the expression on his face, she added, "Of course, it's not like the entire Sahara is nothing but ergs. After all, the damned thing's nine million square kilometers . . . as big as the United States. It's not all sand."

"No?"

"No," she said cheerfully. "Some places it's pebbles and gravel."

"Oh, well . . . that makes all the difference," Sulu acknowledged.

"So . . . what will I laugh at?"

"Oh." He'd hoped she'd forgotten. "Uhm . . . you're not going to find this easy to believe . . . but the whole thing back at the city? I thought it was a put-on."

"Put-on?" She shook her head, not understanding.

"I thought . . ." He sighed. "I was visiting with a friend . . . and I'd been complaining that there was no adventure to be had on Earth. That it couldn't possibly compare to the kinds of excitement that we encountered in space exploration. And what with the timing of all of this . . . and the outrageousness, the mysteriousness of it all . . . I was convinced he'd set it up. Demora is filled with people who are employees, or freelancers who are willing to be hired to perform some sort of bizarre adventure play. They were the evil villains, you were the mystery woman with the vague and exotic background. That's what I thought was going on here. Up until . . ." He paused and looked down again at the stain on his jacket that represented some of the remains of Kelles. "Well . . . I know better now."

"So when you went after Taine and the others that first time . . . you thought they were actors."

He paused, remembering. "Not when I first approached them, no. I thought they were following you to try and hurt you. It was only later, as matters escalated, that I thought it was faked."

"So you tried to help me initially believing that I was in trouble . . . and eventually, upon discovering your error, you then leaped to the rescue in a shuttle, engaged in a daring high-speed chase across the desert, battled hand to hand with a man who was trying to kill you, then hurled us to safety with a makeshift sled . . . and now you're concerned I'll laugh at you."

Sulu stared at her. "Well . . . I wouldn't have put it quite that way but, essentially . . . yes, that's right."

And to his utter astonishment she leaned over and kissed him full on the lips. It was brief, sweet, and refreshing, like a summer shower that comes from nowhere, vanishes to the same place, and leaves you feeling invigorated.

She looked at him and he would have sworn that the twinkling stars from overhead were reflected in her eyes.

"You are so cute," she told him. Then she patted him on the knee. "Come on. Let's go."

"By all means," he said, and pulled his boots back on.

She took his hand as they started up the next erg. They made it to the top, slid down the other side, and continued walking. His fingers interlaced with hers as they kept moving, slowly but steadily.

Neither of them complained, both remaining stoic about the situation. But as hour piled upon hour, their progress was nowhere near as rapid as either of them would have liked, and the lack of water was starting to get to them. Plus unspoken was the simple fact that time was against them. Sooner or later, the sun would rise. No one was more aware of that than Sulu. As the sun rose the heat would begin to rise as well, the temperature driven upward, going as high as 110 degrees Fahrenheit. It was incumbent upon them to get as far as they possibly could during the night, but it wasn't as if they'd already had the most restful of days.

As they scaled and then slid down dunes, no discussion passed between them. During the plateaus, however, they would talk. Sulu discussed his youth in San Francisco, and his Starfleet career, which began in physics but then switched to navigation and helm. His family, his friends.

And Ling, for her part, listened. She didn't volunteer much in the way of her own personal history, and when he pressed her she smiled and demurred. "Oh, come now, Sulu. Don't you remember? The mystery woman. What good would be served by knowing too much about the mystery woman."

"But you're not really."

"Oh, but I am. At least, I am now. I rather like it, I must admit." She smiled. "Understand, I don't think of myself that way. I'm just a hard worker, with a background that would sound rather mundane if I went into it. But being a 'mystery woman,' well . . . that's an honor. Even a responsibility."

"How is it a . . ." He stopped and pointed. "Look."

She followed where he was pointing, certain that they couldn't possibly be within view of the city. The shuttle had taken them too far, too fast. They couldn't have covered the distance that quickly. . . .

Then she saw it.

"An oasis," she said.

"At first I thought it might be a mirage."

"Not at night. Come on."

There were some ninety large oases throughout the Sahara, and many smaller ones. This was definitely one of the smaller ones, too small to support any sort of large settlement. But the vegetation, while not copious, was still lush, and the water was flowing from an underground spring. They drank of it greedily, for although they were nowhere near as dehydrated as they would have been had it been daytime, their thirst was nevertheless a very real thing.

Sulu let the water run over his parched lips, splashing it in his face, closing his eyes and letting it run over his head. He wavered slightly and realized that closing his eyes wasn't the best of ideas; he was that fatigued. He forced them open and looked at Ling Sui.

She had removed her shirt, revealing a black halter top beneath. Her arms were muscular, even more so than Sulu would have surmised. He could see the curve of her breasts beneath the halter; they looked small and firm. If she was aware of his gaze moving across her, she gave no indication of it. She soaked the shirt in the small spring and then draped it over herself.

"You didn't need me," he said after a time.

She looked up at him questioningly. "Pardon?"

"You seem familiar with the Sahara. From the bottoms of your feet it's clear that you've done a ton of walking. I'd wager you'd have no trouble looking at the stars and figuring out which way to go."

She smiled and looked down. "If you wagered it, your money would be safe."

"Then why . . . ?"

"Why?" She feigned surprise. "Why, don't you remember? I'm your mystery woman now."

He laughed softly.

"Oh, now you scoff," she said. "Obviously you don't really know anything about it."

"I don't?"

"No, you don't." She pulled her legs up and wrapped her arms around them. And she sounded very sincere as she said, "Every man—particularly every man of adventure— should have one mystery woman in his life, Sulu. That woman who enters his sphere like a comet. Who creates her own reality around him and swallows him up in it. Who 'gets' to him, inflaming his senses, heightening the sheer experience of living so that from then on, when he wakes up each morning ever after, the world seems a little different to him because he knows that she's somewhere out there in it.

"That woman whom he thinks about, wonders about . . . wonders if, sooner or later, she'll pop back into his life just as abruptly as she entered it before. With some new adventure in tow, some new villains seeking to do her in. It doesn't happen, of course, because such things never happen more than once, really. You can't have a string of mystery women; it's unfair to all those pathetic wretches who, in fact, never do get a mystery woman. And years into the future, when he murmurs her name in his sleep, his wife asks him about it in the morning and he shrugs and says, 'It was just a dream, honey. It's not supposed to make sense.'"

"You've got my entire life planned out for me, then? You come into it, you disappear from it, and I marry someone else and think of you now and then in fleeting moments?"

She looked at him sadly. "I hope not."

They were silent for a time, and then Ling Sui glanced around and said, "Do you think we should start walking again?" But she didn't sound tremendously enthused by the notion.

Nor was Sulu for that matter. He shook his head. "I don't know about you, but I've had a rather long day," he said wryly. "I don't think it'll be all that long until sunrise. And I doubt that we'd luck into another oasis right when the sun's coming up. But if we stay here . . ."

"Then we rest, recuperate, and start walking again tomorrow night." She nodded. "You're right, that's probably the way to go."

He nodded, then removed his jacket, rolling it up into a makeshift pillow that he positioned beneath his head. Ling Sui didn't seem to need any such contrivance, merely lying back with her head resting on the vegetation, her hands interlaced behind her head.

"Are you married, mystery woman?" he asked. "Or affianced, or in some way connected to someone else at the moment?"

"Oh, come on, Sulu," she chided. "Do I seem like that kind of woman?"

"I don't know what kind of woman you seem like. You're a mystery woman, remember."

"Right. That's right. Forgive me . . . this rarefied status is still new to me." Then, her voice soft and devoid of her cockiness, she said, "No. No husband. No fiancé. No one. You?"

"No one," he echoed.

"Ever feel lonely?"

"I have my friends. And I have the stars. We live in a galaxy so teeming with life . . . and I look up at the stars, knowing there are planets out there with alien life-forms that are likely looking right back at me. With all that, how can one ever be lonely."

"Oh, I feel exactly the same way. I've done my share of starhopping. Not on par with yours, of course, but I've gotten around. Seen a lot of things. Been up to my neck in one thing or another. Frankly, I don't even have time to be lonely."

"Same here."

"Ditto."

"Couldn't agree more."

She paused. "Ever feel lonely?" she asked again.

"Yes. A lot. You?"

"The same."

"Any regrets?"

He paused a moment, considering. "Do you want to wade through the same unconvincing rationalizations, or should we go straight for the truth."

"Oh, let's chance it."

"Regrets, yes."

"Same here. Although . . . it's not too late, you know. You're relatively young. So am I. We could each decide that's there more to life than running around and adventuring."

"Not too late?"

"No."

He gave it some thought and then sighed. "No, you're wrong. It's too late."

"I was afraid of that," she said.

They were quiet for a time more. It was so still, so silent

111

around them, and Sulu became very aware of her breathing . . . and, curiously, he thought he could hear the steady rhythm of his own heart. . . .

"Why'd you switch?" she asked.

"Pardon?"

She rolled over, propping her head up on one hand. "Why did you switch?" she asked again. "From physics to helm. Aren't you just a . . . a chauffeur with delusions of grandeur?"

He chuckled softly at the metaphor. "Well, I'm in charge of weapons and tactical as well . . . plus, helming a starship is a bit more complicated than steering a vehicle."

"But that's not why."

"No, it's not." He hadn't stopped looking at the stars. "It's because, as I spent time in the lab, I suddenly came to the realization that, in that part of the service, I'd continue to spend my time in labs. Labs on a science vessel, labs on a starship . . . didn't matter. I'd be down in the bowels of the ship somewhere doing reports, making studies, passing answers on to the captain, who'd be up on the bridge doing whatever was necessary for the survival of the ship and crew.

"And I was talking with my mother one day, and I told her what I was learning at the Academy. And maybe she sensed somehow that I wasn't entirely happy with it. Part of what had drawn me to physics was that my father was a physicist, and so I just felt the inclination to follow in his footsteps. And she said to me—I suspect in hopes of prompting me to stay Earthbound—'I don't understand why you have to be out in space to be a physicist.' And I tried to have an answer for that . . . I think I even muttered something, although it was something clever such as 'You wouldn't understand.' But the fact was that she was right. There was no reason. Not really. Oh, there were experiments certainly that could only be conducted in space, but . . . was that sufficient reason? And I realized to me, at least, it wasn't.

"But helmsman . . . steering the ship . . . looking straight ahead and seeing the stars clustered in front of you . . .

that's what I was really going out there for, Ling. For the stars. To go out and there lose myself in them."

"A helmsman who wants to lose himself? Doesn't sound promising."

He yawned and said, "There's no problem with losing yourself . . . as long as you can always find your way back."

"I suppose you're right," she said. "I suppose that—"

But the rest of what she said began to haze out to him and, almost before he realized it, he was asleep.

He was in that place where waking and dreaming intersect. . . . Stars seemed to float about him, and he was unsure of whether he was at the helm of the Enterprise or staring up into the night skies above the Sahara. It was an odd sensation, because usually one isn't aware that one is dreaming, and yet here he was, feeling as if the stars were rushing past him as he sped toward some odd destiny.

Star clusters were swirling in front of him, surrounded by blackness, and then they seemed to regroup and form the outline of a face . . .

Her face . . .

"Your mystery woman," she said to him, and she brought her lips to his. She tasted so sweet . . . she tasted like wild abandon, and youth, and adventure, and forbidden fruit that he could not resist here in the garden, and he told her all this, and she laughed. "Tasted all that before, have you, so you could compare?" she said teasingly. . . . And her hands were everywhere, she was everywhere in the dream, in the reality, the stars surrounding them and he had no idea if he was sleeping or awake or both. . . .

"Let this ease both our loneliness, at least for a little while," she whispered, her breath warm in his ear, and whether he was sleeping or awake he didn't care because it felt too good, what she was doing to him; too good, the muscular body moving against his and the heat, God, the heat was . . .

. . . pounding on him.

He sat up, blinking against the sun, suddenly aware that he was baking in it.

It was high above him, so high that he thought it might be

around noon or so. The growth around him had protected him for a time, but the sun had moved into position so that it was shining down on him now.

He rolled over, his joints stiff, and he splashed water on his face from the stream.

"Ling Sui," he started to say, and looked up.

She wasn't there.

At first it didn't register on him that she was gone. He thought he was just looking in the wrong direction, but when he rolled over he saw that he was, in fact, alone.

He got to his feet, his legs wavering slightly. *"Ling Sui!"* he called again, his voice sounding hoarse.

No reply came except the echo of his own voice.

No sound except the nothingness of the desert . . . and the cries of Sulu shouting a name over and over.

Chapter Twelve

THE MAN WHO WAS KNOWN in the city of Demora as Mr. Molo, designated the Magistrate (and who was known to the creators of the city of Demora as Arnold Brinkman, and was designated on-site manager) let smoke curl lazily from the (fake) cigarette he held delicately between his large fingers. His suit was white, his fez was red, and his ceiling fan was broken.

He was staring across the spotless surface of his desk at the disheveled Asian gentleman seated directly across from him. He had an associate who was a bit younger and not remotely disheveled.

Staying consistent with the ambience of Demora as a whole, Mr. Molo was taking notes on a notepad with a scratchy pencil. "So let's see if I understand this," he said softly, looking over what he'd written. "You were chatting with a young woman, Lieutenant Commander Sulu . . . and suddenly people began shooting . . . you panicked, leaped into a nearby vehicle, and fled, eventually crashing the vehicle in the desert. You walked for a time with the young lady, found an oasis . . . the young lady disappeared during

115

the night . . ." He turned his attention to Chekov. "And then you found him?"

"I vas concerned," said Chekov. "He vas out all night." He looked at Sulu with a deadpan. "You know how I vorry."

Sulu's face was inscrutable. With no comment, Mr. Molo continued, "You rented out a shuttle, began combing the desert, and stumbled over him? That was fairly lucky."

"Lucky?" Chekov looked indignant. "I'll have you know, Meester Molo, that I've piloted shuttlecrafts through ion storms searching for lost landing parties on a planet of active wolcanoes. Spotting Meester Sulu vas child's play."

Mr. Molo took a long drag on his cigarette, then turned his swivel chair in preparation to heft his bulk to a standing position. His back was momentarily to the Starfleet officers, and Sulu took the opportunity to turn to Chekov and mouth, *Active volcanoes?*

Chekov shrugged. Damn, but it had sounded impressive.

"But you were less successful finding the young woman."

"Ve continued the search in an expanding radius. We searched for several hours. There was no sign of her."

"Where do you think she went?"

Chekov gave him a slightly patronizing look. "If I had an idea of vere she vent, ve vould have gone there and gotten her. Yes?"

Apparently unfazed, Molo turned his attention back to Sulu. "What were you doing in the Thieves Quarter?"

"Being shot at. I told you."

"Were they shooting at you? Or at the young woman?"

"I didn't stop to ask them. They didn't seem the type to be generous with providing information."

"And you never saw the woman before that?"

"Never."

"And did the young woman tell you her name?"

Sulu seemed to hesitate a moment, and then said, "Yes."

His pencil poised over his notepad, Mr. Molo prompted, "And that name would be?"

"Moo."

Mr. Molo blinked. "Would that be a first name or last name?"

"First."

"Most unusual."

"I believe she said she grew up on a farm."

"All right," said Mr. Molo, and he carefully wrote the name, *Moo.* "Last name?"

"Shu pork."

Chekov cleared his throat loudly, giving him the opportunity to put his hand carefully over his mouth to cover his smile. Sulu remained expressionless.

Mr. Molo allowed the pencil point to hover over the notepad for a moment before he laid the pencil down gently. He steepled his fingers. "Do you think you're funny, Lieutenant Commander? Do you think that a complaint to Starfleet over your questionable conduct in our city would be as amusing as you?"

Slowly Sulu leaned forward, his eyes unblinking. "What I think, Mr. Molo, is that I'm hot. I'm tired. I'm parched. What I think"—and then his voice became low and hoarse, and there was an edge to it that could have carved diamond—"what I think is that you're dirty. Filthy, in fact. I think there are things that go on in this town that are illegal and immoral, and payoffs are made, all of which go into your pocket. I think this lovely little fantasy city has developed its own dark underbelly, just like the cities it was created to imitate. I think you provide information to whoever wants it for the right price. That you don't give a damn about anyone or anything except lining your own pocket. Or maybe it goes higher, to your employer's organization. And if you want to start investigations in Starfleet of me, then you'd better be ready to withstand some heavy-duty investigating directed right back at you. Take your best shot, and I'll take mine, and we'll see who's left standing."

There was a long, deathly silence.

Then, very slowly, Mr. Molo slid open his desk drawer and placed his notepad into it. His pencil went into a pencil holder.

"I apologize for the inconveniences you've encountered, Lieutenant Commander," he said. "I've already sent word to your hotel that all charges are to be considered compliments of management."

Sulu made no motion. Not a nod, or even a blink of an eyebrow. He might as well have been carved from marble.

Chekov rose from his chair and said levelly, "Ve appreciate the gesture."

They started for the door, and as they approached it Mr. Molo said, "Oh, and gentlemen . . ."

They turned to him and waited.

". . . your business is so joyous to have, that I think it would be criminal to keep it all to ourselves. I think you should consider bringing future business to as many other places as possible. Share the wealth, as it were."

"Other places besides here," said Chekov.

"Actually, I was thinking any place but here."

Sulu nodded slowly. "So was I." And they walked out.

Their bags sat on the bed, packed and waiting for the bellman to come upstairs. Sulu stood on the porch, watching the sun halfway up in the sky.

They had stayed one more night, made one more sweep of the desert. But there had been no sign of her. They had also gone exploring in the Thieves Quarter, this time quietly armed with phasers that Chekov had acquired through means that he didn't volunteer and Sulu didn't inquire about. Still no sign. The mention of her name drew blank stares.

Sulu found where her apartment had been. It was vacant. He found the warehouse where he'd been imprisoned. Empty.

"I swear to you, I didn't arrange it," Chekov had said to him. He didn't have to work hard to convince Sulu of that; Sulu was already a believer.

Now, on the veranda, Sulu let out a sigh. Chekov was doing one of his usual last-minute checks of drawers to make sure nothing had been overlooked. He paused and glanced over at his friend. "If you like, ve can stay longer. See if . . ."

Sulu shook his head. "No. She's gone because she wants to be gone. No trace of her footprints in the sand. No trace of her. Gone. All gone."

"As if none of it mattered."

"Oh," Sulu said, "it mattered. It mattered to me. Whatever happens with her now . . . it's out of my control. That's always a difficult thing for a helmsman to admit: that he's not steering the vessel."

"It's not like you to give up."

"Give up?" Sulu looked at him in surprise. "It has nothing to do with giving up, Chekov. It's simply the end, that's all."

"The end?"

"Of course. Someone once said . . . I don't remember who . . . that the entire trick to ending a story is to know where to end it. Saying 'They lived happily ever after' only works because you've ended the story at a high point. If you continue it beyond that point, eventually the hero and heroine grow old and die. Every story really has an unhappy ending. It's all in the timing. Ling Sui . . . she knew the timing called for her to mysteriously disappear. What else was she supposed to do? Stick with me, marry me, grow old and die with me? No no, Pav . . . that would be all wrong. All wrong. This story ends where it has to: on a note of mystery. Anything else would be . . . inappropriate."

There was a knock at the door. The bellman entered, picking up their bags and heading down to the lobby. Chekov walked over to Sulu, stood next to him for a moment, looking out at the sun, and then said, "Those things you vere just saying . . ."

"Yes?"

"You do realize, of course, that I have absolutely no idea vat you vere talking about."

"Of course."

"I mean, it makes no sense at all."

Sulu patted him on the arm and said, "It's just a dream, honey. It's not supposed to make sense." He walked out the door.

" 'Honey'?" Chekov muttered. Then he shrugged. "Oh vell," he said, and headed out after Sulu.

SECTION THREE

MEMORIAL

Chapter Thirteen

THE FUNERAL WAS SO PACKED that for a moment Sulu thought he wouldn't be able to get in.

He recognized a number of people from his own crew, and it seemed as if the entire crew of the *Enterprise* 1701-B had shown up as well. He had no idea what the maximum capacity in the Starfleet memorial chapel was, but whatever that magic number might be, it had to be pushing at the seams by this point.

He stood outside it a moment, looking off to the right. The Golden Gate Bridge gleamed in the morning sun. He remembered when he'd attended Starfleet, he'd always considered the view of the bridge symbolic. The Academy was supposed to be the bridge to the stars. Somehow that seemed consistent with the Academy's motto of "Ex astris, scientia"—"From the stars, knowledge."

Knowledge.

He'd been staring at the stars a great deal lately. Watching them move past from the rarefied position of his command chair rather than the helm. Looking to them for answers. For knowledge.

The stars, which had told him so much in the past, had stopped talking to him. If they had knowledge or understanding of his daughter's fate, they were mute.

Stars didn't twinkle in space, of course. They simply sat there against their black velvet backdrop, unblinking. Staring at him. Laughing at him. Keeping their secrets to themselves.

He'd looked to the stars when James Kirk had died. Looking for answers, looking for understanding. Seeking to grasp what justice there was in Kirk's abrupt and pointless demise while saving lives.

The stars had responded with silence then, too. Yet he had divined answers from them. The notion that Kirk was never meant to die quietly of old age on some bed somewhere. Despite his nominal roles as diplomat and explorer, what he was was, first and foremost, a warrior (he'd referred to himself as a soldier on more than one occasion). Yes, a warrior, battling against ignorance. Against fear. Against death. He'd gone out the way he would have wanted, indeed the only way it was possible for him to go.

But Demora . . . ?

She'd barely begun. She'd had none of the experiences, none of the opportunities that Kirk had had. All she'd had were dreams and hopes. Seated at the helm of the *Enterprise* . . . or at least the ship bearing the name *Enterprise* . . . ready to follow her father's path.

Except her father's path had taken him to great and glorious adventures, to the command of a starship, to . . . who knew where?

And hers had taken her to a pointless and confusing death.

He'd looked to the stars for answers, and gotten no reply at all. And this time, when the stars stared unblinkingly and silently at him, it hadn't seemed profound. He'd garnered nothing from it. It had just angered him, as if they knew something they weren't telling him.

A hand rested on his shoulder, startling him slightly. He turned and found himself looking into the face of Uhura. Standing just behind her was Chekov. They were in their dress uniforms.

Uhura's eyes were red. "I'm so sorry," she whispered, and held him close.

"I know."

"If there's anything I can do . . ." It was the type of thing one said in such circumstances, even though helplessness was the theme of the day. Chekov, grim-faced, nodded in agreement with Uhura's sentiments.

"I appreciate that," said Sulu, and he truly did. He knew from personal experience that these were the sort of people who would willingly walk into the fires of hell for him if he told them that, by doing so, Demora would be returned to him.

"It's not fair," said Chekov through gritted teeth. There was so much anger radiating from him that it was palpable.

"No. It's not," agreed Sulu.

"We . . . weren't able to let Scotty know in time," Uhura said apologetically. "We got a message out to the *Jenolen*. It's transporting him to a retirement community at the Norpin Colony. We haven't heard back yet."

"That's all right," said Sulu. "If anyone is entitled to an undisturbed retirement, it's Scotty."

"Meester Spock is on some sort of diplomatic mission," Chekov said. "Ve got vord to Dr. McCoy, but he's ill at the moment."

Sulu looked up in concern. "Anything we should worry about?"

"He said it was nothing a transplant wouldn't be curing. Fortunately he's got several cloned organs in the bank. He'll be fine."

"That's good to know."

Uhura looked him in the eyes and was concerned. He didn't look like . . . himself.

"Are you sure you're all right?" she asked doubtfully.

"Yes. I'm sure."

Sulu turned away then and started into the chapel. As he approached, he was immediately recognized. Despite the density of the crowd, a path seemed to melt away for him.

Uhura didn't follow immediately, and Chekov looked to her questioningly. "Vat is it?" he asked.

She paused and then said, "You know . . . when we look at stars, we're really not seeing what's there."

"Of course." He shrugged. "Because of the time the light takes to travel. A star can be dead, but ve still see the light from it." He stared at her uncomprehendingly. "So?"

"So . . . so that's what Sulu seemed like just now. There was something in his eyes . . . some faint glimmer of life . . . but it was as if the point of origin was dead. As if part of him had simply . . . disconnected."

"I don't blame him," said Chekov, and then he added darkly, "But I know who I do blame."

Captain John Harriman stepped up to the podium at the front of the chapel and looked out at the assembled Starfleet personnel.

Behind him, in an urn, were the mortal remains of Demora Sulu. Harriman couldn't quite bring himself to turn and look at them.

He began to speak and, to his horror, found that his throat had completely closed up. All he made was the slightest of gagging noises. He hoped that no one noticed; that the sea of faces looking up at him wasn't aware that inside he was shaking.

Because he'd killed her. He'd shot her and shot her until she stopped moving.

He hadn't slept since that moment. Minutes here and there, floating in the gray area of drowsiness, was all he had managed to snag.

He'd replayed the moment over and over in his mind, the entire sequence of events that had led up to the nude, unmoving body of Demora Sulu lying dead on the planet surface. He had tried to figure out what other way he could have handled it. What action he could have taken so that she might have lived and he would not feel like a murderer.

If he'd been faster . . .

. . . stronger . . .

. . . smarter, better . . .

. . . better, that's what it came down to, didn't it. His drive to be the best. The drive that had brought him the captaincy of the flagship of the fleet.

Was he all will and no skill?

He saw Hikaru Sulu.

He hadn't spotted him at first. He hated to admit it, but there had been a sense of relief. Looking Hikaru Sulu in the face was going to be the hardest part of all this.

The faces of his crew members had been tough enough. The looks, the sidelong glances, the conversations that would mysteriously dry up the moment that Harriman came within earshot.

But Sulu . . .

It had been tough enough at the *Enterprise* launch, with the eyes of three living legends drilling into the back of his neck. But, good lord, having Hikaru Sulu staring straight at him . . . he'd gone from living legends to living hell.

A moment passed between the two men, and it was as if Harriman projected a thought to him. And the thought was, *Perhaps you should come up here and do this. . . .*

And it was clear that Sulu had gotten the "message," because he gave an almost imperceptible shake of his head. He didn't want to get up in front of this audience. He was going to sit there unmoving, unspeaking, in the eighth row, and Harriman was going to hang out there all by himself. Which was certainly no less than Harriman felt he deserved.

All of it—Harriman's hesitation, his strangled cough, his reflection on what life had been like for him recently, and the entire silent communication with Sulu—it had all taken place in just over a second or two.

He squared his shoulders and began again, and this time—thankfully—his voice emerged firm and confident, belying the inner turmoil he felt.

"When we sign on for our exploratory service . . . we know the risk involved. We know how fragile is our existence, surrounded by a crushing vacuum, encountering unknowns at every turn. But we take that risk, we embrace that risk, because we want to. We need to.

"Nevertheless, acknowledging the inevitability of death and facing it are two different things. Especially when the circumstances are as . . . unfortunate and tragic as Demora Sulu's passing was.

"Demora Sulu was liked and admired aboard the *Enter-*

prise. She was a good friend. She was a good officer. She deserved better than what happened. And the fact that we will never fully understand what happened makes it all the more frustrating. We want answers. And the hard truth of the universe we live in is that answers are not only not always forthcoming, but oftentimes they're in short supply.

"She was eager and willing to learn. Her bravery was unquestioned. And she was unfailingly cheerful. She would always have a smile on her face, and she seemed to greet each day with unrestrained joy.

"She was fond of chocolate, saying she loved it more than it loved her. She was a gifted athlete, something of a gymnast. She was a . . ." He actually smiled slightly in spite of himself. "She was an abominable poker player, which made her rather popular. She liked to sing, her enthusiasm outstripping her actual musical skill. And that was part of her charm as well. It is a source of tremendous frustration that we didn't spend more time with her. Didn't have the opportunity to get to know her better.

"As is routine, she specified disposition of her remains in the event of . . ." And for the first time he forced himself to look at the urn. ". . . this. It is her wish that her ashes be scattered into Earth's sun so that . . . according to her will . . . she could keep an eye on what was going on here."

This actually prompted smiles from several in the audience. Soft chuckles of people remembering Demora's rather unique thought process.

"We will honor her request. And, in this ceremony, we will honor her memory. I invite anyone who wishes to share recollections of her to come up and say something about her."

There was a pause, that always uncomfortable moment when no one is sure what anyone else is doing. People glancing at one another, trying to determine through some sort of silent divining who's going to be first up.

More than one pair of eyes turned to Hikaru Sulu.

He didn't move.

Chekov, however, did. He rose at about the same time that Maggie Thompson did. But Thompson immediately sat when she saw who had risen.

Chekov's footsteps seemed to echo in the otherwise silent chapel. He reached the front, turned to face the assemblage, and began to speak.

He spoke of Demora's life. Of the honor he'd felt being made her godfather. Anecdotes that alternately brought smiles and tears to the faces of the mourners.

He was, in short, in excellent form. Never better, in fact. In every way, he rose to the occasion.

Hikaru Sulu didn't hear a word of it.

Instead he was staring intently, unblinkingly at Harriman. Every so often Harriman would glance Sulu's way, seemingly just to check if Sulu was still watching him.

He was.

It was as if he was trying to drill a hole into the man's mind. To see what was in there, to determine firsthand how remorseful he was. To see whether he was devastated, eaten up, or simply accepting of the concept that, hey, she knew what the risks were. That's just simply the way it plays out sometimes.

Harriman felt his soul beginning to wither under the intense scrutiny. And then, slowly, his fatigue, his frustration, his own soul-searching and acute self-examination began to rally. Damn it, he felt guilty enough. He didn't need to feel more so, and even if this was Demora's father, and even if he was legendary, right up there with Kirk, still . . . where did Sulu get off staring at him relentlessly, remorselessly.

He hadn't meant to kill her. It was an accident. The whole thing was a grotesque, outlandish accident, and if Hikaru Sulu had been in the exact same position he'd have done the exact same thing, so *get the hell out of my head*, thought Harriman.

After Chekov was done, other crewmen came up, one by one, to talk about Demora. But Harriman went through the rest of the memorial service on autopilot. Instead he felt as if he were busy fighting a silent war. It was a war against a man who was certainly no stranger to battle, but Harriman had reserves of strength that he had not even begun to tap.

And if Demora Sulu deserved better, well . . . so did he.

* * *

The congregants were gathering in the courtyard outside the chapel. Since Demora had already been cremated, there was obviously no cemetery to go to. The service with the ashes being delivered into the heart of Sol would take place aboard the *Enterprise* as the ship prepared to leave orbit.

Chekov, Sulu, and Uhura were gathered in a small group, talking among themselves. Every so often officers or friends of Demora's would drift past and offer their condolences. Sulu nodded gravely, shook hands, accepted the kind words.

Harriman watched, fatigue and his own gnawing guilt (although he wouldn't have recognized it as such, most likely) pushing at him. He squared his shoulders and strode over toward the former *Enterprise* officers. They looked up as he approached, and he noted that Uhura took a step closer to Sulu in an almost protective posture. Chekov stood his ground. Sulu didn't move at all; a mannequin would have shown more life.

"Captain Sulu . . . I just wish you to know . . . I share your loss," said Harriman. And then he braced himself. Braced himself for the likely invective that would flow forth. The grief and anguish of a father who'd had his only child gunned down, face-to-face with the man who pulled the trigger.

Sulu's eyes flashed for just a moment. Uhura seemed to react to it, as if she'd noticed something she hadn't before. But then Sulu reined himself in, brushing aside the anger and frustration that threatened to overwhelm him.

"It's . . . never easy to lose a crew member," Sulu said. "Under circumstances like these . . ." His voice trailed off and then he cleared his throat and said, "You . . . did the best you could. It's all right."

Inwardly, Harriman let out a sigh. Sulu could have said anything. Could even have walked away, cold-shouldered him. Relief flooded through Harriman.

"I . . . appreciate that, sir," he said. "The responsibility is mine. I know that you can empathize with that. Hell . . . even Captain Kirk lost his share of crew members. I doubt it ever got easier for him."

Sulu nodded, his face impassive.

And then Chekov muttered something.

Harriman hadn't quite heard it, and his head snapped around to lock gazes with Chekov. And whereas Sulu had seemed self-possessed, even slightly removed . . . Chekov was glaring at him with all the anger and fury that Harriman had been inflicting on himself.

And Harriman bristled.

"Did you say something to me, sir?"

"Not a thing," Chekov replied.

For a moment the air between them was electric. Then Harriman started to turn away, and then Chekov was right in front of him, right in his face, anger to the boiling point and beyond.

"Keptin Kirk vould have found another way."

"Would he," said Harriman icily.

"An unarmed girl . . . and you found no other vay to stop her than to shoot her down like a dog." Chekov's voice was rising with fury. Sulu put a hand on Chekov's shoulder, trying to calm him, but Chekov shrugged it off.

"You weren't there."

"No, I vasn't. Because if I had been there . . . if he had been there," and he pointed at Sulu, then gestured to Uhura, "if she had been there . . . if anyone else had been there, Demora would be alive. But no! It vas you! Ve served vit Keptin Kirk, and ve survived five-year mission after five-year mission!"

"Pavel," and now Uhura was trying to calm him, but it wasn't helping. His voice rose, thunderous, and now everyone was looking at him. Officers, diplomats, everyone was watching in thunderstruck amazement.

"But not Demora Sulu! No, she didn't survive five years. Not even five months on your *Enterprise!* And Keptin Kirk? He didn't even survive *five minutes!* And you call yourself a keptin?!"

Harriman was trembling within as he said in low fury, "I don't think you're exactly the best person to hold me up to opprobrium, *Commander*. With all *due* respect . . . it's Starfleet that calls me a captain, and a starship commander. Something, I should point out, that they have never, and will never, call you."

Harriman was approximately a head taller and fifteen years younger than Chekov. That made no difference, however, because Chekov's left-handed punch hit him squarely on the point of his chin.

Fortunately for Harriman, he did not go down, but instead only staggered.

Unfortunately for Harriman, Chekov was by nature right-handed. And a split second after Chekov had tagged him with his left, he hauled back and dropped him with his right.

Harriman went down, his lip split, slightly dazed.

Now everyone was shouting, trying to pull Chekov away. He was unleashing a string of profanities in Russian.

"Pavel, calm down! This isn't helping!" Sulu was shouting.

But Harriman was back on his feet, and the world seemed to haze red in front of him. He felt as if the surface of Askalon V were crunching beneath him once more, and he drove forward and crashed into Chekov. Chekov met the charge and they shoved against each other even as people tried to pull them apart. They tore at each other's jackets, decorum forgotten, the solemnity of the moment forgotten. The only thing that mattered was doing something about the anger that both of them felt. Anger directed from Chekov at Harriman, and anger directed from Harriman at . . . himself.

"*Stop it!*" Sulu bellowed, coming between them, shoving them away from each other. "Do you think she would *want* this? Do you? *Do you?!*"

Chekov and Harriman glared at each other, chests heaving. They said nothing, for, indeed, what was there *to* say?

They turned away from each other and walked away in opposite directions, leaving silence hanging over the assemblage.

Chapter Fourteen

HARRIMAN SAT in his quarters aboard the *Enterprise,* studying his face in the mirror. The swelling had gone down somewhat, which was fortunate.

His door chime beeped. He wasn't especially in the mood to receive visitors; on the other hand, he didn't want anyone to accuse him of hiding in his stateroom. "Come," he called.

The door slid open and Harriman was literally stunned to see who'd entered.

It was a Starfleet admiral, square-shouldered, barrel-chested, white hair trimmed in a buzz cut. He stood half a head taller than Harriman and the room seemed to expand to incorporate his presence.

"Admiral!" Harriman was immediately on his feet. "I wasn't expecting you! I'd have . . . have arranged for a detail to . . ."

The admiral made a dismissive wave. "No need to worry, son. Some people my age like to stand on ceremony, and others like to walk around it. Me, hell . . . I run around it."

He stuck out a hand and Harriman shook it firmly. "How you feeling, son?"

Harriman sighed. "I won't lie; it's been rough, Father."

Admiral Blackjack Harriman nodded sympathetically. Technically speaking, he was John Harriman, Senior, making his son Junior. But he'd been called Jack for as long as he could remember, and Blackjack since his Academy days wherein his card playing skills became legendary.

"Glad you're not lying, son," said the admiral. "You never could lie to me, you know. Never."

"Sit down, sir, please."

Blackjack took his son's chin and turned his head this way and that. "Chekov really tore into you, didn't he," said Blackjack. "Starfleet's all abuzz about it. He didn't do himself much good with that little stunt."

"Well, I can't exactly say that I've done myself all that much good either," admitted Harriman.

Blackjack sighed, his meaty fingers resting on his lap. "Well, let's get the simple stuff out of the way. The main reason I'm here is that I'm going to be attending that reception on Donatti Two. Scientifically advanced society, good strategic location . . . and, as it so happens, their sovereign emperor is a nut about Earth card games." He winked broadly. "I'll try not to fleece him too badly, for the sake of interstellar harmony. In any event, I was going to be hitching a transport out there . . . but since you rerouted *Enterprise* here, Starfleet decided I might as well arrive in style. Seemed like the ideal opportunity to catch a lift from my only son."

"It's an honor to have you aboard, sir."

The admiral leaned forward, his face darkening. "Having a rough time of it, aren't you, son."

"You could say that, sir. I'm . . ." He sighed. "I'm afraid I'm being regarded as something of a jinx."

"Listen, son. There's something I want you to understand, and it goes no further than this room. Get it?"

Harriman nodded.

"Because," continued Blackjack, "I know Kirk had a lot of friends. And hell, I'll admit his accomplishments were not inconsiderable. But a good officer, John, he was not."

"But . . . this isn't about Kirk."

"Oh, yes it is," said Blackjack. "What happened to the girl is tragic, sure, but tragedies happen all the time. Yeah . . . you killed her. Guess what, son. Every time a commander ever sent troops into a situation, knowing that most of 'em wouldn't be coming back except in pieces, that commander was killing those people. They all had folks, and they all had friends, and they were all dead. And that's just the way of it, is all.

"But what's giving this thing its subtext is the Kirk connection. And I'm telling you right now—and I can say this as an admiral, not as your father—that you're ten times the officer Kirk ever was. Kirk was a cowboy, a troublemaker. Thought he owned the galaxy. Thought he had all the answers. Second-guessed regs all the time, did what he felt like doing and managed to come up smelling like a rose because he had admirers in the right places. That, and people who were willing to tolerate his activities as long as it didn't backfire. They gave him the rope, and maybe he tripped on it every now and then, but he never hung himself with it.

"And what's frightening to me as an officer in Starfleet is the notion that some young officers might see him as a role model. That's not what we need, Johnny. We need officers with smarts . . . and respect . . . and an awareness that Starfleet is a unit, and must function with that sort of respect for the order of things. You understand that. Kirk never understood it, and none of Kirk's officers ever understood it. That's why Commander Chekov vented his spleen. I'm just sorry you had to be the recipient of it."

"I'm sorry, too, sir."

Blackjack stood and clapped Harriman on the shoulder. "I'm gonna go grab some chow. Join me?"

Harriman shrugged and then nodded. "Whatever you say, sir. Wouldn't want to buck a senior officer."

"That's my boy!" laughed the admiral, and they headed down to the officers' lounge.

* * *

Chekov paced Sulu's apartment, holding a coldpak against his eye. Uhura was seated nearby and looking at him accusingly. At a table, Sulu was calmly pouring out tea.

"Do you have any idea what a fool you made of yourself?" Uhura demanded.

"I'd do it again," shot back Chekov.

"Oh, I see. Well, you're not a fool, then. You're a damned fool."

"I appreciate the wote of confidence."

"Appreciate this then, too," Uhura told him. "Whether you like it or not, Chekov, the fact is that Starfleet has reviewed the facts regarding Demora's death, taken depositions from the other crew members involved, and concluded that Captain Harriman acted properly."

"Oh, acted properly, yes. Paragon of wirtue, that one." He shook his head, removed the coldpak, and examined his face in a mirror. "He has the nerve to stand there and say he takes responsibility for vat happened. Takes responsibility how, precisely? Ven Keptin Kirk took responsibility for his actions, he brought us all back from Vulcan, stood before the Federation Council, took full culpability for all actions, and vas busted in rank. Harriman takes responsibility, and it's business as usual." He shook his head. "Vat a joke. Vat a sick joke." Then Chekov turned to Sulu. "Vat about you?"

"Me?" Sulu looked up at him calmly. "What about me?"

"I did it for you, too."

As always, Sulu's face remained impassive. "I don't recall asking you to take a swing . . ."

"Two swings," Uhura pointed out.

"Two swings at Captain Harriman."

"You didn't have to. I could tell."

"You could tell I wanted you, at my daughter's memorial service, to get into a fistfight with her commander?"

Chekov strode toward him and leaned forward on the table. "I could tell that you were angry. That you were furious. This man, this . . . 'keptin' . . . lost Keptin Kirk for us. Lost Demora for us. Lost her? Killed her! And you stood there and gave him absolution! That's vat he vanted, that's vat you gave him! As if vat he did was acceptable! And it vas not! Not to me! And it should not have been to you!"

And Sulu slammed his open palm on the table so hard that the tea service rattled. One of the cups overturned, spilling a thin trail of liquid down the center of the table.

"She was my daughter, Chekov. Your goddaughter, but my child. I will honor her in my own way. And let me tell you that trying to knock out her captain . . . whether we like him or not, whether we accept what he did or not . . . is *not* how I choose to respect her memory. Is that understood?"

"And how do you choose to respect it, then."

"None of your business."

Chekov and Uhura exchanged glances. Then Uhura slowly stepped forward and said, "Sulu . . . I don't think what Chekov did was any more right than you do. But . . . after everything we've been through together, now you claim something is none of our business. Sulu! I thought we were beyond that."

"Beyond a right to privacy? Beyond a right to deal with grief however we wish?" Sulu shook his head. "I don't think we ever move beyond that."

He rose and went to the window, leaning against the plexi. "I'll be returning to the *Excelsior* shortly. You each have assignments to get to. I'd recommend you get to them."

Uhura and Chekov exchanged glances. "Aren't you . . . aren't you going to the ceremony?" asked Uhura.

"You mean hurling her ashes into the sun?" Sulu said evenly.

"Of course."

Sulu shrugged. "It's pointless. She's not going to know or care. She's gone, Uhura. She's gone. Those ashes in that urn aren't her, any more than the urn itself is. We say we're doing it to honor her wishes, but it's . . . it's nonsense. Her wish would have been to live. That's all. To live. And since we couldn't honor that wish, what does any of the rest of it matter? Ceremonies like that, they're for the living, not the dead. They're for survivors to find a way that they can . . . let go . . . of the departed. Well, I let go in my own way. And my way doesn't include standing there in maudlin assemblage while a corpse's ashes . . ."

Uhura slapped him.

She did it even before she'd realized her hand was in motion. She gasped as she did so, as if she'd been the one who'd been struck.

Sulu stood there, his cheek flushed red from the impact. With the slightest hint of amusement, he said, "And you were chewing out Chekov."

Uhura folded her hands and looked down. "I'm sorry," she said softly. "I'm sorry because I know that you're not . . . not acting like yourself. I know you too well to believe that you're this . . . this dispassionate. You're simply . . . I don't know . . . unwilling to accept what's happened. Or unable. Whatever the reason, you're simply not dealing with it. So you're shutting us out. Shutting out emotion, as if you were Spock."

"He has been on my mind recently, yes," Sulu admitted. "And Captain Kirk, as well."

"Don't you see, then?" She took him by the arms, as if she could squeeze emotion into him. "Don't you see what's happening? We've reached an age, Sulu, where it starts to feel like all we're going to experience from here on in is death. We're going to make no more new friends, bond with no more loved ones. Instead we're just going to watch old friends and lovers die, one by one. But we can't just shut down, just disconnect as you're doing. You'll die inside if you do, be less of a human being. . . ."

Sulu met her gaze and, just for a moment, she thought she saw something stirring in his eyes. But then he seemed to just fade away from her once more, and he replied, "I appreciate the sentiment, Uhura. I do. And I'm going to be fine. Truly."

There was a sharp beep from his personal computer station. "That's probably a call I've been waiting for," said Sulu. "If both of you don't mind, I'd . . . like to be alone now. Gather my thoughts. That sort of thing."

Chekov and Uhura nodded in what they hoped was understanding. Sulu moved with them to the door, accepting their muttered condolences once more, nodding in acquiescence to their offers of emotional support. They would both be there for him, that they made quite clear, and he acknowledged it and expressed all the requisite gratitude for their sentiments.

The moment they were out the door, Sulu pivoted and headed back for the computer station. If Chekov or Uhura had still been watching, they would have noticed a subtle but significant change in Sulu's manner. Sharper, decisive, the almost suffocating lethargy lifted from him like the removal of a shroud.

The screen blinked on and there was the image of Admiral LaVelle. LaVelle had a round face, with dark curly hair tinged with gray. "Captain," she said without preamble, her voice echoing a faint Southern drawl, "first allow me to extend condolences once more, both for myself and behalf of Starfleet, on your loss."

"Appreciated, Admiral."

"Regarding your inquiry as to the status of Askalon Five, site of your daughter's death"—LaVelle was clearly glancing at another screen off to the side—"Captain Harriman has quarantined it. You know the regs regarding a quarantine once it's been set in place."

"Yes, ma'am. Quarantine cannot be lifted, nor any contact made with the planet, until a quarantine team has been sent in to discover the source of infection, dispatch it if possible, and then observe the planet for one month to make certain that no sign of the reason for the quarantine remains."

"You know this, then."

"Yes, ma'am."

"Yet you request permission for the *Excelsior* to go to Askalon Five. You've already put this request in to Admiral Paul over in the quarantine division and, when she said no, you had the request pushed up to me."

"That is correct, ma'am."

LaVelle smiled sympathetically. "Captain . . . I appreciate your concerns . . . but regulations were put into place specifically for this sort of situation. A situation where our emotional impulses might prompt us to take some sort of action that could have serious repercussions. At the time when we most want to get around or ignore regulations is the moment when we must, most faithfully, adhere to them. You understand that, correct?"

"Absolutely, Admiral." He nodded respectfully. "I was simply proceeding up the chain of command in pursuing a query."

"And that is perfectly acceptable. But the query will end here. We understand that, Captain Sulu?"

"Yes, ma'am, we do. A question, though. At what point will a quarantine team be dispatched to make its initial inquiries?"

"I thought you might ask that. At the moment, Captain, our resources are somewhat stretched. The collapse of the Klingon Empire has strained the Federation's capabilities. We're dealing with situations that have greater immediacy than that of Askalon Five. We can't pull a team off Cygnus Three, for example, where a virus is ravaging an entire colony, to investigate where there are no inhabitants. We're trying to prevent people dying, Captain, and shifting a team to see what the problem is on Askalon Five will not bring back your daughter, and may even cost lives if the time could have been better spent elsewhere."

"I appreciate and understand all that, Admiral," Sulu said evenly. "I simply wish to have a projected date."

LaVelle let out a sigh and once again checked a screen that Sulu couldn't see. "Eight . . . nine months, perhaps. Could be a little sooner, I imagine. Could also be considerably later. We do the best we can, Captain."

"Yes, ma'am. We all do."

"Good. Now . . . have you been apprised of the situation on Centrelis?"

"Yes, Admiral. Newly admitted to the Federation, and just beyond the outskirts of Tholian space . . ."

"Correct, and the Tholian assembly is claiming that the planet's orbit brings it into Tholian space thirty percent of the Centrelian year . . . and therefore is making noise that the Centrelians should turn over thirty percent of the planet's resources. We're endeavoring to handle it through diplomatic channels, but the diplomats have requested the presence of a starship as backup."

"The theory being that it will cut down on Tholian saber-rattling."

"Exactly. You, Captain, have the most experience with the Tholians. So you're elected to handle this."

" 'Elected.' You make it sound like a democracy, Admiral."

"That we most definitely are not. You will proceed to Centrelis with all due haste and stay on-station there until the situation is resolved. Good luck in your mission, Captain. And again . . . my condolences."

"Thank you, Admiral," said Sulu.

The screen blinked out.

Sulu stared for a long time at the computer. Then he leaned forward and said, "Computer . . . prepare to record a message."

"Ready," said the computer.

He steepled his fingers for a moment, and then he began to speak.

"By the time you receive this," he said, "I may very well have thrown away my captaincy. For all I know, I may even be dead."

And he continued. As he did so, his gaze settled on a small holopicture that sat on the desk just to the right of the screen.

It was one of those special ones called a Lifeshot. Taken over a series of years, the Lifeshot took the subject at the youngest age photographed, and merged it sequentially with the next shot and the next and so on. The simple routine on the Lifeshot's computer created a tasteful wardrobe, clothing the image. The morphing program did the rest.

The result was that the Lifeshot gave a visual progression of the subject, at varying speeds depending upon the viewer's preference.

Sulu watched the Lifeshot, ranging from Demora's smiling six-year-old face to the final shot that had been taken of her when she was about twenty. He'd taken her regularly every year until the point where he'd assumed command of the *Excelsior*. He'd asked her to keep up with it while he was gone, but she'd hemmed and hawed and finally told him that she just didn't want to anymore. He hadn't argued with her because, frankly, arguing with Demora could often be a losing proposition. Once she'd made her mind up, that was pretty much that.

The transition on the Lifeshot took about a minute. Sulu sat there and watched her grow from child to blossoming adolescence, and from there to a young woman . . . nine inches high, to be sure, but there was nothing diminutive about the memories or the feelings.

He was surprised how steady his voice was as he recorded. It really shouldn't have been surprising, because he really wasn't giving much thought to what he was saying. His thoughts, his emotions . . . his soul, he realized . . . were a million miles away. Or, to be more specific . . . thirteen years ago. . . .

SECTION FOUR

PARENTHOOD

Chapter Fifteen

IT HELPED TO HAVE friends in the office of the Surgeon General in Starfleet, and those Leonard McCoy had in abundance. So when the rather curious "situation" arose, it was McCoy who was summoned in for a consult out of deference to his long-standing relationship with the . . . as it was delicately put . . . "person in question."

He wished that Jim were around to handle this, but he was off doing that damned fool diving of his. Kirk had regaled him with tales of deep-sea explorations, wearing antiquated gear and a bathing suit rather than proper insulated suits with their built-in fail-safe oxygen supplies. "That's not really undersea diving," he'd sniffed. "You don't feel like you're part of the sea."

"You'll become a permanent part of the sea if you're not careful," McCoy had grumbled at him. But he'd decided not to push it too much; the problem with Kirk was that he'd probably come up with something even more danger-ous to do. That's the kind of guy he was: totally uncaring about personal safety. Under the impression that trivialities such as mortality applied to lesser beings.

Hopefully that would change as soon as Kirk started the faculty assignment at Starfleet Academy. Even that, though, made McCoy apprehensive. There was only one place where Kirk would truly be happy, and that was in the command chair of a starship. But they'd been giving him the full treatment, Starfleet had. Emphasized all the experience he had to share. Convinced him that by teaching at the Academy, he could be improving Starfleet at its core.

And he'd bought it. Blast him, he'd bought it. McCoy knew, in his heart of hearts, that it was going to cost Kirk in the long run. His body might have been on Earth, but his soul was in the stars. He would keep running faster and faster, looking for something that he didn't even know he was missing. And when he finally realized that whatever it was he was searching for was still gone—light-years away and forever beyond his reach—he would start to wither. Wither and die. McCoy could see it clear as anything, but Kirk—home and flush with triumph from his second five-year mission—had been blinded to it. Blinded by the success and accolades. And maybe, God help him, by the legend that was building around him. McCoy had no doubt that, sooner or later, Kirk would realize the hideous mistake. Realize what he'd gotten himself into because he'd believed his own press.

"Damn his ego," he muttered.

"Damn whose ego, Doc?"

McCoy looked up and saw Mr. Sulu standing there, his arms folded across his chest.

"No one's," replied McCoy.

Sulu smiled. "Oh, come on now, Doc. You ask me to come meet you here at the Surgeon General's building . . . you're all mysterious about it . . . and now you won't even tell me what's on your mind?"

"Oh, we'll . . . discuss it," said McCoy. "Uhm . . . sit down, Sulu. How are things going with you?"

Sulu looked at McCoy appraisingly. It was clear he knew something was on the doctor's mind. How could he not, after all? McCoy had summoned him, with some degree of urgency, from Starfleet Headquarters, and obviously had some reason for doing so. But he also knew that McCoy wasn't the type to be rushed. He'd get to it in his own good time, so it was simplest to go along with McCoy at his own speed.

"Things are going fine, Doc," Sulu said as he sank into the chair opposite McCoy. It wasn't McCoy's office, but merely one that he was borrowing. "Have you heard?"

"Heard what?"

"I've been offered the position of first officer aboard the *Bozeman.* Had a subspace meeting with Captain Bateson. He's," and he smiled slightly, "not exactly Captain Kirk. More the . . . cerebral type."

"Funny. For some reason, I have trouble picturing you any place other than the helm of the *Enterprise.*"

"So do I. But let's face it, Doc. The newest *Enterprise* refit will take at least six to eight months . . . I've even heard as much as a year. Plus there's talk about this new *Excelsior* class that will make the *Enterprise* obsolete. I have as much loyalty to the *Enterprise* as the next man, Doc . . . but the writing's on the wall. Two, maybe three years tops, and she'll be retired, and I'll be . . . what? Three years older? Still at helm?" He shook his head. "I have to admit that Admiral's Kirk's decision to teach shook me a bit. At first I was a bit stunned. But then I thought, Well, with the sort of career he's had, he deserves it, right? He's entitled."

McCoy said nothing.

Sulu continued, "Somehow I was perfectly satisfied with the status quo as along as James Kirk was in that command chair. But if I'm going to be out there on my own, Doc, then it's about time I started working on my career, too. Sink or swim, as they say."

"As they say." He paused. "Sulu, do you ever wish there was . . . something else? Something more, besides a career?"

"Wish?" He shrugged. "I've . . . thought of it from time to time, of course. But this is who I am, Doctor. It's what I do. No use complaining about it now."

McCoy shifted uncomfortably in his seat, and Sulu looked at him a bit askance. "Doc . . . ?" He let the prompt hang there in the air. "Doc . . . we've known each other for too long to be shy about things now. If there's something on your mind . . ."

"You know," McCoy said, "no matter how many times I've had to deliver news like this, it doesn't get easier. Sulu . . . Susan Ling is dead."

Sulu stared at him a moment and then said calmly, "I'm . . . sorry to hear that."

McCoy looked surprised. "Don't take this wrong, but . . . I'd have expected even Spock to give more of a reaction than that."

"More of a reaction?"

"Yes! I tell you she's dead, you sit there cool as you please and just tell me you're sorry to hear it."

Sulu was about to reply, then stopped, reconsidered, and started again. "Doc . . . there's something I'm missing here. I feel badly that this friend of yours is—"

"*Mine?* I never . . ." He sighed in exasperation, then turned and said, "Computer—file on Susan Ling."

A file appeared on the screen and McCoy swiveled it around for Sulu to see.

Sulu stared at it . . . and went ashen.

McCoy saw the instant change in Sulu's demeanor, and immediately realized the magnitude of his error. "Oh, God . . . you didn't know her real name, did you?"

Sulu shook his head.

"I'm sorry, Sulu."

He stared at the image on the screen. Ling Sui, as he had known her, stared back at him with that slightly uncomfortable expression one always has when posing for some sort of official photograph. Words ran alongside the picture and he tried to read them, but they blurred together. He rubbed at the bridge of his nose and sat back, trying to compose himself. "How?" he managed to ask.

"Sakuro's disease. Apparently the symptoms first manifested while she was on Marris Three, and their facilities aren't exactly up to Federation standard. She managed to get to a starbase, but by then it was too late."

Sulu looked down at his lap. "I . . . haven't seen her for years. Six . . . maybe seven years, I think."

"Haven't thought about her since then?"

He shook his head, and a small smile touched his lips. "Oh, I've . . . remembered her . . . from time to time. I'll tell you about it sometime . . . although it would help if you had a few drinks in you to make it believable. I wish . . ."

McCoy raised an eyebrow. "What?"

"I was just thinking that . . . Susan . . . was a remarkable woman. Being with her was like trying to snag light rays. And I sometimes wish I'd . . . I'd managed to have more of her than just a fleeting memory."

"Well . . . you're always supposed to be careful of what you wish for, because you may get it."

The comment jogged at Sulu's memory for a moment, and then he recalled. He shook his head slowly. "That's funny."

"There's something funny about this?"

"Well, only in that Chekov said exactly the same thing shortly before I met Susan."

Then, slowly, a tumbler clicked over in Sulu's mind. He looked at McCoy with curiosity and said, "Doc . . . how did you know that I knew her?"

McCoy sighed. "I was wondering when you'd ask. She didn't have a formal will, precisely, but she did leave behind a document and you were named in it."

"What, she left me something?"

"Not some*thing* exactly . . ."

There was a knock at the door, and a soft voice came from the other side. It was female, very young, with a slightly musical lilt to it. "Doctor? I'm lonely in the other room. Can I come in? Is he here yet?"

Sulu and McCoy exchanged glances.

And Sulu knew.

Instantly.

His voice was a hoarse whisper. "You can't be serious."

McCoy nodded.

"But . . ." Sulu felt as if he'd lost physical contact with the rest of his body. "But . . . we just . . . there was just that one time, in the desert . . ."

"A lot about humans has changed over the millenia, but the fact that it only takes once isn't among them," McCoy said dryly. "Would you like to meet her?"

Before Sulu could get out another word, the door slid open.

She was wearing a carefully pressed blue dress. Her hands were interlaced in front of her, her fingernails delicately painted red. Her long black hair was drawn back in a ponytail. Her face . . .

Her face looked like someone had taken Ling Sui's head, shrunk it to child size, and stuck it on a little girl's body.

She studied Sulu carefully.

"Are you my father?" she asked. Her English was carefully spoken and slightly accented. Sulu knew immediately that she was multilingual.

Sulu looked to McCoy. McCoy nodded slowly. "First thing we did," he said softly. "Ran a test cross-matched against your gene files. There's no doubt."

He turned back and stared at her. "It . . . appears so," he said in answer to her question. He was looking for something to say, something memorable, something that he could look back on years from now and marvel at its brilliance and pithiness.

"And you are—?" he asked after a moment.

It wasn't brilliant. It wasn't pithy. It wasn't even especially useful, because she simply stared at him.

Not wanting to leave matters hanging, McCoy said, "Hikaru Sulu . . . this is Demora Ling. Or . . . Demora Sulu, if you . . ."

"Get married?" asked Demora.

Despite the fragility of the situation, McCoy was nonetheless amused. "I was going to say 'arrange an adoption.' But that's pretty much up to you. To both of you."

Sulu felt as if he were reeling. It seemed all a hell of a lot to absorb at one time, and there was Demora simply staring at him with Ling Sui's eyes.

"So . . . you'll be going off on another ship soon, right? The *Bozeman?*"

Sulu nodded.

"That sounds exciting. Have a good time."

Slowly Sulu hunkered down until he was on eye level with her. "Honey," he said slowly, "I'm . . . look, I want you to be a big girl about this . . ."

"You don't have to sound so patronizing," she informed him airily.

"I'm . . . sorry. I didn't mean to. Demora . . . could you wait outside? I know you've been there for a while," he said upon seeing her face start to twist in exasperation. "Just a short while longer. And then we'll go . . ." For want of a better word, he said, "home."

She seemed to be looking straight through to the back of his head. Then she nodded and stepped into the outside room, the doors hissing behind her.

He remained in a crouched position, his back to McCoy. "It's . . . a lot to absorb. You understand, don't you?"

"I wish there had been a smoother way to tell you." He paused. "What are you going to do?"

"I don't know. Not yet. I just . . . need time to think." Slowly he straightened up.

"I know this may sound like an odd thing to say at this time, Sulu, but . . ." McCoy stuck out a hand. "Congratulations. You're a father."

"Thank you, Doctor." Sulu shook the hand. Then he started for the door, stopped, turned back to McCoy, and said once more, with unmistakable incredulity in his voice, "It was just the one time."

"I hope it was worth it," said McCoy.

"Actually . . . I barely remember it. I was half asleep," said Sulu, and he walked out the door.

And McCoy shook his head and muttered to himself, "Well, it's pretty damned obvious which half was awake."

Chapter Sixteen

WHEN THE DOOR to Sulu's apartment slid open, Chekov found himself staring at a young Asian girl in a blue dress. Reflexively he glanced at the apartment number on the assumption that he was at the wrong place. But a quick check proved that he was where he was supposed to be.

"Is Meester Sulu here?" he asked.

She nodded but didn't step aside. "Who are you?"

"Pavel Chekov. Who are you?"

"Demora."

"Demora, like the city?"

"Just like."

"Vell . . . most unusual. I am a friend of Sulu's. Are you?"

She appeared to consider it. "The jury's still out on that, frankly."

He was surprised by her apparent erudition. Then again, Chekov didn't have a great deal of experience with children, so he wasn't entirely certain what to expect.

"May I come in?"

She stepped aside, giving him room to enter.

He'd always liked Sulu's apartment . . . not that Sulu had a great deal of time to spend there, what with being gone for years at a time. Furnished in dark browns, with real wood furniture (lord only knew where Sulu had acquired it). His antique weapons collection, ranging from swords to firearms, was secured behind plexi cabinets. Pictures or portraits of his various ancestors hung on the walls. Sulu was fairly big on families, and could trace his ancestry back centuries.

"Vere is Sulu, do you know?"

She chucked a finger. "In the kitchen. Making dinner."

"I'll just go talk to him then."

"Fine," said Demora with a shrug. She moved over to a couch and sank down into the cushion.

Chekov found Sulu in the kitchen. "So . . . vat mysterious and exotic dish are you preparing?"

Sulu was busy scooping something from a pot and pouring it over rolls. "Chili," he said. "It's what Demora wanted."

"Ah, Demora. Your sentinal at the gate. Interesting little girl. She's . . . vat? Eleven? Twelve?"

"Just turning seven."

"She seems older."

"Well, that's appropriate. I feel older."

"So who is she? Niece?"

"Daughter."

"Whose daughter?"

Sulu stared at him. "Mine."

It was clear that Chekov was having trouble digesting the information. "I'm sorry . . . vat?"

"She's my daughter."

Chekov looked in the direction of the living room, where Demora was seated, and then back to Sulu. He looked stunned. "Your . . . daughter."

"Yes."

"*Your* daughter. Your *daughter?*"

Sulu put the plates down, making no attempt to hide his impatience. He spoke in a low tone to keep their voices from reaching Demora. "Are we going to move past this sentence anytime soon?"

"You have a daughter?" Chekov whispered. "And you never mentioned her to me?"

"I didn't know! I didn't know until a few hours ago."

"Do you know who the mother is?"

"Of *course* I know who the mother is."

"Oh, *now* you say 'Of course.' Considering you didn't know the child existed, the idea of you not knowing who the mother is doesn't seem all that farfetched."

"It's Ling Sui. You remember her."

"Of course I remember her. The woman from . . ." And then he thudded his hand against his forehead. "Of course. From Demora. I should have realized it vasn't simply coincidence." He hesitated. "So . . . so vat do you do now?"

"I don't know," said Sulu in exasperation. "She has no other relatives but me. She's just lost her mother. She doesn't seem especially interested in me. And I'm scheduled to ship out with the *Bozeman.*"

"Does she know that?"

"She knows it, yes."

"Vell, perhaps the reason she's not especially interested is because she doesn't vant to make the emotional investment in someone who is leaving."

Sulu transferred the dishes onto a serving tray. "Since when are you the great child psychiatrist?"

"Since ven are you a father?"

Sulu sighed. "All right. *Touché.*"

As he started to head into the dining room, Chekov stopped him and said, "Uhm . . . you didn't mention to me at the time that you and Ling Sui . . ."

"It was just once."

"That's all it takes."

"So I've heard," said Sulu.

The meal didn't go precisely as planned.

For one thing, Chekov didn't plan for himself and Demora to hit it off as well as they did. He had grown accustomed to thinking of children as odd, separate creatures, rather than simply small humans. Beings with their own rules and own manner of communication to which no adult could be privy.

Demora was quite the opposite. She was, he suspected, very much her mother's daughter. She spoke with intelligence and education about a startling number of topics, ranging from archaeology to the present condition of Federation politics. Chekov found himself becoming quite fond of her during his visit, and he suspected that Demora felt likewise.

Sulu, for his part, kept his own counsel. His gaze would dart from one to the other as they chatted. Chekov interacted with Demora with such ease that Sulu felt torn. On the one hand he was pleased that they were hitting it off so well. On the other hand . . . he was a little jealous.

But he realized why it was that Chekov felt so at ease with her. It was because he was going to be able to leave. This was Sulu's problem, Sulu's situation, and Chekov was just a visitor to it. He could get to know Demora as a person, chat with her, laugh with her . . . and Sulu got to worry about what in hell he was going to do next.

Chekov stayed late into the evening, regaling Demora with stories about his and Sulu's time together in the service. A couple of times Sulu tried to hush him up, but Chekov was not easy to stop. Each anecdote would remind him of another, and he'd say with growing excitement, "And *then* there vas the time . . ."

The hour grew later and later, and finally Sulu said, "Demora . . . I really think it's time for bed. I showed you where the guest bedroom is. . . ."

"That's because I'm a guest?"

He looked from Demora to Chekov and back again. Clearing his throat, he said, "That's . . . just what I'm in the habit of calling it, that's all."

"It's early for me still."

"Well, I think it's time you went to bed."

She squared her shoulders and said, "Mother lets me st . . ."

And then she caught herself, speaking of her mother in the present tense. It was a slip that had a very visible effect on her, and she looked downcast. It was the first time since he'd met her that he'd seen anything from her acknowledging her loss. She certainly pulled herself together quickly, however, as she said, "All right. Good night then." She turned and walked briskly away toward the rear of the apartment, and Sulu had the feeling—probably legitimate—that the reason she retreated so quickly was because she didn't want him to see her cry.

Chekov leaned over and said to Sulu in a low voice, "She's a great kid, isn't she?"

"Oh . . . fabulous," Sulu said. "So how do you suggest I handle this?"

"Vell—" Chekov gave it a moment's thought. "—you could try and talk Starfleet into letting you bring her along."

"You mean on the *Bozeman?* Against regs. Never happen." He looked down, drumming his fingers. "I'm . . . going to make arrangements."

"Vat kind? You'll leave her vith your family?"

"There are schools. I've done some checking. Boarding schools and such that will take care of the child year round. Educate her, feed her. That would be best, I think."

"Vile you're off exploring the galaxy," said Chekov.

"You make it sound trivial."

"I don't mean to," said Chekov. "And you know I don't feel that vay. I'm just saying . . ."

"What? What are you saying?"

He raised his eyes and studied his longtime friend. "I'm saying that here's a child who vill have lost her mother and never really gotten to know her father. And that's a lousy vay to grow up."

"Oh really. How do you know?"

"Because that's how I grew up."

Sulu said nothing for a moment, then went back to tapping his fingers on the coffee table in front of them. "You turned out okay," he said after a time.

"Perhaps. But maybe I could have turned out better. I'll never know."

"And if I leave her, she'll never know. Is that what you're

saying?" Sulu rose, looking down at Chekov. "What are you telling me, Pav? That I should quit? Turn down the first-officer position? Walk away from the thing I know most about in the galaxy so that I can try being a father to an instant family, something about which I assure you I know absolutely nothing? Chekov . . . it's crazy. It wouldn't do her any good, and it certainly wouldn't do me any good."

"Are you sure?"

"Yes, I'm sure!"

"Then I suppose there's nothing more to say."

"Apparently not."

Sulu sat back down. It had never seemed so quiet in the apartment before. It was as if the absence of noise had become an entity unto itself.

"It's just ironic, that's all," Chekov finally said.

"What is?"

"Vell . . . years ago, you were telling me how life on Earth couldn't be exciting. How there was no adventure. And then you were pulled into the entire business vit Ling Sui, and you thought you had found adventure. But that was only a few days. There is no greater adventure than raising a child."

"You're speaking from experience, I gather," he said sarcastically.

"I vish. Just gut instinct. The same instinct that tells me leaving her behind vouldn't be right."

"Maybe you'd feel differently if the situations were reversed."

"Maybe," agreed Chekov. "But . . . they're not. And so I don't."

"What do you want from me, Chekov?" Sulu said in exasperation. "What do you expect me to do? Have some sudden burst of paternal affection that I never had before? Look at this child who is, to all intents and purposes, a stranger to me, and feel so protective of her that I reorder my life around her? Chekov, I . . . I have responsibilities . . ."

"Yes. You do," said Chekov sharply. "And vun of them is

in the 'guest bedroom' right now. So the only question is: Vat are you going to do about it?"

"I'm going to do right by her," Sulu said. "It just may be that you and I have different definitions of what's right."

"Actually," Chekov replied, "I don't think ve do. Ve simply von't both admit to it, that's all."

Chapter Seventeen

SULU AND DEMORA spent the next day walking around San Francisco. Demora was quiet much of the time as he pointed out landmarks to her. She seemed politely interested at most.

He stopped outside one building, pointed, and said, "This is where I grew up."

She cast a quick glance at it. "Your family still live here?" she asked.

He shook his head. "My mother moved to New Tokyo to take care of her sister. The rest of my family . . . they're all going on with their lives in other places." He sighed. "Once upon a time, families lived together in the same house for generations. But it's . . . not like that anymore. It hasn't been for a long, long time. There's too many opportunities out there. Too many directions for people to go."

"And no one wants to be anchored with children."

He stopped and looked down at her. Realizing that candy-coating the truth was going to be a waste of time with this child, he said bluntly, "So . . . how much of my conversation with Chekov did you overhear last night?"

"All of it," she said in that matter-of-fact tone of hers.

"And how do you feel about it?"

She shrugged. She had a very expressive shrug.

"That's it? Just," and he shrugged back.

"Mother brought me with her wherever she went because that's what she felt she had to do to be a good mother. You feel you have to dump me in a school because that's how you'll be a good father. Everyone does what they have to do. One way or another makes no difference to me."

He studied her, trying to see if she was being sarcastic. If she was trying to cover up some sort of deep hurt. But her face was as inscrutable as . . .

. . . as his could be.

"You're being very grown-up," he said.

She raised an eyebrow ever so slightly. "Someone has to be," she replied.

The school that Sulu had in mind was in Washington state, just outside Seattle. Called the Winchester School, it was one of several schools highly recommended to Starfleet personnel who were in similar straits as Sulu (not identical, of course; Sulu's circumstances were rather unusual, even for Starfleet).

They walked around the grounds for a time, visited the dorms, spoke with the teachers. At all times Demora was polite, quiet, respectful.

It made Sulu extremely nervous.

He had long ago learned to trust his gut instinct. For instance, when encountering another ship, he simply *knew* when there was going to be trouble. Before the other ship would put up their shields, before any alerts were sounded . . . Sulu just had a feeling.

He had that feeling now. Her shields had been raised. He wasn't sure what her weapons were, but he dreaded having them fired in his direction.

"Do you like it?" he asked as they stood in the dorm.

She nodded. That was all. Just nodded.

She nodded in the classrooms. She nodded in the library. She nodded in the grassy center square. She nodded so much that Sulu thought her head was going to fall off.

On the flight home, he said to her, "I think you don't like it."

She sighed in exasperation. "I said I did."

"I think you may just be saying what I want to hear."

She looked up at him icily. "How do I know what you want to hear? I hardly know you."

And it's not like you're giving me the chance. She didn't say it in so many words, but he was positive that's what was going through her mind. Either that or it was so strongly on his own mind that he was superimposing it onto her.

"All right. Fair enough," he said. "What would you like to know about me?"

She gave it some consideration.

"Did you love my mother?" she asked.

He wasn't certain what he'd been expecting her to say. On the other hand, he realized, he shouldn't have been the least bit surprised.

But what was he supposed to say? The truth was that he had barely had any time with her mother. They'd had no time to build a relationship, to establish bonds of trust. To create all the things that went into a loving . . .

And then he thought about her. Thought about her smile . . . her laugh . . . her bravery, her grim humor . . . thought about what she had been to him, what she'd represented . . .

. . . thought about the press of their bodies against each other . . .

. . . thought about what she had given him.

And he smiled and said, "Demora . . . I think I loved your mother before I ever met her."

She looked at him slightly askance. "Does that mean yes?"

"It means yes." He hesitated and then said, "Did she love me?"

Again with the shrug. "I guess."

"Did she ever say?"

Demora laughed slightly. "She never even said she loved me. Mother wasn't much for talking; just doing. Are you like that?"

"In a way. Are you?"

"In a way. Besides," she added with that mature air of

hers, "talking about love and everything . . . it's a waste of time, really."

"If it's a waste of time, why'd you bring it up?"

"I felt like wasting time, I guess. I mean, I'm here. You're here. Mother's gone. Love really doesn't much matter in the grand scheme of things, you know? Not in our situation."

"Our situation being—?"

"Well . . . it's like if a meteor is coming toward your planet. You can spend a lot of time wondering where the meteor came from. Maybe it was part of another planet that blew up, and then you wonder if there were people on *that* planet, and what were they like, and did they all die, and all that kind of stuff. But none of it really matters. The only thing that matters is that you have to do something about the meteor—blast it to pieces—because it's a threat to your planet."

"And I'm the planet, and you're the meteor. Is that what you're saying?"

She shrugged once more. Sulu's shoulders were starting to ache just watching her.

"Demora . . . the last thing I want to do is blast you to pieces."

"And what's the first thing you want to do with me?"

He shook his head in confusion. "What?"

She spoke utterly calmly, not appearing the least bit upset. "The first thing you'd want to do with me . . . is wish that I wasn't here. Because then you could go on with your life."

"That's not true."

She looked away.

He put a hand on her shoulder but she pushed it away. "That's not true," he said again.

And with a set jaw and steady gaze she said, "You know it is."

Which, of course, he did.

She was to leave for the Winchester School in the morning. This way she'd have enough time to settle in there, and for Sulu to then board the next outbound transport to take him to the *Bozeman*.

She said nothing as she went off to bed; just nodded her head slightly as he told her that he'd see her bright and early in the morning. He thought he should say more, but decided that there was no reason to do so now. It would seem maudlin and pointless. Plenty of time for goodbyes later.

That night he dreamt of Susan. Or Ling Sui.

He'd dreamt of her before. Some nights aboard the *Enterprise* when sleep didn't come easily, she'd come to him. Rarely was it in the city of Demora, or in the Sahara. Instead they would be at Wrigley's Pleasure Planet together, or cruising the rings of Saturn, or in a jungle paradise. Occasionally moments of danger from their adventure would reappear in fragmented form. But no matter what the forum for their adventure, she was always smiling and loving and set for anything.

But not this time.

This time he was on the bridge of the *Enterprise*. He was seated in the command chair. There was no one else around, and the bridge seemed oddly distended, as if being viewed through a fish-eye lens.

He heard weeping from behind him, a soul in torment. It was echoing through the bridge. He spun in his chair and faced the turbolift.

It sat open. Standing in the lift was Ling Sui. She said nothing, did nothing. She just stood there, with tears flowing down her cheeks, her chest heaving slightly in time to the sobs. Sulu got up from his chair and the turbolift doors slid shut. He crossed to the lift quickly, stepping over a tribble, and walked up to the doors. They didn't open. The crying continued. He jammed his fingers in and worked on prying them wide. They slid open with a low moan rather than their customary hiss.

The turbolift was empty.

The crying continued.

He stepped into the turbolift, trying to find where Ling had vanished to. The doors slid shut, and the turbolift began to move straight down.

It began to accelerate, faster and faster, and still he heard the crying. Except it no longer sounded like that of a grown woman. It had escalated in pitch and now seemed to Sulu like the sobbing of a child.

It was about at that time that he realized the turbolift was dropping faster than it should. Much faster. The floors were streaking past and Sulu suddenly knew that he was in free fall. There was absolutely no way in hell that the turbolift was going to slow down in time to prevent him from being a smear on the bottom of the shaft.

The sobbing was fading, becoming fainter and fainter, and Sulu braced himself for the impact. He wondered if, as they always say, his life would flash before his eyes. He waited and then it came, danced before him, so quick that it was little more than an eyeblink.

It was a child's face.

Sulu snapped awake.

He sat in his room, bare-chested, chest heaving, for quite a while. His hands were flat on his mattress as if trying to reassure him that he was on firm ground instead of being in danger that it would begin to plummet under him.

He checked his chronometer and was surprised to see that it was only 2 A.M. He was wide awake, completely rested . . . if one could call being jostled awake by a horrifying nightmare restful.

He wiped the sweat from his bow and slid his feet to the floor. Then he pulled his robe from his closet and wrapped it around himself.

He padded out into the hallway and walked the short distance to the guest bedroom. He paused a moment, listening for the sound of steady breathing. Then he slipped into the room.

Light from the hallway cascaded through, illuminating the lower half of her bed. She had wound the sheet around her, but even so he could see that she was curled up in a fetal position. The curve of her back was rising and falling erratically. Her head was a bit twisted around and didn't look squarely on the pillow. Somehow it all seemed very uncomfortable.

Sulu went to her and gently started to readjust her head onto the pillow. And as he did so, he felt the pillow's wetness. Very damp, as if . . .

She'd been crying into it.

Coincidental? Or had he heard it distantly in his sleep and it had worked its way into his dream? The latter seemed the more likely somehow.

Crying herself to sleep. Why? Because her mother was gone? Because her father was sending her away? Because she had no home, no place to call her own?

She'd put on a tremendous show of strength, a fabulous show. But there was no dissembling in sleep, no bravado to cover inner fears. There was just a sleeping child with the remnants of her anxiety still damp on the pillow.

"Shields down," he murmured. And he wasn't sure if he was referring to her or to himself.

He went back to his room, took one of the extra pillows on his bed and brought it back to her. Removing the sopping pillow, he substituted the dry one. He slid it under her head gently, then readjusted the blanket around her. Doing so required momentarily moving her hands.

One of her small, delicate hands wrapped around two of his fingers and squeezed tightly.

He pulled gently, trying to disengage, but she wouldn't let go. She wasn't consciously aware of it at all . . .

Tenderly he wrapped the rest of his fingers around her hand, enveloping hers in his.

In her sleep, all unintending, she had launched her weaponry. It wasn't as devastating as a phaser, nor as destructive as a photon torpedo . . . but it cut far deeper and, in its way, was much more effective.

He stood there for some minutes, and saw that her uneven breathing had smoothed out. Her sleep was calm now. Whatever torments had been in her mind had apparently vanished, the strength of a father's hand enough to squeeze them into nothingness.

Once he was positive that she was sleeping soundly, he gently—ever so gently—disengaged his hand from hers. He watched her there some more, bathed in the light from the hallway, and then carefully backed out of the room, never taking his eyes from her.

He remained for a moment or two more, then went to the

bay window in the living room. He stared up at the stars, thought about helming a starship through them.

Thought about standing at the side of a captain.

Thought about his own captaincy.

Thought about the *Enterprise* . . . about what he'd been working for all these years . . . about the mission . . . the credo . . .

Space, the final frontier . . .

How could he turn away from it? It would always be calling to him, pleading with him, scolding him like a spurned lover . . .

To explore strange new worlds . . .

Not to see planet after planet . . . tread on alien soil . . . wonder what new mystery was to unfold before his eyes . . .

To seek out new life . . .

And that was where he stopped.

New life.

A new life. And it *was* new. Six years old, good lord, that wasn't so much as an eyeblink in the history of the galaxy. Not even the beginning of a heartbeat in that endless body of time.

A new life, and he had not sought it out, it had sought him out.

A new life, and he was responsible for it.

Now . . . what the hell was he going to *do* about it?

Captain Morgan Bateson's image flickered slightly over the subspace patch. Sulu had begged a favor from Janice Rand, working the graveyard shift at Starfleet Communicore, to plug into a high-priority signal.

"You owe me for this, Sulu," she had said.

"Anything," he had replied.

"Fine. You make captain, you rescue me out of this lousy detail."

"Done and done," he had assured her.

She'd gotten it through on a priority signal, punching through local traffic, and getting him a direct real-time line to the *Bozeman*.

Captain Bateson, fingers steepled, regarded Sulu with an

obvious air of puzzlement. "According to the incoming computer feed, Commander, it's somewhere in the neighborhood of 0500 hours where you are. Early riser?"

"Sometimes, yes, sir."

"Something is on your mind, I take it."

"Yes, sir." Sulu shifted uncomfortably, not exactly certain how to proceed.

Bateson nodded encouragingly. "Go ahead. I'm listening."

"I . . . regret that I will not be able to serve you as your second-in-command, sir. A circumstance has arisen that precludes my leaving Earth for the foreseeable future."

"I see." Bateson smiled. "Didn't get somebody pregnant, did you?" He was joking.

Sulu blinked in surprise. "Yes, sir." He paused. "Seven years ago."

Now it was Bateson's turn to look surprised. He recovered very quickly, however. "Well, Commander . . . I take it that either the mother has a gestation period exceeded only by the eight-year birth cycle of a Terwilligan Flogg . . . or else this was a fairly recent revelation."

"The latter, sir."

"The mother just sprung this on you?"

"The mother is dead, sir."

"Oh." Bateson pursed his lips slightly. "You could make other arrangements for the . . ." He paused. "Boy or girl?"

"Girl, sir."

"Girl. You could make other arrangements for her, I presume."

"Yes, sir. I choose not to."

"I see. You could also have simply informed me via communiqué through Starfleet Command."

"I know, sir. I also choose not to do that. I . . . feel I owe you a face-to-face explanation, sir."

"What you owe me, mister, is your service as my second-in-command," said Bateson sharply. "I did not make my choice lightly, and I dislike the notion of having to start from scratch."

"Yes, sir. However . . ."

"However, you feel you owe something to your daughter as well." His voice softened. "Must have been a difficult decision for you, Commander."

"None harder, sir."

"Then I'll be damned if I make it any more so for you." He sighed.

"I'm sorry about this, sir."

He actually chuckled slightly. "Save your sympathy for yourself, Commander. All I have to worry about is a temporary inconvenience. You have the far more serious situation on your hands. What's the girl's name, by the way?"

"Demora."

"Demora Sulu. I'll remember that. And you be sure she remembers the name of Morgan Bateson, whom she deprived of a perfectly good first officer."

"I will, sir."

"Good luck, Commander."

"And to you, sir."

"Bozeman out."

And just like that, it was over. The line was cut, the *Bozeman* and all the people aboard with their lives . . .

And Sulu's was about to begin.

Demora Ling rolled over and stretched, blinking against the sunlight coming in through the window.

She sat up, rubbing the sleep from her eyes, and got out of bed. The hem of her nightgown fell down to her ankles as she walked over to the window, yawned, and looked out.

The sun was high in the sky. Too high. They had a reservation for her on an early-morning shuttle. Her suspicion was verified a moment later when she checked the chronometer and saw that it was a few minutes before noon.

She ran out into the living room and found Sulu sitting there, calmly scanning the morning headlines while sipping a cup of tea. He looked at her blandly. "Finally roll out of bed, did you. You always sleep in like this?"

"It's noon," she said.

"Yes, I know. Do you drink tea? I don't have any kid's-type drinks, like hot chocolate or such. Sorry."

"It's noon," she repeated, as if she couldn't quite believe he was that oblivious of the time. "We . . . I have a shuttle to get to."

"We do?"

"And . . . and you have an assignment to get to."

"Ah. Well, there you're right. But the Academy can wait a few days."

She rubbed her eyes, apparently to make sure that she was genuinely awake. "The Academy?"

"Yes, Starfleet Academy. When Admiral Kirk was offered a teaching position there, he made an open offer to myself and several other longtime associates. I've decided to take him up on it."

Her head bobbed up and down slightly, a physical reflection of each new piece of information that was entering her head. "That's . . . that's here."

"Right."

"Here in San Francisco."

"Right."

"Am I still going up to the place up in Washington?"

"Not if you don't want to." He paused. "Do you want to?"

In a very soft voice, she said, "No. I hate it."

"Then why didn't you say so?"

Even more softly, she admitted, "Because I didn't think you'd care."

"Of course I care. I'm your father."

"I know you are. I just . . . I didn't know what that meant. Not really. I'm still not sure."

He put down the teacup. The movement was clumsy, and he hoped it didn't betray his nervousness. Lord, his hands had been steadier when he'd been programming phaser blasts against Klingon ships that had them sighted.

"What it means," he said slowly, "is that after you have some breakfast, we go out and take a Lifeshot, so we can watch you grow up. We go buy you some clothes. Some toys . . ."

"Toys?" she said.

"Okay, a lot of toys. We stop calling the guest room the guest room, and start calling it Demora's room. We put the wheels in motion—if you'd like—for me to officially adopt you. We do right by you."

She seemed to want to say a hundred things at once. Instead the only word the child was able to get out, her eyes wide in wonderment, was "Why?"

He smiled. "A lot of reasons. Only two that really matter: Because I'm your father. And because I love you."

"*Love* me?" she said incredulously. "You don't even *know* me."

"I know. Isn't it the most stupid thing you've ever heard?"

"Yes," she said, her lower lip trembling.

He put out a hand to her, and she took it and started to cry just as she had the previous night, except this time there were strong arms to hold her and comfort her as she said over and over, "It's stupid it's stupid it's stupid . . ."

And somehow, Sulu felt the eyes of Ling Sui upon him.

Wherever you are, you crazy woman . . . I hate you. And by the way . . . thank you . . . thank you forever. . . .

Chapter Eighteen

"DAD . . . CAN I GO with you to the Academy sometime?"

Sulu looked at Demora in surprise while, at the same time, never breaking stride.

The two of them were jogging briskly down Telegraph Hill, the way up always being a bit easier than the way down. The sun was still just in the process of coming up over the horizon, as it usually was during their early-morning runs.

In the early days, when Demora had wanted to run beside him, he'd had to completely alter his route to accommodate her. But over the years, as she'd approached her teen years, she'd had less and less trouble keeping up with him. Consequently he'd started going back to his old running paths. She'd continued to keep up with him, and he started to foresee a time when it would be all *he* could do to keep up with *her*.

"You want to come to the Academy?"

"That's what I said."

Her long hair swung across the small of her back like a

pendulum. They were both wearing T-shirts and shorts as she displayed her ability to maintain pace with her father.

What Demora wasn't was tall . . . a source of great frustration to her, although Sulu kept assuring her that she was in for a growth spurt. Demora would teasingly ask him if he was anticipating a growth spurt for himself, and indeed would occasionally gibe him by calling him Tiny. She meant it affectionately, and he let her get away with it, although he swore that anyone else who ever tried to call him that would sorely regret it.

Indeed, her lack of height made her appear, at first glance, much younger than she was. Her face still had the softness of childhood. Fully dressed, she looked preadolescent. However, in the sweaty shirt plastered to her chest and the shorts, and the shorts revealing legs like those of a young colt, there was no mistaking the fact that she was a youthful woman on the cutting edge of maturity. Sulu noticed young men's eyes turning these days as they jogged along, and he had a sneaking suspicion that he wasn't the one being sized up.

They slowed to a stop at a street corner. Sulu started to stretch, massaging a muscle that was cramping. "You've never asked to before. In fact, the first time I mentioned it, you showed such disinterest I never brought it up again."

She shrugged (some things never changing). "I didn't think you really wanted me to."

He gaped at her. But then he thought better of his first reaction, because if there was one thing he'd come to learn, it was never to accept anything Demora said or did at face value. It had been a long and hard lesson for him. He was used to dealing with adults . . . and outspoken adults, at that, such as Leonard McCoy or Pavel Chekov. People who told you exactly where they stood.

Demora wasn't always as forthcoming. This had worried him at first, but Sulu—being thorough—had researched the subject. He'd read everything he could get his hands on, from recent treatises on child rearing, all the way back to material written centuries before. He remembered a confusing conversation he'd had with Chekov, wherein Sulu had been quoting certain philosophies on parenting and Chekov had asked him who was the authority Sulu was using.

"Spock," Sulu had told him.

Chekov had looked exceedingly confused. "Meester Spock? Vat does he know about children?"

"No, Dr. Spock."

"A doctor?" Chekov was even more befuddled. "Ven did he become a doctor? Does Dr. McCoy know?"

In any event, Sulu had learned not to believe the first thing Demora said . . . or, for that matter, even the second or third necessarily. Speaking with any child was less like a normal conversation and more like peeling an onion: many layers to slice through to get to the core, and not a few tears shed along the way.

"You thought I didn't want you to? Demy . . . come on. You couldn't have thought that. I've told you about it often enough. Encouraged you. You've heard Chekov and me discuss the old days whenever he comes over. So how could you possibly think that I didn't want to share it with you?"

Demora had her foot placed flat against a building and was stretching to touch her toes. She paused and looked to him. "Truth?"

"Beats lies."

She turned and leaned against the building, her arms folded across her budding breasts. "I've been hearing about Starfleet for so long, and how wonderful it is . . . I've almost been afraid of it."

"Afraid of it?" He said it half with a laugh, unsure of what she could possibly be talking about.

"What if I visit the Academy with you . . . meet the cadets, sit in on a class . . . and I find the whole thing . . . I don't know. Dull. Maybe the cadets will be jerks, or the subject matter will bore me stiff."

"Demy! It's a visit, not a career choice."

"It's stepping into your world for the first time. Oh, I certainly was off-planet enough with Mother. But it's . . . it's different somehow. I don't know why, but it just . . . is."

"But now you want to come."

"I've just been doing a lot of thinking lately. I miss

Chekov, for one thing. He sends his letters from the *Reliant,* but it's not the same. It couldn't be. And also there's . . ."

"All right, then," Sulu said. "How about today?"

She looked surprised. "Today?"

"Why not today?"

"No reason not to. I just meant . . . some time in the future."

"Two hours from now is the future, isn't it? That's the wonderful thing about the future. It's whenever you want it to be."

"Okay. Fine. That would be . . . fine," said Demora.

"But Demora . . . promise me something."

"Sure, Dad. What?"

"You'll stay out of trouble."

"Dad!" She looked at him accusingly. "When have I ever . . . ?"

"Let's not cite chapter and verse, all right?" he warned. "You know very well the number of times I've heard it from your teachers about your knack for getting in over your head. I want you to swear to me, on your honor, that you'll stay out of trouble."

"Sure. Whatever."

"I don't want 'whatever.' "

"All right, I swear."

"On your honor?"

"On my honor."

She smiled.

He frowned.

Chapter Nineteen

MAKING ASTRONAVIGATION interesting was not an easy task. There were no subtleties, no deep philosophies, no sprightly discussions about the ethics of the situation or second-guessing the right or wrong of an action. There was just straight memorization and trying to teach students how to think without regard to such irrelevancies as "up" and "down."

So in order to prevent eyes from glazing over, Sulu would tend to intersperse his lectures with his firsthand experiences. This would invariably keep the students' interest, their minds sharp and entertained, so that they wouldn't feel overwhelmed in trying to grasp the many facts that would be necessary for them to survive.

He was in the midst of one now, amused—as always—by the reactions he was getting from his class. "So I brought the *Enterprise* around, full one hundred and eighty degrees . . . and the planet was in front of us *again.*"

There was startled laughter . . . and some looks of outright incredulity . . . from the students.

"I thought that I had forgotten every single thing I'd ever learned about helming a ship," he continued. "I kept looking at the instruments, looking back at the screen, back at the instruments," and he demonstrated, his head bobbing as if it were on a spring, his eyes growing increasingly flummoxed.

"He moved the planet?" asked one cadet. "The whole thing?"

"The whole thing," affirmed Sulu.

"That's the most insane thing I've ever heard," said another.

Sulu figured that he should save for another time the anecdote about the giant hand gripping the saucer section and keeping the entire ship in place.

His eyes swept the room, looking for Demora. She'd been seated toward the back, her hands propping up her head. It was hard to tell if she was interested in what he was lecturing about. It was all somewhat advanced, after all. Not the sort of thing that was normal for a young girl to try and absorb, or even pay attention to.

She wasn't there. Her seat was empty.

He stopped talking for a moment, slightly concerned. Where the hell had she just vanished to? He wondered if he should halt, or even dismiss, the class, and go look for her.

But surely that was an overreaction. They were at Starfleet Academy, after all, not rowing in the Amazon or something. And she'd promised, on her honor, that she would not get into trouble. Demora knew how seriously Sulu took such oaths, and he had every confidence that she would do nothing to violate it.

Everywhere she looked, there was something new.

Galvanized doors, signs pointing the way to various labs and classrooms. Cadets would pass her and react with a brief smile, or a nod of the head. Plus the occasional puzzled frown, of course.

"Excuse me . . . where are you going?" she heard from behind her. She turned to see two cadets, male and female . . . the latter a Vulcan. It was the Vulcan who had spoken to her.

"Just looking around."

"You should not be wandering around," said the Vulcan. "Who are you?"

"Demora Sulu," she replied.

The cadet at the Vulcan's side pulled at her sleeve. "See? She's Commander Sulu's daughter. Come on, Saavik, we're going to be late for class."

"All right, Peter." She cast one more uneasy glance at Demora. "I think it would be best if you returned to your father," she said before she and classmate Peter Preston moved off down the hallway.

Demora, naturally, put the encounter immediately out of her mind, and continued on her way.

A couple of cadets came through a pair of heavy-duty doors, and Demora slipped through them before they shut, so that she never saw the sign that read MARK IV SIMULATOR.

She did, however, notice the freestanding sign a little farther in that read, USE OF THIS FACILITY WITH AUTHORIZED SUPERVISION ONLY. She drummed on it a moment and then continued on her way.

She made her way down the hall, past windows overlooking the gardens. She saw a young man working down there, under the guidance of an older man. The young man was medium height, with closely cut red hair. The older man was bossy and—judging by the younger man's reactions—a bit of a grouch.

Demora watched for a few minutes, and then kept going.

She slowed and then stopped upon finding what appeared to be a large set of double doors. She stepped through them . . . and stopped, slack-jawed.

She'd heard about them, but she'd never seen one before. It was the bridge of a starship.

Oh, she knew it wasn't really, of course. It was some sort of mock-up, a model. Probably designed to show students what they could expect when they finally made it through training and embarked on their career in space.

She entered it, looking around, fascinated by what she was seeing. Everything was lit up, flickering. There was even a starfield displayed on the monitor screen. It didn't take much for her to imagine herself out in the depths of space.

At every station there were readouts of activities throughout the "ship."

Her hand brushed briefly across the command chair, but somehow it didn't seem to hold interest for her. Instead she found her attention drawn to the helm station, the site of so many of her father's stories. The adventures, the battles . . . the incredible sensation of having the mighty starship's heading and weaponry at your fingertips.

She sat down at the helm station, studying the controls. "Commander Demora Sulu, reporting for duty," she said, dropping her voice an octave and trying to sound official.

She started touching controls at random. "Heading at two-ten mark three," she said briskly. "No Romulans. No Kling . . . wait! I see one coming!" She pushed a button. "B-kow! Got you! Hmm! They were guarding that planet! Scanning the planet surface . . . Captain! It appears to be . . . an entirely new race of little blue squishy guys! And . . ."

Suddenly she heard a rumbling. For a brief moment she thought there was an earthquake. Then her head snapped around and she saw the source: The large double doors through which she'd entered had just slid closed.

She froze and looked back at the controls. Had she done that? She didn't think so, but she'd been touching pads and controls pretty much with abandon. "Hello?" she called cautiously, in such a small voice that she almost couldn't hear herself.

Then the air around her crackled and she heard something. It was some sort of message, a voice speaking with tremendous urgency.

"Imperative," it said. "This is the *Kobayashi Maru*, nineteen parsecs out of Altair Six. We've struck a gravitic mine and have lost all power." The transmission was awful, almost impossible to make out. "Our hull is penetrated and we have sustained many casualties . . ."

Demora was frozen in her chair. It certainly sounded like a genuine transmission. Was anyone else hearing it? Of course, they had to be. Perhaps she was somehow picking up something coming through Starfleet Communicore. It wasn't all that far off, after all.

Kobayashi Maru. That name sounded familiar for some reason. Her father had mentioned it at some point, but she couldn't remember exactly when. He'd told her about so many adventures, mentioned so many ships, that sometimes they seemed to blur together. Which one was the *Kobayashi Maru* again . . . ?

She looked toward the console from where the transmission was originating, as it continued, *"Enterprise,* our position is Gamma Hydra Section Ten."

Enterprise? The ship was talking directly to the *Enterprise?* That would explain it. The *Enterprise* was running training maneuvers in the immediate sector. That's pretty much what it was used for these days. Her dad had grumbled about it from time to time, saying that it was a remarkable waste of an incredible ship, and she deserved better. He always called it "she," with enough affection that occasionally Demora even felt a little jealous.

Was she going to hear the *Enterprise's* response? Or was this fluke picking up only one-half of the conversation?

She heard the even fainter voice of the commander of the *Kobayashi Maru* as he said, "Hull penetrated! Life-support systems failing! Can you assist us, *Enterprise?* Can you assist us—?"

Demora desperately wished she could be up there to help them. There was no doubt in her mind that they were going to be okay, however. If the *Enterprise* was on the job, they were as good as saved.

She imagined herself at the helm, bringing the *Enterprise* within range of the stricken ship. "Just stay calm," she said with authority. "The *Enterprise* is on her way. Captain Hikaru Sulu commanding, Commander Demora Sulu at the helm." She punched in several commands at random. "Won't be any problem at—"

The console exploded.

Demora was blown backward and out of her chair, hitting the deck. All around her the lights were blinking red, alert sirens screeching.

Oh my God, I broke it! Dad's gonna kill me! went through her terrified mind.

Another console blew up. Demora shrieked, trying to

back away from it, and then another one went. Smoke was pouring everywhere, flames dancing all around. She didn't know where to look first. The petrified girl clutched the arm of the command chair. *"Heellppppp!"* she howled. "I'm sorry! *I'm sorry! Get me out of here!"*

And from what seemed an infinite distance, a voice said, "There's someone in there. Sir, I think there's someone in there!"

And another voice, stronger, deeper, more authoritative, said, "Open it up. There's not supposed to be anyone there. Open it up, dammit!"

There was the sound of gears shifting, and the double doors began to slide open.

She dashed for them, her legs pumping, her heart pounding. And she ran squarely into someone who appeared to be an instructor . . . at least, she thought he was. Her eyes were tearing from her fear and mortification, not to mention the smoke.

He halted her headlong flight by taking her firmly by the shoulders. "Who are you, young lady?"

"I'm sorry! I'm sorry!" She was frantic.

The red light from the alert was flickering across his face. "What's your name?"

"D . . . Demora . . ."

"Demora. What were you doing in there, Demora?"

"I was . . ." Her body was trembling. "I was pretending I was a helmsman . . . like my father. . . ."

"And your father is . . . ?"

"Going to be so mad!" she wailed. "Excuse me! I'm sorry! I'm sorry!" And she pulled away from him, running at full speed.

The man watched her go, and a technician came up beside him. "I'm sorry, Admiral Kirk. I swear, I had no idea anyone was in there. I'd never have run the pyrotechnics systems check if I'd known that . . ."

"It's all right, Tuchinsky," said Kirk. "She didn't seem hurt. Just scared half out of her mind. Find her, find out who she belongs to, and have her escorted out of the building, if you wouldn't mind."

Kirk shook his head as Tuchinsky headed off after the

frightened young girl. He had a feeling it would be quite a long time before she stuck her nose where it didn't belong.

He glanced at the simulator and sighed. What an image that made: The *Enterprise* bridge with a kid at the helm.

"That'll be the day," murmured Admiral Kirk.

Tuchinsky didn't find Demora, try as he might, even after he searched the entire building. That was possibly because Demora was no longer in the building, which was fine by Tuchinsky. He went back to Admiral Kirk, told him the girl had scampered, and that was more than enough for Kirk. She'd probably gone running back to her parents, tail between her legs, with a valuable lesson learned.

Demora, meantime, was crouched behind a hedge.

She sat there, red-faced and mortified, her legs drawn up under her chin.

"Excuse me."

She looked up.

The young man whom she'd been watching through the window—the groundskeeper—stood over her, looking down with a grave expression. "There's more comfortable places to sit, and a staggering percentage of them won't be in my way," he said sharply. He didn't sound like the type of person who suffered fools gladly.

She didn't say anything. Instead she just got to her feet and began to walk away, her shoulders sloped.

"Don't do that," he snapped.

She stopped and turned, looking at him in confusion. "Don't do what?"

"That defeated look. You're not defeated. You don't know what defeated is. You're too young for that."

"I'm embarrassed. I screwed up."

He stepped forward, took her chin and brusquely snapped her head right and left. "Hey! What're you doing?!" she demanded.

"Looking for pointed ears or antennae or something like that. You got something like that?"

"No!"

"So you're human."

"Yes!"

181

"So you're a human and you screwed up. There's a news item for you." He shook his head and started to walk away.

"Who the hell are you?" she demanded.

"Boothby," he said.

"Boothby. First name or last name?"

"Who cares? Just shout *Boothby*. You either get me or my father, which is who you were looking for in the first place. My father's the groundskeeper here. I help him. Someday I'll be doing it myself. How's that for a legacy? A landscape filled with space cadets who tromp around on the grass or sit around being depressed." He shook his head. "Grumpy old man. Hope if I get like that, somebody just shoots me and puts me out of my misery."

Too late, thought Demora. Out loud she said, "I'm not sitting around being depressed."

"Good." He continued walking away.

And she shouted after him, "And in case you hadn't noticed, I'm not a cadet!"

"Not yet," he snorted, and disappeared around a corner.

A deathly hush hung over dinner.

Demora picked at her food as her father ate in total silence. "This food isn't cooked enough," she said tentatively.

"It's sushi. This is as cooked as it gets" was his flat reply.

She rolled her eyes. "I know, Dad. It was just a joke."

"I don't feel very humorous tonight, if that's all right with you."

"Will you look at me at least!" she said in exasperation.

He looked at her, his face hard and set.

"Okay, look somewhere else," she requested.

But he didn't. Instead he kept his gaze leveled at her as he said, "Tell me, Demora . . . how do you think I reacted when I heard that some girl got into trouble in the Mark IV simulator? That she needlessly endangered her safety? That she plowed into Admiral Kirk when she went running pell-mell out of the simulator? How do you think I felt about that?"

"I don't know."

"I think you do."

She blew air out of her mouth. "Angry. Embarrassed. I don't know."

He leaned forward and said, "You gave me your word of honor. Of *honor,* Demora. Do you have any idea how much that means?"

"I didn't mean to break my promise. It wasn't my fault! I . . ."

And he slammed an open palm down on the table. Demora jumped, startled. In their years together, she had never, *never* seen him this angry. Indeed, hardly ever angry at all. His control, his calm, was truly remarkable. But it seemed to have deserted him now.

"It wasn't just a promise! *It was honor!* And here you are trying to make excuses for it!" He got up from the table so angrily that he banged his knee against it. It caused him to hobble slightly as he pointed at the portraits of ancestors which adorned his wall. "Honor wasn't just a word to them! Not just a cheap promise to be tossed around and broken when they didn't feel like sticking to it! They fought for honor! They *died* for honor! I trusted you, and you proved not worthy of trust!"

"What do you want from me, Dad?!" Demora shot back. "I said I screwed up! I said I was sorry! How many ways am I supposed to apologize, huh? What do you want me to do, throw myself on a sword because I made a mistake?"

"I want you to realize how much the concept means to me, and why I'm so angry and disappointed that you've lived half your lifetime with me without truly understanding it! I've tried to conduct myself with that philosophy my entire adult life, and it means nothing to you! *Nothing!* Honor is why I'm still here! Because I took responsibility for you, which was the only honorable course open to me!"

And it was at that moment that Sulu suddenly realized he'd said the wrong thing. Because Demora took a step back as if she'd been slapped. Her face looked cold and dark, and in a voice that cut to the heart, she said, "I *thought* you stayed because you loved me. Because you *wanted* to be with me, not because you *had* to be."

Sulu, one of the most accomplished tactical officers in Starfleet, suddenly found himself on the defensive. "It was both, Demy," he said.

She glared at him, the affectionate diminutive not having the desired effect. "I don't think it was both. I think it's just what you said it was."

"They go together. There's a poem: 'I could not love thee dear, so much, loved I not honor more.'"

"To hell with poetry." She pointed a trembling finger at the wall of portraits. "And to hell with them! You care more about a bunch of dead people than you do about me!"

"That's not true."

"It is!" She stomped her foot. "You should have just dumped me at that place up in Washington and been done with me!" And she stormed off into her room.

"Sounds like a problem," said Uhura.

Sulu looked at her image on the screen. Uhura was on Mars at the moment. As a lark, she had taken a brief leave of absence from Starfleet to take a job on a broadcast station on Mars's capital of Ares City.

Sulu was speaking via direct link to her home. "So what do I do?" he asked.

"You're asking me?"

"Well . . . you're a woman."

"Sulu! That's the nicest thing you've ever said to me." She flashed that high-voltage smile of hers.

"I'm not sure what to say to her."

"Tell her you know she's sorry, and you respect her feelings."

"I don't know if that's going to be quite enough. What's the best way to let a female know you love her?"

"Vertically or horizontally?"

He gave her a dour look. "Vertically. Horizontally, and we're playing out a Greek tragedy."

"Just tell her, Sulu."

"She might feel I'm just saying it to try and mend fences."

"Are you?"

He paused. "Of course not."

At that, Uhura paused. "Sulu . . . a suggestion. Protestations of love that are preceded by hesitancy are not the most convincing. 'Do you love me?' 'Ummmmm . . . yes.' You see how that can be a bit off-putting."

"I know."

"Talk to the girl. More important . . . listen to the girl. Reassure her. Just . . . work your way through it. You're dealing with a budding teenager. The explosions you get from matter and antimatter combining are nothing compared to parents clashing with adolescents. Understood?"

"Understood." He nodded.

"Good. Now go make peace with your daughter. After all, she's the only one you've got."

He nodded as Uhura's picture blinked out. Then he rose, walked down the hallway, and knocked on Demora's door.

"Yeah?" came from within.

"Demora. I want to talk."

"Who is it?"

He glanced heavenward for strength. "It's your father."

There was silence for a moment. Then the door slid open and Sulu walked in.

Demora was lying on the bed, head propped up on her hands. Out of reflex, Sulu glanced at the pillow. No tearstains. Well, at least they were past that part.

"Demy," he began.

"I want to be in Starfleet."

He still had his mouth open. It was left hanging that way for a moment before he remembered to close it. "Pardon?"

"I said I want to be in Starfleet."

He cleared off some scattered clothes from a chair and sat. "Since when, may I ask?"

"Since for a long time. But . . . because of two things. First . . . because even though it was fake, still . . . when I was sitting at the helm of the *Enterprise*," and she made quotation marks with her fingers around the word *"Enterprise,"* and continued, "I felt as if I . . . belonged there somehow. And I was thinking about what it would be like to really be up there, out there . . . trying to help people, or explore space . . . I think it's an incredible way to spend your life."

"It is," he sighed. "And . . . the second reason?"

"Because," she said evenly, "I want to make you proud of me."

He stared at her. "That's not necessary. I mean . . . I'll be proud of you no matter what you do."

"I know. But I think I want to do this."

"Well, fortunately enough, it's not like this has to be decided today. It's food for thought at the moment. But I . . . appreciate the gesture."

She went to him then, and they embraced. He'd never felt closer to his daughter than he did at that moment.

And since he didn't see the sadness in her eyes, he didn't realize that he'd never been farther away.

Chapter Twenty

"HE *STOLE* THE *Enterprise?*"

She stared at Janice Rand. They were in a park, seated on a bench, and Janice gestured for her to keep her voice down. When Demora had gotten out of school that day, Janice had been waiting for her. She'd met Janice a couple of times in the past, had brief and pleasant chats with her. None of those casual social interactions, however, had remotely prepared Demora for anything like this.

Demora was fifteen years old. The growth spurt had kicked in a couple of years earlier, as her father had long predicted. She was a half a foot taller, and her body no longer could be mistaken for preadolescent, even if she'd been clothed in a potato sack. Her face had also lost the babyish look, and now had the sculpted features of a striking young woman. Now, though, Janice was worried that the teen was on the verge of an apoplectic seizure that would preclude her ever seeing sixteen.

"He stole the *Enterprise?*" Demora said again. This time she managed to keep her voice to an appalled whisper.

"What do you mean, *stole*. You can't just steal a starship. It's . . ."

Clearly she was having trouble fully grasping the notion. It was hardly surprising, considering the hellacious past couple of months they'd had. She'd heard chapter and verse about the routine training mission that had turned into a duel to the death with a twentieth-century madman named Khan. She'd remembered the blood draining from her face as Chekov had described (over Sulu's protestations) their nail-biting escape from the Genesis torpedo . . . an escape made only at the cost of Mr. Spock's life.

Maybe it had all been too much for him. Her father was out of practice for such life-and-death struggles.

"We can say it was stress," Demora said quickly.

Rand stared at her, confused. "What?"

"Stress. You know. After that training mission, and Spock's death . . . then he found out that they were planning to decommission the *Enterprise,* and he just . . . snapped. Temporary insanity."

But Janice was shaking her head. "Demora, it wasn't like that. It wasn't just some impulse thing. It was carefully planned."

"You mean he planned out a whole—"

"It wasn't just him."

"It wasn't." Demora paused a moment, her face clouding. "Let me guess: the usual suspects."

Rand nodded. "It had something to do with Spock . . . and with Dr. McCoy. I'm still a little hazy on the details. . . ."

"Oh my God," said Demora, her face in her hands. "But . . . but how? You can't just waltz into spacedock and leave with a starship. Shouldn't someone have tried to stop them?"

"Someone did try. Captain Styles of the *Excelsior.* But the *Enterprise* got away."

"Got away? From the *Excelsior?* How did . . . ?" Her face went ashen. "They . . . they didn't fire on it, did they? Didn't get into a fight . . . ?"

"No, no. Nothing like that. They just . . ." Rand cleared her throat. "They broke it."

Demora stared at her, not sure she'd heard right. "I beg your pardon?"

"They broke it."

"How do you *break* a starship?"

Janice waved her hands in exasperation. "They shot the hamster running on the little treadmill that makes it go. *I* don't know what they did! They broke it. The *Excelsior* went about ten meters and then the engines conked out. Captain Styles isn't real happy about it. Made him look like a fool. They're already calling him Styles Without Substance. No, not happy at all, that one."

Birds overhead, recognizing Demora as a customary easy touch for food, settled down near her. "Scram!" she shouted and shooed them away.

"Okay," she said after a moment, "okay . . . maybe this won't be so bad. No property's been really damaged. No one's been killed. Maybe this is salvageable. If . . . if Dad and the others just . . . just bring the *Enterprise* back . . . considering their record, maybe this can all go away. They just need a real good lawyer. Maybe that Cogley guy . . ."

Then she saw that Janice was shaking her head. "No Cogley?"

"That's not the problem. The problem is bringing back the *Enterprise.*"

Demora's voice was deathly cold. "What . . . happened to the *Enterprise.*"

"They broke it," said Rand.

"You mean broke it like shooting the hamster?"

"I mean broke it like into a million pieces. Admiral Kirk blew it up."

Demora, feeling ill, put her head between her legs. "Why did he blow it up?" she asked, her voice so faint that Janice could barely hear it.

"I don't know. I'm sure he had a reason."

"Of course he had a reason. The reason was *to drive me insane!*"

Clearly she was making no attempt to keep her voice down anymore. Passersby in the park glanced her way briefly and then hurried on about their business.

"Where's Dad now? Is he okay? He . . ." Suddenly she

was struck by the horrible thought that maybe this was a long, labored way of breaking the news to her gently. . . .

"He's fine," Janice said quickly, patting her on the hand. "I swear, he's fine. He's on Vulcan."

"Vulcan? What's he doing on Vulcan?"

"I'm a little confused on that part myself. Believe it or not . . . I think he's there with Spock."

"With Spock? Spock's dead."

"He . . ." Janice fished for words and couldn't find any good ones. ". . . he got better," she said.

Demora stood. "I'm going home now," she announced. "I'm going home . . . I'm going to crawl under the blankets . . . and when I wake up, I'll find out this was all an insane dream."

"Close. You'll go home and pack your stuff, and then you're coming to my place."

"Your place? Why?"

"Because the message your father managed to get out to me said that's what he wanted. Demora . . . you have to understand. Sulu, the admiral, all of them . . . they're criminals now. Wanted fugitives. They're under protection by the Vulcan Council, but they can't budge from the planet without risking immediate arrest."

Demora couldn't believe it. She felt as if her world had tilted at a forty-five-degree angle.

"It's not the kind of circumstance that allows a genuine freeflow of communication, you know? Sulu was able to get a brief message out to me, slipping it through Communicore. But that's the best he could do, and it's not likely we'll be hearing from him again until this whole business is settled."

"Which will be . . . when?"

"I don't know," said Janice Rand, not recalling a time in her life when she'd felt quite this helpless.

"All . . . all right. All right, Janice. I'll get my stuff . . . I'll lock up the apartment . . . and I'll room with you. If that's okay."

"That's fine," said Janice. "Really."

Demora stood, shaking her head. "I don't understand

why . . . or *how* . . . he could have done this to me. I just don't."

"Actually . . . he asked me to relay something to you. Something he said he hoped would help you understand. He said to tell you that it was a matter of honor."

Demora sighed. "Yes. I had a feeling that's what he'd say."

Chapter Twenty-one

THE END OF THE WORLD was nigh, and Demora Sulu knew beyond any doubt that she was going to die alone.

Janice wasn't there with her. This, in and of itself, was nothing unusual. Rand's days had been more busy lately since she'd been transferred to Starfleet Command. It had meant longer hours, but a step up in responsibility. And she did usually get home while Demora was still awake; indeed, oftentimes Demora would have dinner waiting for her. The situation made Janice laugh occasionally as she wondered just exactly who was supposed to be taking care of whom.

But Janice hadn't been home for nearly sixteen hours, and Demora . . . along with everyone else on the planet . . . was painfully aware why.

Pictures of the Probe had been broadcast across all Earth bands. Demora had had trouble taking it seriously at first; it reminded her of nothing so much as a giant pecan log. "Give me a fork and a really big glass of milk, I can take care of that thing no problem at all," she'd said.

But there were no jokes now, no amused observations.

No safety.

No hope.

It had drawn closer and closer to Earth, its reason a complete puzzlement. It didn't seem to want to destroy anything. On the other hand, it didn't seem inclined *not* to destroy anything. It just . . . was. Speculation was that it seemed to be searching for someone or something, although Demora was damned if she could figure out what it was. In that respect, the Probe was like a small child tearing apart a room while searching for something. Even if the object (whatever it was) was eventually located, the result was a trashed room.

And Earth was on the verge of becoming a trashed planet.

She couldn't see it in the skies overhead, for it hung above the Earth's atmosphere. But she felt as if she could sense it. Sense its presence, its power. She heard it screech with a noise that chilled her. In response, the Earth seemed determined to tear itself apart.

Janice Rand, Demora knew, was busy coordinating Earth's emergency operations at Starfleet Command. A fat lot of good that was going to do. The Probe couldn't be slowed down or stopped. It was like a force of nature, and confronting it was like standing on a shoreline and spitting at an incoming tidal wave.

Demora hadn't wanted to die in Janice's apartment. Because when all was said and done—despite it having been Demora's place of residence for three months—it was still Janice's apartment. She wanted her home. She wanted to be in her place.

So that was where she had headed. It hadn't made tremendous sense when viewed with a dispassionate frame of mind. She was leaving one apartment to brave the wind, the rain, the trembling of the Earth's crust beneath her feet, all for the purpose of getting to . . . another apartment.

The only thing it accomplished was making her feel—rightly or wrongly—that she was doing *something*. Making some sort of headway, indulging in some sort of activity that was, ultimately, preferable to simply waiting around for the end. If (when) she died, at least she could say to herself, "I didn't die in someone else's home . . . I died in my own."

It was cold comfort, but when your planet was being shaken apart by a lethal probe, you took what you could get.

She went to the bay window and looked out. In the distance was the Golden Gate Bridge. She could see the waves crashing against it, getting higher and higher, and it seemed only a matter of time before the entire span came crashing down. And there she stood, helpless and alone.

And all she could think about was her father.

Part of her was relieved for him. She knew the trajectory of the Probe very well from the news reports, and was aware that it had passed nowhere near Vulcan. So he was safe. Hiding away in exile, with the Federation Council making pronouncements against him and his friends, and now they were going to have the last laugh. His accusers were trapped on Earth, and he was high and dry on an alien world. He was going to survive and, after all, what good was served if both of them died?

And the other part hated him. Hated him with a passion.

She looked at the photographs and representations of his ancestors . . . hers, too, of course. They stared at her with varying degrees of sullenness and inscrutability, and she felt a rage building up inside her.

All that talk about honor. About family. About commitment. And in the end, in the final analysis, what had it meant? What had any of it meant?

"Damn you," she whispered, and then she practically screamed, *"Damn you!"*

She ran to the wall and, her fingers curved into claws, she ripped them off the wall. She tore them off the wall, sending them flying everywhere. Her heart pounded against her ribs, and she yanked so violently that she sent herself tumbling over a chair and crashing to the floor. She lay there curled up, sobbing, feeling like a child again as she tore at the shag carpet with her fingernails.

"You abandoned me, you son of a bitch!" she howled, even though her voice couldn't even be heard above the crashing of the water outside. Rain was pouring down in torrents. It was becoming impossible to see anything at all.

Yes, abandoned her. Run off on an insane, criminal mission to help Spock. And he hadn't said anything to her about it, not a damned thing. He'd sat there, cool as a cucumber on what now appeared to have been the last night they'd ever spend together, and the most deeply moving thing he'd said to her was "Pass the rice." Hadn't said boo to her. Hadn't whispered a word of what he was going to do.

Because he still considered her a child. Still considered her "not worthy" somehow. That was it, of course. Four damned years ago, and he was still angry at her. She couldn't believe it. She was never going to live up to what he wanted, never be what he wanted her to be. Because he didn't want her to be human. It's just like that landscaper—Booby, or whatever the hell his name was. It was just like he'd said. She was human and she screwed up, but her father didn't expect her to be human. He expected her to be this . . . this perfect little thing, this robot, wind her up, set her loose, and watch her never do a single thing wrong and flawlessly live up to some code of honor that was centuries old and as cold and unforgiving as the water pounding outside.

So he hadn't trusted her, and he'd abandoned her without caring if he'd ever see her again. And he was off on Vulcan probably laughing his ass off while the entire world sank under the most cataclysmic flood since Noah had looked skyward and remarked that it looked like showers.

She heard the Probe, getting louder and louder. It was the only noise that managed to surpass the unbridled fury of the storm outside. There was a deafening screech over and over, and she screamed, *"Shut up! Shut up! Just kill us already and get it over with, okay?"*

The wind bashed against the bay window. It shattered, pieces flying everywhere. Demora was positioned behind a couch as it so happened, and that's what saved her life. Shards embedded themselves in the cushion, and a few landed in her hair. If she'd still been standing in front of the window, she would have been dead instantly.

The wind howled through the apartment, knocking over all the contents. Swords fell off the walls, antique guns went tumbling.

This was it. She knew this was it. And she seized upon the mostly demented notion that if she was going to die, then she was going to go down fighting. It didn't matter that the enemy was a soulless Probe orbiting the Earth . . . or the wind blasting her backward. It didn't matter that there was no thinking entity to combat, no villain to triumph over.

She would fight against death itself. She would fight against all the anger, all the disappointment in her life, all the fear that threatened to overwhelm her.

She crawled across the floor and grabbed a samurai sword, one that her father had told her once belonged to a great samurai ancestor. She imagined that she could feel strength flowing through the hilt. Her grip on it alone was enough to empower her.

She pulled it from its scabbard, and the scrape of metal was oddly satisfying. Then Demora staggered to her feet, the blade poised. She stood facing the window, staggering from the power of the gale.

Never in her life had she felt so completely melodramatic. But what the hell. There was no one else around. She was about to die, and if she was going to go, then let it be with some style.

"You want me?" she shouted at Death, waving her sword in the wind. *"Come and get me!"*

And then she saw it.

Death, streaking through the sky in the shape of a great dark bird. It was as if no doubt was being left. Death had made itself visible to the people of Earth, its massive wings moving slowly, like a massive bird of prey. . . .

Bird of . . .

"Wait a minute . . . what the hell?" Her eyes narrowed.

It was. It was a Klingon bird-of-prey. But what the hell was it doing here? The entire Klingon contingent had stormed out of the Federation Council and left Earth a couple of days ago. It had been on all the news. The ambassador and delegation had withdrawn in a snit because the UFP hadn't honored their demands for Kirk's head on a silver platter. At the time no one had doubted that, sooner or later, the Klingons would return, if for no other reason than to harass the council some more.

But there was no way that they would have chosen *now* to return. Nor could it have been by accident: A planetary distress signal had gone out, warning away anyone who might even think about heading toward Earth.

Yet here was a Klingon bird-of-prey, big as life, twice as ugly, crashing into the surging water beneath the Golden Gate Bridge, disappearing in the clouds and blasts of rain that were everywhere in this moment of ultimate cataclysm. Who in hell would be so totally devoid of sanity—or, perhaps, of fear—that they would pilot a warship directly into the heart of the storm, facing certain death and . . .

"Oh, my God," she whispered.

They—Dad, Kirk, and the others—they had stolen a Klingon bird-of-prey. That was one of the things the ambassador had complained about, according to news reports as the facts of the entire affair had come to light.

It was her father.

He'd come home to die with her.

Tears ran down her face as she thought, *That is so sweet.* . . .

Long minutes passed, during which time an odd calm descended on her. She watched the clouds rolling, watched the waves leaping ever higher, and yet there was a certain . . . rightness about it all. She'd found an inner peace, although her hands were gripping the hilt of the sword so tightly that her knuckles had turned white.

It was all going to come to a head within the next seconds, she was certain of that. What would happen? Would a giant wave crash into the building? Would the Earth simply open and swallow them? Would a beam of force blast them to bits?

She was so calm, she realized she didn't even have to wait to find out. Her father, in a final display of honor and integrity, had been willing to perform a final suicidal act rather than outlive his native planet. Perhaps it was an example that she should have the bravery to emulate.

She reversed the sword, put it to her chest, gripping it firmly and taking a deep breath. She tried to find the strength and resolve to drive it home. It was becoming easier and easier for her to concentrate on her intention, thanks to the wind dying down and . . .

"Dying down?"

Startled at the realization, she looked out the window and couldn't believe what she was seeing.

The storm clouds were blowing out to sea. It was as if someone had taken a vid of it and started rolling it backward. The Pacific was smoothing out, the waves lapping around the supports of the Golden Gate descending to their normal height. Demora watched the phenomenon with growing incredulity.

The sun was coming out. And high above, she saw a shuttle angling around and descending toward where the Klingon bird-of-prey had gone into the drink.

Within five minutes of the arrival of the bird-of-prey, the impending armageddon was not only no longer impending . . . it was, in fact, history.

"What happened?" she wondered out loud.

"What happened was, we were cleared."

It was Hikaru Sulu's first meal home in three months, and the events leading up to it had been nothing short of impressive.

Demora hadn't had a chance to see him at first. The shuttle that had plucked Sulu and the others from the water had brought them straight to Starfleet Headquarters. Suspecting that that's where they would be, Demora had headed straight over there. Her efforts to get in to see her father had been herculean. She'd tried every possible means of ingress, tried to talk her way past more guards than she would have believed conceivable. She offered every excuse, up to and including that she was dying and only had a very short time to live. ("Bring a doctor's note," one amused guard instructed.)

None of it had worked. Despite Demora's best tries, the *Enterprise* seven had been kept under wraps. The only ones who might have gotten in to see them were legal counsel, but the accused had all refused the option (Scotty had been the most outspoken about that: "Lawyers. As if we dinna have enough problems"), until the council of the UFP had been able to convene and discuss the situation.

The outcome of that discussion had been made public. It had been less than an hour ago when the renegades from the

Enterprise had faced the council in closed session. Then the session had ended and the outlaws-turned-heroes had separated to return to home and loved ones.

When Sulu had walked in, Demora had been waiting for him. She'd made desperate endeavors to clean up the apartment, but there were still many signs of the damage that the storm had wreaked. Sulu hadn't cared, however. His booted feet had crunched on the broken glass in the carpet as he walked quickly to his daughter and embraced her.

"Did you miss me?" he asked her.

"Why, did you go somewhere?" she replied with her typical breeziness.

Now they sat at the hastily cobbled-together dinner that Demora had managed to prepare for them. Many systems were still out of whack. It was going to take some time for everything to be restored to normal. Sulu made a point of saying that he didn't care, that being with her was all that mattered.

"They said that due to 'extenuating circumstances,' they were forgiving us our transgressions, basically," Sulu explained to her.

"The circumstances being that you saved the Earth."

"I'd have to say that's correct. The only one they came down on was the admiral . . . and they busted him back to captain."

She winced. "That must have hurt."

"Not really. Between you and me, I don't think he was ever really happy as an admiral. As captain, he can—and will—be back in command of a starship. That's where he belongs."

"From everything you've said about him, I'd have to agree. Of course, the Klingons are still angry with him."

"True enough," Sulu agreed, twirling thin noodles onto his fork.

"Not a problem," said Demora. "All he has to do is save the Klingons from some big catastrophe, and then they'll forgive him, too."

"Part of me wants to say that that's too absurd for words," Sulu said. "On the other hand, I've learned never to underestimate the adm . . . the captain." He sighed and looked around the apartment. "My my, what a mess."

"I know. The storm was kind of hard on it."

He glanced at the far wall. "Even knocked down all the pictures of my family."

"Oh yes," she said quickly. "It was vicious. Just everything came down."

"Well, you did your best."

"Dad . . . I have to tell you something . . ."

He waited, eyebrows raised.

"When I saw your ship . . . I thought that that was going to be it for you. That there was no way you could possibly . . ." Her voice trailed off.

"Oh, come now, Demy," he chided her. "You should have more faith. I was at the helm, remember. It was my job to bring her in safely. I'm a helmsman, not a kamikaze. We came plowing into that bay with a plan and a crew to pull it off. I don't dispute that it was tricky, but believe you me, Demy . . . and you never have to worry about this . . . one thing I most definitely am not is suicidal."

He said it with amusement in his voice. Laughing at the concept. Laughing at her.

Sure, now, in the light of calm skies and the ebbing of her fears, it seemed laughable enough. But not at the time. Not only that, but her faulty reasoning had almost . . .

. . . almost . . .

"No, of course you're not suicidal, Dad. I wouldn't even suggest such a thing."

Her fork dangled over the noodles. There was so much she wanted to say. So much that angered her, frustrated her, frightened her. So many unresolved sentiments that had been brought to the surface by Sulu's long absence. She wanted to bring it up, but she didn't even know where to begin.

"Janice treated you well, I assume," said Sulu.

"Oh yes." She nodded. "Yes, very well."

"Good," said Sulu. He reached over and patted her hand. "I knew I could count on her. Just like I knew I could count on you to be a grown-up. You're getting so big, Demy."

"Thanks, Dad." She cleared her throat. "And it's . . . it's

great to have you home. I can't begin to tell you how. And there's a lot I'd—"

The front door chimed. Demora started to rise, but Sulu said, "No, no, I'll get it." He went to the door as Demora remained in her seat.

Chekov walked in, brimming with excitement. "Now" was all he said.

Sulu looked surprised. "Now?"

"Now. Ve're to report to the spacedock shuttle immediately. I vould have called ahead, but comm is still out in this section of town."

"What's going on?" Demora asked.

Chekov crossed quickly to her and kissed her on the cheek. "Good to see you again, darling. Vat a mess, eh?" He turned back to Sulu. "So? Vat are you vaiting for?"

Despite Chekov's acknowledgment of her presence, she still felt as if she were invisible. "Excuse me. He just got back. Dad, you just got back. . . ."

He paused, and then took her by the hands. "Demy . . . I'm sure it won't be for too long."

"What 'it'? What's going on?"

"They're putting the captain back in charge of a starship. I told you that. Taking a guess, the *Excelsior*. And we're going to be his command crew . . . just for the shakedown cruise, that's all. I'm sure it won't be for too long."

She stared at him and thought, *How can you be so sure? The moment you get out there, anything can happen at any moment. Isn't that what you've always said? Another probe, another madman, another threat . . . and it'll be another three months? A year? Five? You just came back!*

He squeezed her hand tightly and said, "Demy . . . if you have a problem with it . . ."

But she could see it in his eyes. He didn't want her to say anything unless it was approval. He didn't want to hear everything that was going through her mind, not really.

And she knew, right then. Knew that all her suspicions, all her guilt since she was a kid, was justified. Given a choice between her and the stars, there was simply no contest. He was meant to be a creature in flight and ever since she had first shown up, she'd handicapped him. He'd been a crippled, wretched bird flapping around, as destined for a crash as that Klingon bird-of-prey had been. It was all her fault, and the guilt and self-recrimination hardened into a wall surrounding her heart.

And at that moment she swore herself an oath . . . that she would never again say or do anything to hamper him. Here was a man who had just helped save the Earth. *Save the Earth,* for God's sake. And she was going to start trying to tie him down again? To heap guilt on him, make him feel he owed her something? She saw the excitement in his eyes over the prospect of getting right back out there again.

More: She saw the future. Suddenly it revealed itself to her, clear as the new day that had dawned on the salvaged Earth. The explorer, the space adventurer within Hikaru Sulu had reawoken with a ferocious appetite. The years with her had been wasted ones. All the times he'd commented that saddling James Kirk with a teaching job was a waste of material, he could just as easily have been saying that about himself.

He would pursue more adventures, she knew that now. She saw him at the helm of a ship . . . hell, she saw him in a command chair. Fulfiling a destiny that had been side-tracked by the unexpected addition of a young girl. Sulu was meant to save planets, not be tied down to one.

And she would follow him. She would. Within two years she'd be eligible to enroll at Starfleet Academy. The final frontier pulled at her just as it did her father. Even more strongly, in fact, because joining Starfleet would enable her to become the only thing that he could ever respect: someone just like him.

"It's okay, Dad," she said, in the greatest acting performance of her life. "Really. It's okay. I'm not a kid anymore, like you said. If there's any problems, I've got Janice as back-up, but hey . . . gotta start being independent sometime. And after everything you've been through . . . you deserve it. Go. I'll be here when you get back. Hell, if you're gone long enough, I'll be through the Academy and be coming out after you."

Despite her resolve, just for a moment, she desperately wanted him to see through it. To validate for her their years together. To say, *Don't be ridiculous. We could so easily have lost each other forever. I'm going to stay with you right here, by your side, and we're going to talk and heal our relationship and* . . .

He held her tightly. "I knew you'd understand," he said.

She smiled gamely. "Hey, what are daughters for?"

Then it was another hug, a quick kiss, a hurried farewell, and he and Chekov were out the door. Demora sat at the table for a long time after that, staring at the cooling bowl of noodles. Then, of their own volition it seemed, Demora's hands reached out, grabbed the bowl, and hurled it against the wall. The bowl shattered, noodles all over the wall and sliding down it in a large smear.

It was a mess. But then again, what was one more mess in her life . . . more or less.

SECTION FIVE

LIFE AFTER DEATH

Chapter Twenty-two

CHEKOV CAME OUT of the disciplinary hearing smarting a bit, but otherwise intact. Uhura, who had stood by him during the hearing, had given an impassioned speech which, frankly, had Chekov less than thrilled. She had painted him as so totally devastated by the shock of recent events—first his beloved captain, then his beloved goddaughter—that he had simply come unhinged. Temporary insanity, as it were. That was why, she said, he had hauled off and attacked Captain Harriman at Demora Sulu's memorial service.

The disciplinary committee conferred and finally settled for a slap on the wrist—an official reprimand (which Chekov had no problem with) and an official written apology from Chekov to Captain Harriman (which Chekov did have a problem with).

They walked back to his place, Chekov complaining all the way. "I'd like to apologize, all right," he said tersely. "Apologize vit a brick through that thick skull of his."

"Look, Pavel, you'd better own up to the fact that you got off lucky," Uhura informed him. "Lucky that you got a hearing board that was somewhat sympathetic to your state of mind. And lucky that Harriman decided not to press the matter. Otherwise it could have gone extremely badly for you."

Chekov gave a derisive snort, but Uhura could tell that he knew she had a point. By the time they got back to Chekov's home, Uhura was already suggesting language for the apology that Chekov was admitting he could live with.

Upon entering, Chekov immediately noticed that there was a message waiting for him. "You know where everything is." Chekov gestured.

"I know where the vodka is," replied Uhura. "That's about all you keep around here."

"I think of it as having priorities," he said archly as he punched up the message at his computer station.

Uhura managed to turn up some fruit juice, and she sat down on the couch to sip it delicately. "Chekov," she said after a moment, sounding fairly glum, "you want to hear something really depressing? I mean, I probably shouldn't be saying this, all things considered. But I think about everything we've accomplished . . . and what we're leaving behind. Except . . . the captain's dead. His son is dead. Sulu's daughter is dead. I have no family, nor do you or Scotty. I feel as if we're going, one by one, like characters in a murder mystery. And when it's all over, all we'll be are names in Starfleet texts somewhere. We struggled and risked so much, and in end . . . maybe we'll be remembered. But there will be no one left to really love us. Was it all worth it, Chekov? Was it?"

He didn't say anything in response. She turned. "Chekov?"

He was seated at his computer screen, and now he turned to Uhura and gestured quickly. "Come here."

"Were you listening to anything I said?"

"Not a vord. Uhura . . ."

"Well, I'm certainly glad I told you what was on my mi—"

"Uhura, *now!*" he said with such urgency that it brought her full attention upon him. She went quickly to him and bent over his shoulder to see what he was looking at.

There was an image of Sulu, frozen on the screen. "What's going on?" she asked.

"I'll play it again," he said. "Vatch."

Sulu stayed immobile for a moment more, and then he said, "By the time you receive this, I may very well have thrown away my captaincy. For all I know, I may even be dead. But it's important to me that you, Chekov, and you, Uhura, understand what I'm doing and why I'm doing it."

"He sent the exact same message to both of us, I'd guess," said Chekov. "That's vy . . ."

"I figured that out, Chekov," she said dryly.

"I refuse to accept the mystery of Demora's death so easily," continued Sulu. "I've barely eaten, barely slept . . . barely been able to function since I learned of it. Captain Harriman's quarantine action, while understandable— even regulation—is not one that I can tolerate. I can't wait around for months, even years, to find out why my daughter's life is ashes. Indeed . . . I can't wait around so much as a week. I have to know, for Demora's sake . . . and for mine. Because in those moments where I do barely drift to sleep . . . in those twilight seconds . . . I still feel like I hear her calling to me. I can't abandon her to an enigma. I can't.

"I am therefore intending to bring the *Excelsior* directly to Askalon Five. Doing this will be not only a direct violation of the quarantine regs, but directly ignoring the orders of Admiral LaVelle. I suspect the recriminations may be severe, but it cannot be helped. I have to do this. I have to.

"On the other hand, I knew I could not tell you . . . my friends . . . because I knew there would be no preventing you from joining me on this potentially career-ending quest. Only a couple of years ago, we came together to help Dr. McCoy rejoin Spock's soul to his body. We emerged from that situation unscathed, largely due to the potentially disastrous—yet, ironically, lucky—problem with the Probe. The timing of that bordered on the supernatural. If we'd arrived days earlier, we'd have been serving sentences on a mining colony somewhere. Days, even hours later . . . and Earth would have been destroyed.

"So it appears that Captain Kirk had some powerful gods watching over him. But it would seem that even those gods have finally abandoned him, and if they weren't there for him . . . it's a good bet they won't be there for us. Based on that, I cannot and will not risk your coming along.

"Instead I have decided to handle this matter in the way that Mr. Spock did in the Talos Four affair. By taking these actions on myself, by myself, to shield you from potential recriminations. It's my problem. And she was . . . my daughter.

"But it is important to me that you know and understand my need for subterfuge, so that you won't think the less of me. Losing your respect would pain me almost as much as losing Demora . . . and," he said with a grim smile, "I don't think I can handle much more loss right now.

"So . . . that is the situation. It's my situation. Wish me good luck, and a hope that whatever gods protected James Kirk for so well and so long . . . cast a brief and favorable glance my way. Sulu out."

The picture blinked off, leaving Chekov and Uhura staring at the blank screen for a long moment.

"I cannot believe he did that," Chekov said. "I cannot believe he left us behind."

"I can," Uhura replied. "I can believe it, for the exact reasons he said. This is something he had to do. He needs to find peace of mind. And I guess he couldn't do that if part of his mind was on us."

"So vat happens now? Ve pretend that everything is normal? Go on with our lives?"

"That's right," said Uhura. "That's exactly what we do. Oh . . . and one other thing."

"Vat?"

"We pray."

She floated in a haze of confusion . . .

She thought she heard voices talking . . . unfamiliar voices . . .

There was liquid everywhere . . . she was submerged in some sort of gelatinous mass. She should have been drowning, but she wasn't . . . it filled her nose, her lungs, every part of her, but instead of suffocating her, it nourished her . . .

It was like being back in the womb . . .

. . . whose womb . . . someone's womb . . .

. . . her recollection was nonexistent, her awareness of who or where she was at best a distant thing . . .

. . . she wanted someone . . . someone to come to her . . . someone to save her . . . but she didn't know what or who she needed to be saved from . . . or who could possibly find her . . .

Chapter Twenty-three

NO ONE HAD WANTED to be the first to say anything.

Not Anik of Matern, the first officer, who heard the order given. Not Lojur, the Kothan navigator who laid in the course. Not Lieutenant Shandra Docksey at helm as she sent the *Excelsior* hurtling in a direction that was not remotely akin to the one that she had thought she'd be following. Not even Commander Rand at communications.

Nevertheless, somebody had to say something. At first it looked like it was going to be Rand, thanks to her long association with Captain Sulu. But Anik took it upon herself to do it. She stepped forward on her delicate legs, cleared her throat and said, "Captain . . ."

He turned in his chair and looked remarkably calm. They both knew exactly what she was going to say, so it was just a matter of her saying it.

"The course you've indicated for us is not the course to Centrelis."

"Not necessarily, Commander," he said reasonably.

Anik seemed momentarily confused, as if uncertain he'd heard the statement. "Sir . . . ?"

"It's simply not the shortest route to Centrelis. I've decided we're going to take the scenic route."

"The . . . scenic route, sir?"

"That's right, Commander. Life is too short not to take time to savor the pretty things in life. Don't you agree?"

Docksey and Lojur exchanged glances.

Anik looked at him suspiciously. "Sir . . ."

"The course is as I ordered it, Commander. On my responsibility. Do you have a problem with that?"

"Sir . . . it's not whether I have a problem with it or not. It's whether Starfleet will have a problem with it."

"Are you lecturing me, Commander?"

The bridge had gotten very quiet. Anik had that ethereal look, but no one doubted her strength of character or spirit. She was not someone who would permit herself to be intimidated or pushed around.

Sulu met Anik's level gaze, and then said with exceeding calm, "I know what I'm doing, Commander."

"Yes, Captain. I think we all know what you're doing," Anik replied. "And it is my recommendation that—"

It was at that moment that the distress signal came.

"Captain," said Rand urgently. "Call for assistance coming in." It was a fair guess that never, in the history of Starfleet, had news of a ship in trouble been greeted with such relief. "Cargo ship *Burton* in sector two-nine-J, with a malfunctioning warp coil. They need to abandon ship and are requesting immediate assistance."

"Signal that—" He paused . . . looked at Anik . . . and then smiled. "Signal that we anticipated their request, and will rendezvous with them at . . ." He looked to Lojur, eyebrows raised questioningly.

"We can be there in"—Lojur checked his instruments—"forty-seven minutes, sir."

"In forty-seven minutes," Sulu said. "We will off-load the crew and cargo to *Excelsior,* and transport them to Starbase Nine."

"Yes, sir," she said, and turned to her comm board to relay the message.

As she did so, Sulu looked evenly at Anik. "Satisfied, Commander?"

There were a few things that occurred to Anik, but instead of saying any of them she just smiled thinly. "Perfectly, Captain."

The rescue went off without problems. The *Burton* was not unsalvageable. By the time the crew and cargo had been removed from the cargo ship, the warp-coil breach had poisoned the interior of the vessel. Still, it could easily be decontaminated, so the *Excelsior* took the ship in tow.

The crew of the *Burton* was duly impressed by the *Excelsior*. Most of the crew members had spent their entire careers on small ships, and had never seen anything like the *Excelsior* except in pictures. The crew of the *Excelsior* was polite and cooperative, and no one from the *Burton* would possibly have been able to guess that the *Excelsior*'s crew was preoccupied and concerned with the situation regarding the captain.

In short order the starship arrived at Starbase 9, where the *Burton*'s crew and cargo was removed with relative ease. All things considered, it was easily one of the more routine, even pedestrian, missions that the *Excelsior* had ever undertaken.

As it happened, it also turned out to be one of the costliest.

The *Excelsior* was still in orbit around Starbase 9, just finishing up the transfer, when Janice Rand turned from her communications panel and looked to Sulu. He was in his command chair, staring resolutely at the screen. He seemed as if he were ever so slightly out of phase: aware of the world around him and yet just a bit removed from it. But somehow he seemed to sense that Rand had to say something to him before she actually said it. He turned to face her before she'd had the opportunity to open her mouth.

"Incoming communication, sir. Admiral LaVelle."

The bridge crew reacted to this. LaVelle was pretty high up on the food chain. If, as they had already come to suspect, this little jaunt was unauthorized, then they were going to hear about it now. The immediate thought on all their minds was that Sulu was going to get up from his command chair and ask that the call be transferred to his quarters, where he could take it in privacy.

So there was collective, if unspoken, surprise when he said, "On-screen, Commander."

Rand, along with the others, had thought he would want the shield of his quarters to conduct the call. "Sir—?" she began.

But he was calm, certain. "On-screen, Commander." And, making sure that she knew he was aware of what was going through her mind, he added, "I have nothing to hide."

With a small uncertain nod of her head that seemed to say, *Oooookay, if you say so,* she transferred the signal to the main screen.

The image of Starbase 9 vanished from the screen, to be replaced by the concerned face of Admiral LaVelle. Even she seemed surprised to be on an open channel. "Captain Sulu, a more private forum might be preferable for you," she said.

"I have no secrets from my crew, Admiral," Sulu replied sanguinely.

"Very well. Then I'll simply ask you what the hell you think you're doing?"

"What I have to, Admiral. That's all anyone does," he said evenly.

"What anyone does in Starfleet is obey orders," said LaVelle. "Your orders have you going to Centrelis. And regulations having you staying away from Askalon Five. I commend you for stopping along your one-way voyage-to-court-martial to help the transport ship *Burton.* You must have known that the command of Starbase Nine would routinely inform Starfleet of the aid provided by *Excelsior.*"

"Yes, Admiral, I was quite aware."

"So you gave up the additional time you might have had to reach Askalon Five before we found out about it. As I said, commendable. Out of respect to your act of self-sacrifice, I will give you this one opportunity to rectify the situation. I am perfectly willing to write up this little detour as a response to a distress signal. You can walk away from this incident with a nice little notation on your file. That will give us ample opportunity to go on with our lives and forget that there was any . . . 'irregularity' in anyone's conduct. What do you say?" she asked with a touch of hopefulness in her voice.

"I say I'm most appreciative of the offer, Admiral."

LaVelle nodded slowly. "You're continuing on your heading to Askalon Five, aren't you."

"Yes, Admiral."

"In that case, Captain, the penalties will be quite harsh, and immediate measures, with prejudice, will have to be taken. Do you understand that?"

There was deathly silence in the bridge upon that pronouncement.

"Yes, Admiral. I understand that you're doing what you have to," Sulu said levelly. "I guess that doesn't make you all that different from me, does it."

"It does in one major respect, Captain. You see . . . one of us isn't in trouble."

She allowed that pronouncement to hang there, and then her image blinked off the screen.

All eyes were upon Sulu, waiting for him to say something . . . *anything*. Waiting, preferably, for him to say something that indicated he was steering himself away from this potentially self-destructive course.

Slowly he surveyed his command crew.

"Who's going to relieve me of command?" he asked.

There was strength in his voice, challenge. A gauntlet thrown down, which no one was especially eager to pick up. Sulu seemed to radiate confidence and conviction.

"Listen to me carefully, people," he said. "I am not crazy. I have not lost my mind, nor have I become drunk with power. We've been down this road before, with far higher stakes. When I told Captain Kirk the location of the Khitomer conference, I was aiding and abetting a convicted criminal. I could have been brought up on charges of treason. But I acted out of loyalty and out of honor, being willing to betray my country rather than betray my friend. It's out of that same sense of honor that I act now."

"But sir," said Rand as gently as she could, "it's not the

same. This is a useless risk of your career because . . . because . . ."

"Because Demora is dead."

"Yes, sir," Anik spoke up.

"That may very well be," Sulu agreed. "But her memory is still very much alive. And what I'm doing, I'm doing on behalf of her memory. That, and because I'm determined to find out what sort of circumstance on Askalon Five could have led to her death. She didn't simply take a wrong step and fall off a cliff, or die because some native creature leaped out from hiding and attacked her. Demora went berserk. She died naked and savage, shot down by her own commander. And I will know why." His voice began to rise with unexpected vehemence. "Not ten months from now, or a year from now, or six years from now. I will know *right now*. I owe her that. And if Starfleet feels they don't owe me that, then that will be between Starfleet and me. Do we understand each other?"

There was a long moment when everyone looked to each other to see how they were responding. It was as if the command crew needed to be of one mind so that they could function.

And then Anik said simply, "Aye, sir."

"Aye, sir," echoed Janice Rand.

One by one, the votes of confidence came. Sulu nodded to each one individually. And then he said, "Helm . . . best speed to Askalon Five."

"Best speed," echoed Docksey, even as she thought to herself, *We are in so much trouble. . . .*

The *Excelsior* whipped around and hurtled away from Starbase 9.

And light-years away, the call went out to the nearest starship in a position to stop them. . . .

"You really think you're going to be saved, don't you. You really think you have a prayer. . . ."

The voice floated through her head as aimlessly as she herself floated in the ooze. She tried to reject what she was hearing, but it permeated her at every level. There was no escape from it, no defense she could erect. . . .

"You're all alone. You're mine, just like your mother was, and this time you're not going to get away . . . you're going to stay mine, and maybe I'll let you out eventually before I wipe your memory and put you back so you can float in bewilderment some more, always wondering, always confused . . . maybe I've already done it . . . maybe I'm doing it right now and you're too muddled to realize it . . . you don't know up, down, or sideways, everything's gone, and you know what? We can give it all back to you and then take it away again, and you'll never know . . . you'll never ever know. . . ."

And the thought came to her, the thought of salvation . . . and curiously that most fleeting of thoughts was not of her captain, of her shipmates, of anyone whom she considered a close friend. . . .

Like the child she had once been, one word drifted through her mind . . .

Daddy . . .

Chapter Twenty-four

"FATHER, you can't be serious."

Admiral Blackjack Harriman paced the interior of his son's quarters. He nodded his head, his expression grim. "I'm afraid I am serious, son. Word came directly from Admiral LaVelle herself."

Captain Harriman looked confused. "They want us to go after *Excelsior*?"

"That's right, Johnny. And you are authorized to use any and all means to get *Excelsior* to back off, up to and including force. The fact is, Starfleet is simply unwilling to countenance these types of shenanigans and displays of disrespect. Kirk made a career out of it; his associates are simply not going to be allowed to continue that tradition."

"But . . ."

"Captain Sulu is in clear violation of regs, son," said Blackjack. "Not only that, but Sulu is acting in direct contradiction of LaVelle's orders. This simply cannot be tolerated, and this ship has been chosen to teach *Excelsior* a lesson. I admit that there's some irony involved . . . a vessel named *Enterprise* hunting down Sulu. But we can't worry about that. The order has been given and the duty is clear."

Harriman stared at the far wall. "You're aware, Father, this is my fault. If—"

"We're not going through that again, son," said Blackjack. "That way lies madness. We're just going to get the job done."

He looked up at his father, his eyes narrowed to slits. "Tell me one thing, though. Why did Admiral LaVelle contact you, rather than me? This is my ship. If we're being given a new assignment, it should come through me."

"Admiral LaVelle and I go all the way back to the Academy, son." He shrugged. "Perhaps she simply felt more comfortable filtering the order through me. Besides, it's not contrary to protocol. I do happen to be the ranking officer on board. This was just Starfleet's call. It's not up to us to start second-guessing superior officers, son. That's what Sulu is doing. And that's how he's managed to land himself in a world of trouble. I assume we understand each other."

"Yes, sir. Perfectly."

But there was something in his voice. Something that the admiral found vaguely disturbing. As Captain Harriman headed for the door, Blackjack stepped partially into his way, just enough to block his exit. They looked at each other for a moment, and then the captain dropped his gaze, suddenly intensely interested in the tops of his boots.

"You're not going to have a problem with this, are you, son? I'd hate to think that you'd allow sentiment or some sort of," and his voice took on a distasteful edge, "weak-kneed attitude to cloud your judgment."

"My knees are just fine, sir, thank you," said Harriman tightly. "I know my orders, and I know my duty. Do you have reason to believe otherwise?"

"No."

"Then kindly step aside, sir, and let me do my job."

Blackjack nodded approvingly. "Yes, sir, Captain."

Harriman walked out the door, turned left, and headed briskly down the corridor. By the time his father caught up,

Harriman had already reached a turbolift and was on his way to the bridge.

He stepped out onto the bridge. Dane snapped off one of her customary salutes. For some reason he felt even less tolerant of her quirks today than he did under regular circumstances.

"Mr. Magnus, plot course for Askalon Five," he said.

Magnus turned in his chair, making no attempt to hide his surprise. "Askalon Five, sir?" he asked.

"That's correct. I thought the order was clear enough. You understood it, didn't you?"

"Sir," Dane spoke up, "Askalon Five is under quarantine."

"No one is more aware of that than I am, Dane," said Harriman. "I am also acutely aware that I dislike repeating orders. You aren't going to require me to do that, are you?"

"No, sir," said Magnus with a shrug. "Course plotted and laid in, sir." He glanced over at Lieutenant Chaput next to him, a fire-headed helmswoman who looked no less confused than Magnus.

"Helm has the course, sir," Chaput confirmed. "Awaiting your orders."

"Best speed to Askalon Five, helm," said Harriman and, with a brisk rap of his knuckles, added, "Engage."

The *Enterprise* leaped into warp space, hurtling toward Askalon V with all due haste.

As it did so, Commander Dane took a step away from her station and said, "Captain . . . if I may ask . . . ?"

"Why are we returning to Askalon?" He sat there for a moment, grim faced, and then said, "Because, Commander . . . we have orders. We are to intercept another starship which has taken it upon herself to go to Askalon Five, contravening both Starfleet orders and quarantine regulations. My precise orders are that we are to take whatever steps are necessary to make this vessel realize the folly of its actions."

"Does that include force, sir?"

"It does indeed."

There was silence for a moment. And then Dane said, "Captain . . . is this about Demora?"

"Considering that Captain Sulu is involved, I'd say that's a safe assumption."

And that was when Harriman heard something murmured from the direction of the science station. He turned slowly to face Lieutenant Maggie Thompson. "You have something to say, Lieutenant?" he asked.

"No, sir," she replied.

"I think you do. And I would appreciate your being forthright enough to say what's on your mind rather than muttering under your breath."

She looked at him with unmistakable defiance. "If they're going to try and do something to help Demora, then we should be helping them, not hunting them."

"Is it necessary for me to painfully remind you, Lieutenant, that Ensign Demora Sulu is deceased? I pushed the button that fired her ashes into the sun myself. She is beyond help, and *Excelsior* is beyond the bounds of acceptable behavior for a starship. But if you have a problem with that, and feel that you cannot function up to full capacity due to the emotional dynamics involved, then I cordially invite you to relieve yourself of duty."

"I would prefer not, sir," she said. The words were deferential, but the tone was most definitely not.

If Harriman took any note of that tone, he didn't let on. Instead he looked to the rest of the command crew. "That applies to the rest of you as well. If there's anyone here who feels they won't be able to perform to their usual high standards of excellence . . . I invite them to leave the bridge now. There will be no black mark against you, no stain on your record. But if any of you feel that this duty is going to be too emotionally . . . incendiary . . . speak up now."

No one did, of course . . . even though several of them did indeed want to get up and walk off. But it simply wasn't the sort of situation that permitted an indulgence of one's true feelings. Not for any of the bridge crew. Not even for the ship's commander.

"Sir," Dane ventured, "if we are to prepare for a possible battle situation . . ."

"I'm ahead of you, Commander. Signal yellow alert. Maintain battle readiness."

"Signaling yellow alert," Z'on said from his station.

Harriman realized that he'd been standing the entire time. Slowly he settled into his command chair, watching the stars fly past. And, allowing a bit of wistfulness to creep into his voice, he said, "It's moments like this when I wish I could be facing something simple . . . like a horde of rampaging Blumbergs."

Despite the seriousness of the situation, the comment actually drew smiles from several of the crewmen . . . and an utterly confused look from Lieutenant Chaput, who turned to Magnus and said, "A horde of what?"

"Don't ask," advised Magnus. "Believe me, if you know what's good for you . . . don't ask."

Chaput didn't ask.

Chapter Twenty-five

ASKALON V filled the screen like a canker.

For long moments no one on the bridge of the *Excelsior* said anything. Sulu stared at the planet, certain that he could feel sensations of evil and foulness rolling off the world's surface. Would it be likely that he'd feel that way if Demora hadn't met her end there? Not likely. He was impressing his own views, shaped through the tragedy, upon the planet.

None of which stopped him from feeling basically repulsed just looking at the place.

The others regarded the planet as well, but they were seeing it differently than Sulu was. They looked at it and saw the world that was serving as the Waterloo for the captain whom they'd come to admire and respect. None of them had the slightest doubt that this decision was going to cost him dearly. Cost him his command, perhaps even his career. And in exchange for this high price, the reward was meager if not nonexistent. Nothing could bring his daughter back, and there was certainly no guarantee that even the answers he craved would be forthcoming.

Nonetheless, they stood in respectful silence.

"Commander Anik," he said after a time, "ready a shuttlecraft, please."

Anik nodded, feeling a bit relieved that another potential argument had been avoided. At least Sulu wasn't totally dismissing or ignoring the fact that the planet was under quarantine. When Captain Harriman and the rest of the landing party had beamed back aboard the *Enterprise,* the transporter had automatically screened and cleared them of any potentially harmful germs that they might have contracted on the planet . . . including the possible whatever-it-was that had had such a fatal effect on Demora.

But if Sulu was going down there, he was going to be exposed to whatever viruses or germs might be awaiting him. The smart thing to do, therefore, was to cruise the surface via shuttle while making preliminary readings, rather than simply beaming down into a conceivably lethal situation.

"Shuttlecraft *Galileo* will be ready for you in five minutes, sir," said Anik.

Upon hearing this, Janice Rand winced. Not the *Galileo.* Anything but the *Galileo.* Hadn't anyone noticed that the damned shuttle was jinxed? It was always crashing, burning, and making all manner of unfortunate and oftentimes catastrophic landings. She hoped that Sulu would ask for another craft.

"Excellent," he said.

Lord, he really did believe in tempting fate. Not willing to send Sulu off to disaster all by himself, Rand stood. "Permission to accompany you, sir," she said.

"I appreciate the offer, Commander, but no." He rose from his chair. "This is my responsibility. My decision. And my business. No one else is going to take a risk as a result of it except me."

She nodded, but she didn't look happy about it. Not unsympathetically, Sulu put a hand on her shoulder and said, "I appreciate the thought, Janice. Hold the fort. I'll be back before you know it."

"Will do, sir," she said gamely . . . wondering if she was ever going to see him again.

Sulu, meantime, turned to Anik. And in a low voice he said, "If I were Starfleet, I'd be sending another ship out to spank us. Keep sensors on maximum, and don't hesitate for a moment to back off. Leave me if necessary."

"Captain, we wouldn't . . ."

"You would and you should, if it means the alternative is standing your ground and fighting another starship. You have your orders, Anik. I expect you to carry them out."

"Yes, sir," said Anik, not looking especially happy about it.

He headed for the turbolift, and behind him various crew members echoed each other as they said, "Good luck." He stopped and nodded to them in response.

"Good luck to us all," he said. "I have no doubt we'll all need it."

He stopped at the armory, not wanting to take any chances. By the time he got to the shuttlecraft, Anik was waiting for him.

They stood facing each other, Sulu's arms draped behind his back. "Here to wish me bon voyage, Commander?"

"Sir . . . I am asking you one more time not to do this."

"And why are you asking me this, when you know I have already made up my mind?"

Anik looked somewhat self-conscious. "Because I'm being selfish, sir."

He raised an eyebrow. "Selfish?"

"Yes. Because when I was coming up through the Academy, the exploits of Captain Kirk and his command crew were already . . . there's no other way to put it, sir . . . legendary. And my greatest hope, my goal, was to be able to serve under one of those remarkable people. You people were . . . are . . . my heroes. So when your previous number one, Commander Valtane, requested transfer off the *Excelsior . . .*"

"Valtane was a good officer," admitted Sulu, "but the crew never warmed to him."

"Yes, well . . . his loss was my gain. You have no idea, Captain, how many strings I pulled, favors I called in . . . how hard I lobbied for this assignment. And I achieved my goal. I am living my dream. I try not to make a point of it because, frankly"—she shifted uncomfortably—"I don't consider it a terribly professional attitude to have. But there it is, and it's mine."

"So what you're saying is that you feel I'm taking a needless risk and, therefore, jeopardizing your dream."

"Yes, sir."

"Doesn't that seem a bit self-centered to you?"

"Yes, sir," she said again, not sounding the least bit repentant.

"Well, Commander . . . I guess you'll find that just because one rises to the rank of captain, that doesn't necessarily mean that one becomes any less self-centered." He paused. "I remember an incident with Captain Kirk, about ten years ago . . . he was Admiral Kirk at the time. We'd been caught completely flat-footed by Khan . . . you might have heard about it."

"I was in my last year at the Academy. The students who came back, who . . . survived . . . called it the training mission from hell."

"That's fairly accurate. In any event, we were helpless, taken off guard by the *Reliant.* Power out, weapons down. Not a hope in the world. And we got a subspace transmission from the *Reliant* . . . and I'll never forget this, as long as I live. Uhura turned to the admiral and said we were receiving terms of surrender. It was as if she'd spoken the foulest obscenity. Nobody moved. Nobody breathed. When the admiral told her to put it on-screen, it was as if we'd all been stabbed because this was James T. Kirk, and he didn't surrender while he was alive. And he wound up stalling for time and outsmarting Khan. He'd done it. Even though he blamed himself, called himself 'senile,' nevertheless . . . he sent the *Reliant* running. It was as if all was right with the galaxy once more. So I suppose . . . I learned that from him. To never surrender until the last card is played. And even though Demora is out of the game, I still have a few hands I'm going to play out. Do you understand?"

Anik sighed. "Not really, I guess, since I still would prefer you didn't have to go."

"I'd prefer it too." He headed toward the shuttle, then

turned and said, "Anik. I should remind you that an attractive young yeoman served with Captain Kirk in his first five-year mission. One Janice Rand by name. She wasn't with him quite as long as I was, but . . . I suppose it could have been considered quality time. So if it's the spirit of us 'legends' that so motivated you, well . . . you'll find that there's legends everywhere you look. They are what we make of them."

She nodded and stepped back as Sulu climbed into the shuttlecraft *Galileo*. "Good luck, Captain. We'll be waiting for you."

"Keep a light burning," he replied as the door sealed him in. Moments later, the shuttlecraft lifted out of the bay and angled around and down toward the surface of Askalon V.

She heard the voices, and they sounded concerned.

They reached her as if from a great distance, and she sensed that, this time, they weren't directed at her. They were talking with each other, although she felt as if they were slowly moving toward her like the sun's rays creeping over the horizon. . . .

"They're in orbit. What are they doing here?"

"What do you think they're doing here?"

"He knows."

"He couldn't know!"

"He does, somehow he does."

"I say we take him. I owe him."

"Don't be an .idiot. We have the girl. That was risk enough. He's a damned starship captain. There will be questions. . . ."

"Let there be questions. There's always questions. What there won't be is answers. I want him."

"No."

"I said . . ."

"I said no! We've indulged it this far! Any more would be suicide! I said . . . no!"

None of the conversation meant anything to her. It all blended together, one voice with another. All of it having a blur of incoherency to it.

But still . . .

But still . . .

Vague bits of comprehension began to creep back to her. Self-awareness. Understanding. Slowly she became aware that she was more than just a mind floating in a pool of nothingness. She had a name. She had a being. She had a purpose.

She had to get out. . . .

Chapter Twenty-six

THE SHUTTLECRAFT skimmed the surface of Askalon V. The ions in the atmosphere caused the vessel to buck under Sulu's hand, but it wasn't anything he couldn't handle.

He had studied Harriman's reports on the event thoroughly, and was able to pilot the shuttle to the exact coordinates where the final, fatal encounter with Demora took place a week ago.

What he was pleased to see was that the surface of the planet was apparently going to cooperate in his investigations. Because of its thick, claylike texture, all the prints had remained exactly—or close to exactly—the way that they had been. He nosed the shuttle downward to within ten meters of the surface, then brought a tight view of the area up on the screen so that he could inspect the prints. Sure enough, there they were. Clear signs of a scuffle, with dirt kicked up, tossed around. He could see the remains of the distress beacon, which had been quite thoroughly smashed during the scuffle. Close up, he could even make out blood on the dirt, although he didn't like to think about whose it might be. It certainly backed up what Harriman had put in his report; it had been a vicious fight. The fact that Demora had been bare-handed . . . indeed, bare naked . . . had done nothing to lessen the ferocity of the encounter.

Naked and . . . barefoot.

He zoomed in the exterior monitors on the shuttlecraft, looking for signs of unclad feet. It took him a few moments to pin it down, but there it was. Footprints left behind by Demora's bare feet. He brought the shuttlecraft to a slightly higher elevation, so that he was now about twenty meters high.

There. There to the west, he saw the footprints leading off. He eased the shuttlecraft in the direction that the prints had come from in order to track them to their point of origin.

It took a few moments for him to backtrack, although not too long. Certainly a shuttle could cover distance much more rapidly than a woman on foot. Even if she was running, which Sulu could now tell that she had been doing. At least that's what she'd been doing at first, because her footprints weren't flat. Rather they were weight-distributed in such a way that clearly only the balls of her feet were making an impression. Not only that, but they were farther apart, the wider gait of someone taking long, loping strides.

He thought briefly of all the times they'd gone running together. What a nightmarish contrast this sordid world was to the times they had jogged side by side through San Francisco's sloping streets.

Then he noticed something else. He saw booted footprints coming in from the side and roughly paralleling the running prints of Demora. But the booted prints were going in the other direction.

From the size of the booted prints, Sulu suspected that they likewise belonged to Demora. And the angle that they came from would be consistent with the landing party's original arrival. In other words, Demora had come from the general area of the northwest, moved in this general direction . . . and then something had happened, reducing her to naked savagery, and she'd come hightailing it in a straight easterly direction until running into, and attacking, Harriman and his people.

So all Sulu had to do was get to the point where the

encounter had been . . . find what happened there . . . and then he would have the answer.

Or at the very least, he'd have even more questions.

The shuttle continued its course. In the distance, Sulu spotted the ruined city that had been mentioned in Harriman's reports. What had the inhabitants been like, he wondered. Had some outlandish virus swept over them, turning them all into mindless berserkers such as what Demora had become? Had they been reduced to predator and prey, tearing each other apart until there was nothing left?

And what had happened to Demora, then, was some sort of residual disease left floating in the air?

But if that were the case, why hadn't Harriman and the others been affected? Why just Demora?

Why her?

Why her? Well . . . that was the question, wasn't it. That's what this was all about. Sulu had to admit that this was more than just an exploratory probe to find out what had happened. He was looking for some sort of cosmic answer. Something that would explain to him precisely why his little girl had been singled out to be overtaken by, and fall prey to, this awful demise.

In short . . . he wanted the universe to make sense.

He had traveled the stars for so long that he had almost begun to believe that he could see the barest meaning behind it all. Sometimes he thought that right there, just beyond human consciousness . . . there were the answers that every creature sought in order to *understand*. To seek knowledge. To boldly go, and all that. Just past the horizon line of understanding, he thought he could glimpse the start of comprehension.

And then Kirk had been snatched away . . . and then Demora had been taken from him . . . and just like that, the two great constants of his life had evaporated.

Nature abhors a vacuum.

The loss of Kirk, and now Demora, had left a great airless, souless void within him, and he was trying to fill it up again. Fill it with answers . . . with cognizance . . . with something, dammit. Anything.

The footprints stopped.

Sulu brought the shuttlecraft to a slow halt, hovering above the area that now seemed to serve as the origin point of the tracks.

At first glance, there was nothing particularly remarkable about this stretch of land. It was slightly hillier than other places, but the terrain was that same claylike texture. No shrubbery or brush, flora or fauna.

What there was was the beginning of the barefoot tracks . . . and the end of the booted tracks. Apparently Demora had gotten to this geographic point . . . removed her clothes . . . run back in the general direction of the landing party and tried to kill them. Right where they met, the dirt was a bit disturbed, although nothing too disorderly. As if there had been a very brief scuffle there.

There were no other prints around, which seemed to undercut the notion that some animal had bitten her, giving her an unknown and fast acting version of rabies. Still, it could have been airborne. How many diseases had been transmitted by insects, after all?

There was . . .

"Wait a minute," said Sulu.

Tracks, to and from. No other tracks around. No brush. No place to hide. His view in all directions was unobstructed.

"Where are her clothes?" he asked himself. "Where the hell are her clothes?"

The dirt around where the footprints intersected was in disarray, but it didn't seem dug up. So apparently she hadn't buried her clothes. She could have phasered them into nonexistence . . . but then where was the phaser? Could have set the phaser to self-destruct . . . but *someone* in the landing party would certainly have heard the blast, plus there would be some sort of scorch marks somewhere.

He used shipboard sensors to scan the area where the footprints came together. The atmosphere precluded reliable sensor scans from orbit, but here the readings were a bit clearer. Not much, though.

Sulu chewed on his lower lip for a moment, and then angled the shuttlecraft downward. He landed the *Galileo* not right on the spot where he was suspicious, but instead fifty meters away.

He sat in the shuttle for a long moment, his mind working, trying to anticipate. Then he leaned forward and began to program a course for the shuttlecraft to follow. He set distance, speed, angle. And then he said, "Computer."

"Working," replied the calm female voice.

He gave instructions in quick, clear sentences. The computer acknowledged the instructions in its inflectionless tone. The thing he liked about dealing with a computer was that it didn't bother to point out to him that the orders he was giving seemed, on the surface, crazy bordering on suicidal. There was no deep philosophical discussion. It was just a matter of, "Do this," to which the computer would respond, "Okay."

Sulu was all for spirited arguments, but every so often it was nice to have things go simply.

He ran an atmosphere check as a precaution and found nothing unusual. Nevertheless, just to play it safe, he placed a filtration mask over the lower half of his face. He took a deep breath to make sure that the mask was functioning as it was supposed to. Then he slipped on his field jacket to protect against the chill, opened up the shuttlecraft, and stepped out onto the terrain.

His feet sank a bit into it, but it wasn't anything he couldn't handle. His phaser was strapped to his belt, and he was holding his tricorder as he studied the readouts.

The filtration mask went a long way toward alleviating the breathing problems that the landing party from the *Enterprise* had experienced. Nonetheless, the deceptively chilled wind that flittered across the planet's surface was certainly nasty enough to give him pause, even though he was wearing his field jacket. He stretched to work kinks out of his muscles as he felt his joints freezing up. *Getting old,* he thought.

Slowly, carefully, he walked over to the area where Demora had undergone her startling transformation. He circled it, frowning. There was something, according to the tricorder . . . something beneath the ground. He couldn't quite make it out, however. He was still getting interference with the tricorders scanning circuitry. But was it possible that it was still the atmosphere . . . ?

No. No, he began to suspect the exact opposite. He walked the perimeter, clutching the tricorder as if it were a life preserver, or even the Holy Grail. Something was . . . was *generating* interference. Was mucking with the tricorder's ability to fully apprise him of the area.

He stepped closer to the footprints and where they intersected, taking care not to tread directly on them. He didn't want to obliterate them in case he needed to—

And the ground went out from under him.

He'd had no warning at all, except for the slightest grinding of motors from somewhere he couldn't pinpoint. The ground beneath him opened up quickly and he felt something tugging at his legs. Immediately he realized what it was: a rushing of air like a vacuum, as if he were being sucked down into some great black tube. In the brief time that he had to register an impression, all he could make out was blackness.

All that happened in just under a second and then Sulu disappeared. He cried out as he plummeted into the darkness, but the sounds of his shout were cut off as the ground closed up over him.

Not that there would have been anyone to hear him anyway.

He fell out of control, Alice down the rabbit hole.

Alice . . . the rabbit hole

The amusement park planet . . .

Even as he fell, even as blackness surrounded him, his mind was racing as he realized . . .

. . . the amusement park planet in the Omicron Delta region . . . where things had come up from underground . . . where beings and objects were instantly manufactured . . . beings like the White Rabbit . . . and Alice . . . and the black knight, and that revolver with a seemingly infinite supply of bullets . . . and the samurai . . . and

Demora . . .

The name whispered in his mind, and then he slammed to a halt as unconsciousness claimed him.

* * *

It was very still on the bridge of the *Excelsior*. Anik sat in the command chair, watching the screen steadily. The planet, its secrets still carefully maintained, sat on the screen as the starship orbited it.

The bridge crew went about their duties in a hushed, almost apprehensive manner. There was the usual hum from the instrumentation, the quiet chatter among the crew. But overall there was an air of restraint. Part of their attention was on their work, but most of their minds was on the surface with Captain Sulu.

"Any word yet from the captain?" asked Anik.

"No. But he's not overdue . . . yet," said Rand.

There followed another awkward silence. Finding it intolerable, Anik turned to Janice Rand, whose calm demeanor went a long way toward hiding her inner turmoil. "Commander Rand," she said slowly, "if you don't mind my asking . . . what was it like?"

Janice looked at her with a polite air of confusion. "It? What it?"

"Serving with Captain Sulu back when he was at helm. What was he like?"

"Oh . . . much like he is now. He had his hobbies. A plant named Beauregard that was his pride and joy. And his fencing. Once he became ill and went nuts, chasing people all over the place with a sword. It was . . . odd."

"And Captain Kirk? You were his yeoman. What was it like serving with him . . . with all of them."

Rand sat back slightly, and she smiled. "It was . . . a remarkable time. It was . . ." She blushed. "This will sound awful."

"Go on, Commander," Docksey prompted from helm. The crew was sharp and alert, but on the other hand there was nothing like calm chatter to keep everyone on even keel.

"We were . . . we were the best ship in the fleet. And the best crew. And we knew it somehow. Starfleet knew it, too, probably because we were able to prove ourselves time and time again." She smiled, remembering what it was like. Remembering the joy and excitement of exploration.

She rose from her station and went to Anik, crouching down with one arm resting on the command chair while adopting a masculine swagger. Anik grinned as Janice dropped her voice a couple of octaves and intoned in mock-serious fashion, sounding vaguely like a Starfleet admiral, "There's a problem that needs solving? A major threat to security? Only one man for the job, ladies and gentlemen: James Kirk. Only one ship to handle the situation: the *Enterprise.* Who do you want to have standing between you and a planet killer? It's the *Enterprise.* What, the Klingons are stirring up trouble and we need a starship to go in and show them what's what? It's the *Enterprise.* What's that you say? A giant amoeba is heading your way and a starship is needed to face insurmountable odds? It's the *Enterprise.*"

And suddenly from the science station, Lieutenant Tom Chafin—a muscular, handsome Terran with thick brown hair—reported, "Commander Anik, a ship appears to be dropping out of warp. . . ."

"Confirmed," Lojur now put in. "Vessel bearing two-five-three mark four. It appears to be . . ."

Space warped ahead of them and a massive vessel slid into normal space ten thousand kilometers to starboard.

"One of ours. Federation starship, *Excelsior* class," continued Lojur.

"Which one?" said Anik.

And Janice Rand, back at her station, looked up from her communications board as an incoming hail identified them.

"It's the *Enterprise,*" she said tonelessly.

Chapter Twenty-seven

THE WORLD WAS BLACKNESS, and then a low mocking voice said, "So . . . it's been quite a while, hasn't it, L.C.?"

Sulu reached out, feeling the cool smoothness of the floor beneath him. Slowly he opened his eyes, then squinted against the intensity of the light. Around him he could hear a soft humming and burbling, as if he were surrounded by large vats of liquid.

He lifted his head up and looked around. He was surrounded by large vats of liquid.

Every so often, things *were* what they seemed.

The vats lined the room, and there seemed to be hundreds of them. In either direction, they seemed to stretch unto infinity, like a tunnel. Sulu had no clue as to how large the place might be. At the far end he thought he spied some additional machinery, like a massive engine or power source of some kind, but he was too far away to make it out clearly.

The room itself had silver walls that curved upward into a cathedral ceiling, which seemed almost a mile high at its peak. In a way, the room had a feeling of a holy place, which struck Sulu as being slightly ironic.

Then he saw a pair of boots standing a few feet away. He craned his head and followed the track of the legs, up to the face. He knew, however, what he would see.

"Taine," he said.

His hair was longer, and he had a thick mustache tinged with gray. He'd gotten slightly jowly, but he still looked hard and lean, and the years had not diminished the cold fury in his eyes when he stared at Sulu. He was dressed in green, his pants flared at the cuffs, his shirt hanging loosely.

"You remember my name. I'm flattered."

"Don't be. I once had Vegan maringitis for a week and had to be hospitalized. I remember that name, too." He paused. "Are your flunkies still with you?"

"My associates, you mean? Rogers and Thor, yes. Ours has been a fruitful, if occasionally bumpy, partnership."

"And I was one of the bumps."

"Ohhh," said Taine softly, "you were a very large bump, yes, L.C. Oh, but it's not Lieutenant Commander anymore, is it. It's Captain, isn't it. Captain Sulu. Very, very impressive."

"What are you doing here?" he demanded. "And why did you do it?"

"Do what?" asked Taine, all innocence.

And Sulu felt his control slipping away. "Demora," he said in a harsh whisper. "Why did you . . . did you destroy her? What kind of creature are you that you would do that to . . . to . . ."

His hands convulsed in fury, and then he could hold himself back no longer. He lunged at Taine, hands outstretched.

He didn't get far. To be precise, he got all of a foot before a heavy hand clamped on the back of his jacket and lifted him clear of the floor. He had just enough time to think *Thor* before he was hurled across the room, crashing into one of the vats.

"Are you all right, Captain?" Taine asked with mock concern.

Rocky, Sulu tried to pull himself to his feet. He felt blood trickling down the side of his face, but he didn't wipe it away. He didn't want to acknowledge the dull ache he felt. "What are you doing here . . . and *why did you kill her?*"

Taine, leaning against one of the vats, laughed coarsely. "Her? Oh! You mean Demora! We didn't kill her, Captain."

"I know, Harriman did. But you changed her. You made her over into some . . . some beast. *You* were *responsible!*"

Thor, his massive arms hanging at his sides, stepped next to Taine. Taine was shaking his head. "You're not listening to me, Captain. No, not listening at all." He inclined his head slightly to Thor. Thor, apparently understanding Taine's desire, reached an arm into the vat that Taine was leaning against. He seemed to be fishing around for something, and then found it. He pulled it up and out. . . .

Her eyes were closed, her face almost unrecognizable since it was covered with the thick liquid that coagulated in the vat. Her hair, which Thor was gripping in his meaty hands, was thick with it as well.

She wasn't breathing.

Then, all of a sudden her lungs seemed to contract and she vomited up thick white liquid. It splashed out onto the floor, some of it getting on Taine's boots. He stepped back distastefully.

"Could this be who you're looking for?" asked Taine, chucking a thumb at her.

Sulu stared in disbelief, unable to speak. And then, finally, he managed to push out a word:

"Demora," he whispered.

She vomited once more, fingers clutching the edge of the vat spasmodically. Her eyes were caked shut with the liquid from the vat.

And then, the years falling away, sounding like a child of six, she said, "Daddy . . . I don't feel so good. . . ."

"Incoming hail from the *Enterprise,*" said Rand tonelessly.

Anik of Matern didn't seem particularly inclined to jump to it immediately. She'd had a feeling that this moment was inevitable and, now that it had arrived, she was oddly calm. "Scan them, Mr. Chafin," she said.

"Scanning," said Chafin. After a moment, he announced, "They're on yellow alert. Their defensive systems are charged."

"They're hailing again," Rand told her. "They sound impatient."

Anik pursed her lips and stared at the screen a moment more. "All right. Put them on," she said.

The bridge of the *Enterprise* appeared on the screen. Captain John Harriman was there, standing, his arms draped behind his back. Anik immediately noticed someone else there as well, someone who didn't appear to belong with the rest of the bridge crew. It was an older man, an admiral. Then she recognized him: Admiral "Blackjack" Harriman. The captain's father.

Ohhh, this is not good, thought Anik.

"Excelsior, this is Captain Harriman of the *Enterprise.* I would have appreciated a faster response," said Harriman.

"Our apologies," Anik said evenly. "This is Commander Anik. May we be of assistance."

"Yes, you may. You can start by allowing me to speak with Captain Sulu."

"I regret that he's indisposed."

"Indisposed? How?"

"A flare-up of an old condition," deadpanned Anik. "He's . . ." She hesitated, looking briefly at Rand. Janice shrugged. Anik turned back to Harriman and said, "He's chasing people around with a sword. We hope to alleviate the situation shortly."

Harriman was silent for a moment. "Commander, I'm not interested in playing games," he said. "If you do not bring Captain Sulu to speak to me, I will go on the assumption that he on the planet's surface. Would that be a safe assumption, Commander?"

Anik said nothing.

"Commander . . ." Harriman said warningly.

"Captain Sulu . . . is not available."

Harriman sighed and rubbed the bridge of his nose with

his thumb and forefinger. "All right, Commander . . . have it your way. The captain is not available. That being the case, I must warn you that I have been empowered by Starfleet to order you to leave this vicinity immediately."

"I . . . regret that I cannot comply at this time," said Anik.

"Why not?"

"Orders."

"Whose?"

"Captain Sulu's."

"Really," said Harriman, unimpressed. "Then I wish to speak to him, now."

"Captain Sulu is not available," Anik told them.

Harriman started to make a response, but abruptly Admiral Harriman stepped forward into the foreground. "Commander . . . this is Admiral Harriman."

"Good day, Admiral," she said evenly.

Janice Rand watched Anik with growing admiration. The Maternian looked fragile owing to her nearly transparent skin, but there was absolutely no denying her iron force of will. She was not one to be easily intimidated.

"I'm not interested in playing word games, Commander," he said brusquely. "It's important that you understand the dynamics here. I will tell you what's going on, and you can deny it if you wish, but I'll appreciate wasting no more of anyone's time. Captain Sulu has violated Starfleet orders and quarantine regs by bringing your ship to Askalon Five and then going to the surface himself. His behavior will not be tolerated. You're acting in good conscience as his subordinate, and that's fine. But now I am giving you a direct order as a Starfleet admiral: Return Captain Sulu to the *Excelsior* and then proceed to Starbase Nine, where Captain Sulu will be placed under arrest. Do you understand?"

Anik drew herself up straighter. "I do not know if that will be possible, sir."

"I suggest you make it possible, Commander. Because if you defy me, that will be on your own head. You have five minutes to retrieve him. *Enterprise* out."

The screen blinked out, but the *Enterprise* hung there in space, looking for all the world like it meant business.

"Commander Rand," Anik said softly, "raise Captain Sulu. At the very least, he should be apprised of the situation."

Rand nodded and immediately sent a signal to Sulu's wrist communicator . . .

. . . which was, at that moment, being ground underneath a large heel of an even larger foot.

On the surface of Askalon V, the shuttlecraft *Galileo* sat unmoving and, apparently, ineffectual.

Inside, the computer kept careful track of the passage of time.

Thor stepped back from the communicator, examining the busted equipment with pride.

Rogers, who had just entered the room, nodded approvingly. He had a very sizable phaser rifle strapped to his back, and it looked very impressive.

"We have an arsenal down here as well," Taine informed Sulu. "Some charming toys."

Sulu wasn't listening. He was crouched on the floor, clutching the gasping body of Demora to him. Nude, she had been trembling with cold, and Sulu had removed his jacket and wrapped it around her. Her teeth were chattering so violently she couldn't even say another word.

There was so much he wanted to say to her . . . so much he couldn't believe. He thought she'd been dead. He'd been at her funeral, for God's sake, her body reduced to ashes. He'd come to Askalon V seeking some sort of cosmic truth and understanding, and instead he'd gotten an insane riddle. She was alive, shaking in his arms, and he was so overwrought with emotion that he had no idea how to begin to handle it. He settled for patting her hair, feeling all the time as if he were treating her like a puppy. He couldn't let the depth of his feelings be displayed in these circumstances; not until he and Demora were safely out of it.

Rogers looked less than happy with the situation, and he gave Taine a sufficiently angry glance that Sulu could discern his mind-set immediately. "This whole thing is getting worse and worse," he muttered to Taine.

"You worry too much," Taine replied. "Their instruments won't be able to detect life readings, and his communicator is dead. If they send more people to look for him, they won't find him. And that will be the end of the illustrious career of Captain Sulu."

"You're insane," said Sulu.

Taine smiled slightly. "No. I'm in charge. So . . . do you remember years ago, Captain, when you expected me to explain to you the details behind my 'schemes.' Do you?"

"Yes."

"And I didn't, did I. However . . . time has passed. I've mellowed somewhat. Surviving the near-fatal crash of a shuttlecraft years ago tends to do that to you . . . tends to change your outlook."

"You don't have to tell me. I know what's going on." He tried to steady Demora's trembling.

"Really?" said Taine in surprise. "Now, that would be a switch. The hero giving the villain the secret behind the plot. Those are our respective positions, are they not? You the valiant hero, I the hissable villain. Tell me, O hero . . . what's going on."

"This . . . all this," Sulu said, gesturing to the vats and the vast room, "is similar to the mechanisms on an amusement-park planet where I took shore leave twenty-odd years ago. They create cellular castings of people or objects, with built-in mechanisms capable of reading the thoughts of the subjects and developing them to order."

"Close," said Taine. "Not quite, however. You have heard, I presume, of cloning?"

"Of course. Growing a genetic copy from a cell." He thought of Dr. McCoy's recent health problems. "Mostly it's used to supply new organs; organ banks with vital organs cloned from the originals keep them available for recipients."

"Not ambitious enough. Nowhere near ambitious enough. All this," Taine said, gesturing around, "was created, we believe, by an offshoot race from the same one who created that 'amusement park' planet you speak so fondly of. But they were a warlike, conquest-minded race. They were not interested in using their technology to develop harmless, cellular cast synthetic creatures. They wanted genuine, living, breathing beings. They wanted clones that they could develop into an army. An army of workers. An army of soldiers. Whatever they were needed for, they could do.

"The drawback with cloning has always been the length of time involved. If you want a twenty-year-old, you have to take twenty years to grow one. It doesn't spring up overnight, at least not in all modern science.

"But here . . . oh, but here . . . it does. As instantly as whatever you encountered on the amusement-park planet did."

Sulu cast his mind back, remembering how the samurai, for instance, had leaped into full-blown existence literally seconds after Sulu's thoughts had drifted that way.

"Sturdier, more dynamic . . . in every way, superior to the simple castings of the artificial beings. As near as we can determine, the practice of unrestrained cloning led to a great war on this world. By the time it was done, the city was in ruins, and only the clones survived . . . to die off after a time, or kill each other off.

"Because the clones were not perfect, you see. They had no restraint. They were uncivilized. They were ideal if you wanted an attack by a pack of mad dogs. Anything of greater restraint or finesse than that . . . and there were problems. I suspect that was their downfall. Oh, this is all speculation, you understand." He made a dismissive gesture. "But speculation based on our research. Research made in other worlds, at other sites. Hints, references, all manner of indications as to where this world might be. When Ling Sui . . ."

"You mean Susan," corrected Sulu. For some reason the correction made him feel a little smug.

But Taine looked at him archly. "Ling Sui. Susan Ling. Any of the other half-dozen names she used. I doubt she even remembered what her real name was anymore by the time she died." He leaned forward, looking at Sulu contemplatively. "You really know so very, very little.

Don't you get it yet? Ling Sui and I were partners. Explorers. We went from world to world, working various digs, taking what we could find and selling it to the highest bidder. And in one world we found key information about the cloning technology hidden on another world.

"But Ling Sui decided to get greedy, to try and cut me out. She thought she would sell the information to the highest bidder all on her own. But I caught up with her . . . caught up with her in the city of Demora. You interfered and delayed things, but I eventually caught up with her. Oh yes, I did, before she could sell it."

And from around his neck he removed a locket. Sulu recognized it instantly: It was the locket that Ling Sui had been wearing. It glittered green at him, as green as her eyes had been.

"We . . . renewed our partnership shortly thereafter, for the brief time it took for me to retrieve what she had stolen from me. Ultimately, there were no hard feelings, even though we went our separate ways after that . . . she to continue exploring and turning up new things to sell. And myself on the quest that eventually led me here, a year ago. It took that long, Captain. It's rare that you see that sort of dedication. We've spent a year exploring everything that was down here, discoveries that would amaze you. Getting the equipment up and running. Producing experiments in cloning, using our own genetic material as the sample. Some experiments have been more successful than others, I'll grant you, and we had many early failures. But we've been learning. At this point we can grow a clone to full growth in just under two minutes. Unfortunately they're difficult—impossible—to control. Furthermore, their cellular make-up tends to decay after about ten Earth days and they decompose. Not good for the long term. But we're getting there."

"And what's your plan?" said Sulu sarcastically. "To conquer the galaxy with a horde of clone warriors?"

"Oh, hardly anything so grandiose. However, a Tholian faction is most interested. We've had initial contact with them, opened the lines of communication. They're taken by the notion of armies upon armies of clone warriors. Of course, the Tholians keep trying to give us deadlines, and complain when we don't meet them. They're such sticklers for punctuality."

"I never thought I'd say this," said Sulu, "but Ling Sui was fortunate to have passed away when she did. Certainly preferable to being caught up in any more of your insanity."

"We were two of a kind, Ling Sui and I. At core, we both understood that. You see, Captain . . . what you got involved with was nothing more than a heightened lovers' quarrel."

Sulu looked at him oddly. "Lovers' quarrel? You were trying to kill each other."

"Of course. In case you didn't notice, Ling Sui was not one for half measures. But the fact is that I had prior claim to her, Captain . . . not to mention subsequent claim. Or haven't you figured it out yet."

"Figured out what?"

And Taine grinned lopsidedly. "Demora is my daughter. Not yours. Mine."

Janice Rand looked up from the comm board. "No response, Anik," she said, making no effort to hide her concern.

"Scan for life-forms," Anik instructed.

"Scanning," said Chafin. "Not picking up anything. Could be interference. Could be . . ."

"Could be he's dead," said Anik tonelessly.

The *Starship Enterprise* sat there in front of them, looking like she meant serious business.

On the bridge of the *Enterprise,* the tension was rather palpable. And it was solidly between the admiral and the captain.

"Hope I didn't overstep my bounds, Captain," said the admiral formally. From his tone, he probably thought he was being tongue-in-cheek. To his mild surprise, however, Captain Harriman didn't seem to share in the amusement.

"I am aware that, as senior officer on this vessel, you have the privilege of stepping in where you see fit," said Harriman. "I would appreciate some restraint, however, when possible."

The admiral blinked in surprise, and then his eyes narrowed slightly. "I have no problem with that," he said flatly, "as long as you get the job done."

"Don't be concerned on that score, Admiral."

"Don't give me need to be, Captain."

Upon hearing the exchange, Magnus and Chaput exchanged slightly nervous looks.

Commander Dane shifted uneasily in her chair, and Science Officer Thompson suddenly became intensely interested in the readings from her station.

And both Harrimans turned attention back to the screen.

Chapter Twenty-eight

SULU LAUGHED.

Demora was still clutching him, her mind whirling in confusion. But Taine's claim penetrated the haze. She looked up at Sulu with a mixture of befuddlement and fear, and she was even more puzzled when he started to laugh.

Taine had a variety of responses in mind when he dropped the bombshell on Sulu, but that hadn't been one of them. "What's so funny?" he demanded.

"What's so funny? You're a fool, that's what's so funny."

"I'm not the one who raised the daughter of another man thinking she was my own."

"Neither am I. Doctors did a genetic testing on her when she first came to me. She's mine, Taine. I'm her father; it's incontrovertible."

Rogers looked to Taine, reacting with clear surprise. "You said—"

"Be quiet," he ordered Rogers and looked back to Sulu. "You're lying. I know she's mine."

"You're wrong. What, did you think I would spend all

these years without knowing for sure? I've known since the first day who her father is. And it's not you."

"You're lying!"

Taine lashed out with one booted foot. Sulu raised an arm, managing to ward off part of the blow, catching it on his shoulder. He swayed, but didn't go down.

"She's *mine,*" Taine said in a hoarse whisper. "I recognized her from the moment I saw her picture on the news broadcasts. You remember . . . the ones that went out everywhere when Kirk died. And there was Demora, big as life, shown clutching her fallen comrade next to her on the bridge of the *Enterprise.* The image of her mother, I knew it instantly. And sure enough, her name was reported as Demora Sulu. I laughed over that one, oh, how I laughed." He raised his voice, addressing his associates. "Didn't we laugh, gentlemen?"

Rogers was looking extremely discomfited, and Sulu couldn't blame him. Taine was acting more and more erratically, his sanity being called increasingly into question.

"Look, Taine," he began.

But Taine was paying no attention to him. "So when I discovered that the *Enterprise* was going to be in this sector, I put up a distress beacon I'd picked up during my wanderings and programmed it with Chinese, in the hope that her interest would be piqued. It was a long shot, I'll grant you, but I've spent my life taking long shots. And it worked. You can't argue with success."

"Or dementia," Sulu shot back.

As if Sulu hadn't spoken, Taine said, "We captured her, brought her down here, and replaced her with a clone . . . not quite with the alacrity of your 'amusement-park planet,' but speedily and effectively. Oh, given ten days or so the body would have fallen apart, the fakery revealed. But I was reasonably certain the body would be disposed of, either buried or cremated, so that our little secret remained safe."

Sulu was silent.

"Well, Captain? Nothing to say?"

"Only one thing: How long have I been down here?"

"Oh, under the impression that if you're gone for too long, someone will send help? I wouldn't stake too much to that if I were you. They won't find you down here; we're too well shielded. But in answer to your question . . . it's been precisely fifty-seven minutes. I hope that helps."

"Immensely," replied Sulu.

"It's not helping, Commander," Chafin said, turning from the science station. "I've boosted the gain to the sensor array, but we're still not detecting anything."

"Incoming hail from the *Enterprise*," said Rand.

Anik sighed. "Well, that was inevitable. On-screen."

Captain Harriman's image appeared. "You've been given more than enough time, *Excelsior*. Where's Captain Sulu?"

She drummed her long fingers on the armrest for a moment, weighed the options, and decided to go with the truth. "He's on the planet's surface, but we've been unable to locate him. No life-form readings, no communication. It is my intention to send down a search party."

"Negative," Harriman said flatly. "That will be in direct contravention of Starfleet orders and policy. I submit to you, Commander, the harsh reality that Captain Sulu may very likely already be dead. You weren't on that planet's surface, Commander. I was. Whatever happened to Ensign Sulu very likely has happened to her father as well. Perhaps, in his frenzy, he leaped off a cliff. In any event . . . you will not be sending anyone down after him."

"Captain, you are being unreasonable. . . ."

"Commander, I outrank you, and I have Starfleet's direct orders behind me. Now . . . are you going to comply? Be aware that refusal to do so will make you complicit with Captain Sulu's actions, and there will be severe penalties involved." He paused. "You have a promising career, Commander Anik. I don't suggest you toss it away now."

All eyes on the bridge were upon her. Anik didn't look back at any of them.

"Captain, I regret I cannot comply."

"Very well. You're relieved of command. Who's the next ranking officer there?"

There was deathly silence, and then Janice Rand rose from the communications console. "I am. Commander Janice Rand."

Harriman looked slightly pained. He knew who she was, knew the history that she and Sulu had. "Great," he murmured, as if he knew the answer before he even asked the question. "Commander Rand . . . can I expect you to act in accordance with Starfleet regulations and relieve Anik of command?"

Rand didn't hesitate. "I regret, sir, that you cannot."

"Yes, I surmised that would be the answer," he sighed. He stroked his chin thoughtfully. "Looks like we have a situation on our hands, doesn't it."

"Yes, sir, it does."

And suddenly as if in a tremendous hurry, Harriman said, "You have five minutes to reconsider your position. Use it wisely." And then the screen blinked off.

Anik, Rand and the rest of the bridge crew looked at each other in mild confusion. "That was rushed," said Anik.

"Now what?" asked Rand.

"Now?" Anik grinned lopsidedly. "I don't know about you, but I'll probably start updating my résumé. Apparently it's time for me to start considering a career in the private sector."

"That's an unnecessarily pessimistic view, Commander," said Rand.

Anik looked at her skeptically. "Seems to me, Commander—no offense—that you're a little old to be engaging in fantasies. What's the Earth saying? We've crossed the Ruby Cam."

"Rubicon."

"Whatever it is, we've crossed it. Continue to try and raise Captain Sulu. Ready transporter room to send down a search—"

And suddenly Docksey shouted, "Photon torpedo off to starboard!"

She was right. The *Starship Enterprise* had fired a photon torpedo directly at the *Excelsior*.

"Red alert! Shields up!" called Anik, hoping it would be in time. "All engines, hard to port! Brace for impact!"

The *Excelsior* responded instantly, shields flaring into existence a split second before the photon torpedo smashed directly into the starboard section of the *Excelsior* . . . and shattered harmlessly.

"No impact!" called Lojur.

"Oh, there was impact, all right," said Anik. "But they removed the warhead."

"Son of a bitch was trying to scare us," Rand said.

From helm, Docksey muttered, "Well, it worked."

"Maintain red alert. Docksey, give us some distance."

"Aye, sir. Arm phasers?"

"Not yet. And not until absolutely necessary." Anik shook her head in annoyance. "Fastest five minutes I ever heard of."

And suddenly as if in a tremendous hurry, Harriman said, "You have five minutes to reconsider your position. Use it wisely." And then the screen blinked off.

"Five minutes?" came a voice that sounded like it was choking on fury.

Carefully keeping his back to the Admiral, Harriman said, "Yes, Admiral. Five minutes."

"Captain, five minutes or five hundred minutes isn't going to make a bit of difference. These people are defying you and defying Starfleet. There is no strategic advantage to giving them extra time."

And now Harriman turned to face his father. "Strategic advantage?" he said incredulously. "Admiral . . . that's another starship. One of ours. We're not at war here."

"Oh, yes we are," said the admiral stiffly. "We are at war against disobedience. Against contempt for regulations. Against the theatrics and outright rebellion that James Kirk and the others like him stood for. He spread his philosophies to Captain Sulu, and Sulu gave it to his people. It's like a disease . . . a cancer, eating away at our discipline! You see where this leads, Captain? Anarchy! Defiance! Starfleet cannot function if its officers take it into their heads to do whatever the hell they want!"

"I will handle this in my own way, Admiral," Harriman said sharply.

The air was electric between them. And then, very softly, very deadly, the admiral said, "Captain . . . I am giving you a direct order. I want this situation handled now. Not five minutes from now. Now. Or else."

Harriman felt the blood draining from his face. "Is that a threat, Admiral?"

"Is that a threat? No. This is a threat." Blackjack Harriman turned to Chaput and said, "Helm . . . load an unarmed photon torpedo . . . the kind you use for probes. Then target and fire."

Chaput, stunned, looked to the captain. Captain Harriman was no less stunned. *"What?"*

"You heard me," said the admiral evenly. "It'll just be a warning shot."

"And the next one will be what? For real?"

"If that's what it takes," said the admiral. He turned and was face-to-face with the captain. "Don't make me have to relieve you of duty, Captain."

The muscles of Harriman's jaw twitched furiously. "Helm . . . carry out the order," he said.

"Aye, sir," said Chaput, trying to keep the apprehension out of her voice. "Torpedo locked but not loaded."

"Fire," said Harriman.

"Torpedo away," Chaput said tonelessly.

They watched the streak of light blaze toward the *Excelsior*. The starship tried to get out of the way, but there wasn't enough time or distance between the vessels. The torpedo collided with the starboard warp strut but, since there was no active warhead in it, it simply shattered against it.

"Their shields are up," Dane said from the sensor station.

"Good," the admiral said with satisfaction. "It means they're taking us seriously."

"Apparently this is your game now, Admiral," Harriman told him. "What did you have in mind for the next play?"

Ignoring the sarcasm in Harriman's tone, Blackjack said, "Now, Captain . . . you get to have your five minutes. But it won't be five minutes of them stalling. It'll be five minutes of them sweating. You're no longer dealing from weakness, son. Now you're dealing from strength."

"In some quarters, restraint is considered strength," Harriman said.

The admiral looked at him. "There's no crime handling people with kid gloves, Captain . . . just as long as they know there's a fist of iron inside it. And if you don't have the stomach to deal with this in the proper fashion . . . then I will."

On the surface of the planet, the shuttlecraft sat motionless. But now computer commands began to kick over, and the engines of the *Galileo* began to surge to life.

Slowly but steadily, the shuttle rose into the air.

Thor stood guard over Sulu and Demora, who were still on the floor exactly as they'd been left. Demora had stopped trembling, and was glaring at Thor balefully.

Rogers, meantime, had brought Taine over to another section of the vast room and was talking to him in a low and hurried voice. "Listen to me, Taine," he said. "I've stuck with you through thick and thin, all these years. I always felt I owed you for that time you saved my life back on Castalan Nine. You know that. But between you and me, you haven't been a hundred percent right ever since the crash in the Sahara. Most times you're fine . . . but lately it's . . ."

"What's your point?" said Taine.

"The point is, I think you've got to take a step back. This Sulu guy was a pain in the ass twenty years ago, and I'm the first to admit that I'm as much for painful and agonizing torture as the next sadist. But there's no real percentage in vengeance. This whole taunting thing . . . it's serving no purpose. And this girl you fixated on: Maybe you thought she was your daughter, and that's fine. Or maybe she just reminded you of Ling and, deep down, you felt like you wanted to have her for old time's sake. That's fine, too. I went along with things this far because you never steered me wrong. But Taine . . . Sulu's right. This is crazy. You want to kill them, kill them. You want to indulge yourself with the girl first, then do it. I'll hold her still if you need me to. But you are way over the edge here. You're exposing us to unnecessary risks. It's got to end. So end it."

"You want me to end it," said Taine.

"That's right."

Taine's hand flew, fast and sharp, and speared Rogers in the throat. Rogers gagged as Taine kicked out, catching him in the pit of the stomach and knocking him flat on his back. Before Rogers could sit up, Taine was standing over him with Sulu's phaser rifle cradled in his arms.

"You want me to *end it? I could end you right now!*" He whirled and aimed the phaser at Sulu and Demora. "You want them dead, Rogers? Fine! One piece at a time, though! I'll blast them apart one damned piece at a time!"

The shuttle angled sharply upward, its preencoded course laid in. It reached sufficient height, angled around 180 degrees . . . and then plunged downward in a nosedive.

And Sulu said quietly, in a voice that carried nevertheless, "She must have meant a hell of a lot to you."

"You shut up! You don't know anything!"

"I know more than you could possibly believe," Sulu said confidently. "I know all the things you regret. I know what she meant to you. I know that—"

"I said shut up!" Taine ordered. He approached Sulu, the phaser rifle aimed squarely at him. Sulu had brought the formidable weapon with him because he'd had no idea what to expect and—since he'd been on his own—he figured he would want to pack as much firepower as possible. Now it seemed as if that was going to be a major mistake. "I know why you're doing this," Taine continued. "You hope to make me so mad that I'll simply blow you out of existence. That's what you want, isn't it. A quick, easy painless death, molecules spreading into oblivion so that you never even feel a thing. Or maybe you think there's going to be another rescue. Someone will come plunging through the skylight and save you. Well, Captain, in case you haven't noticed . . ." He gestured upward. *"There's no skylight.* So what are you going to do now, eh?"

"Improvise," replied Sulu.

And the ceiling exploded overhead. Down, down through

the cathedral ceiling smashed the shuttlecraft *Galileo*. Debris fell like hail as the roar of the shuttlecraft's engines filled the massive room.

Thor looked upward just in time to see a huge piece of masonry plunge toward him. He barely had time to throw up his hands in a vain attempt to ward it off before it fell on him, pinning him.

Sulu yanked Demora out of the way of falling rubble as it crashed around them. He heard a phaser whine and, moving more on instinct than anything else, lunged to the left. The phaser crackled over his head as he grabbed up a piece of rock and threw it desperately in Taine's direction.

The rock struck Taine squarely in the temple. He staggered, and the phaser rifle fell to the ground two feet away.

Seeing the opportunity, and knowing it might be their only one, Sulu lunged straight toward the rifle as chunks of the ceiling continued to rain down around him.

Thor intercepted him. Having shoved his way through the rubble, Thor knocked him back with a swing of his huge forearm. He moved after Sulu, rolling in like a thundercloud.

Demora leaped at the rifle and got there just as Taine grabbed it. The powerful weapon was caught between them as they pushed against it and against each other, their mouths drawn back in snarls . . . his contemptuous, hers fierce.

A blast from the phaser rifle ripped loose as Taine's finger found the trigger. It blew out a section of the wall, pieces of metal flying everywhere. One shard went flying in a deadly arc . . . and thudded squarely into the chest of Rogers, who had managed to dodge all of the other rubble only to look down and find a huge piece of metal protruding from his rib cage. He sank to his knees, surprised eyes glassing over.

The shuttlecraft sat serenely, having arrived at its destination and not programmed with any guidance beyond that.

Thor, like the thunder god after which he was named, hammered Sulu. Sulu managed to block a vicious punch that would likely have taken off his head, but a sweep of Thor's massive fist caught him on the side of his arm. The years had done nothing to diminish Thor's strength; if anything, he'd gotten stronger and faster. Sulu wished he could say that for himself.

Another blast ripped from the phaser rifle, and another. Shots were going all over, blasting machinery apart, sending sparks flying. At the far end, where one of the generators stood, a fire erupted.

Taine didn't seem to notice as he tried to rip the phaser rifle from Demora's fingers. But she would not let go. She couldn't have held on to it more strongly if she'd had it in a death grip.

He snarled into Demora's face, *"You should have been mine!"*

"You should have been sucking vacuum at birth!" shot back Demora, and she yanked at the rifle as hard as she could.

Thor stood over Sulu, who was trying to get to his feet. Explosions were rocking the cavern. Thor didn't seem to care. He had picked up a massive block of rubble, and he was about to raise it over his head and bring it slamming down on Sulu.

Only one thing stopped him.

Suddenly he didn't have a head.

A blast from the phaser rifle went squarely between his arms. His head vaporized, blown to ashes. The body remained there for a moment, as if knowing something was wrong but not being entirely sure what it might be. And then it sagged as Sulu rolled out of the way, allowing the body to fall to the ground. Then he got to his feet quickly and tried to get to Demora.

But he couldn't get near. The phaser rifle was still blasting in an arc, and it was all he could do to get the hell out of the way. Vats were blasted open, thick liquid pouring out of them . . .

. . . and bodies. Bodies tumbling out, and Sulu realized with a jolt of horror that they were clones. Clones of Demora. Clones of Taine, or Thor and Rogers. Naked and dripping, growling, trying to figure out where they were, what they were. It was as if Sulu and Demora had stumbled into an old-style horror film.

Demora suddenly rolled onto her back, still gripping the rifle, and Taine had no choice but to follow. And Demora, slamming her feet up into his stomach, sent him flying over her head.

But she lost her grip on the phaser rifle.

He landed in a rapidly growing pool of the white liquid, his grip on the phaser rifle still firm.

"You don't know *anything!*" he howled. "She was mine! She should have been mine and you *ruined everything!*"

Sulu didn't know which "she" Taine was referring to precisely, and it didn't much matter. All he knew was that he and Demora were too far away to do anything except be blown to bits.

And that was when a long piece of metal sliced across Taine's neck.

Taine grabbed at it, confused, reacting more to the sudden warmth jetting from him than from any sensation of pain. He turned, staggering, and saw Rogers directly behind him. Rogers, on the verge of death, but still with enough life in him to have pulled the metal from his chest and used it against Taine.

Taine tried to speak but his vocal cords wouldn't function.

"You . . . you killed us, Taine," Rogers gasped out. "I loved you like a brother . . . and you killed us . . . 'cause you had to have . . . what you couldn't . . . you idiot . . ."

He fell forward onto Taine, knocking Taine onto his back. His finger clutched spasmodically onto the trigger of the phaser rifle one last time and it blew skyward, ripping another gaping hole in the ceiling. Huge chunks of rubble, a mountain of it, fell onto both Taine and Rogers, entombing them.

All around Sulu and Demora, machinery was erupting, the phaser-rifle blasts having set overloads into motion that could not possibly be stopped. "Come on!" Sulu shouted, yanking Demora toward the shuttle.

Clones were starting to stagger to their feet, reaching for the two of them. Sulu kicked them aside and he and his daughter leaped into the shuttle. Within seconds the craft had attained altitude and was rocketing upward through the hole, away from the exploding cavern beneath them.

They'd gotten halfway up before they realized they weren't going to make it.

Admiral Harriman's face appeared on the viewscreen of the *Excelsior*. Without waiting for any niceties, he said flatly, "I assume you realize that we're quite serious, Commander."

"You've made your point abundantly clear, Admiral," Anik said.

"I notice you've brought your shields and weapons on line."

"You've left us no choice in the matter, sir."

Harriman's face reddened ever so slightly. "You indeed do have a choice, young woman. Surrender control over your vessel to *Enterprise*, and follow us to Starbase Nine."

"That is not an option, sir," said Anik. "With all due respect . . . I cannot and will not leave Captain Sulu behind."

Harriman shook his head. "It always amuses me when people do that. When they say, 'With all due respect,' right before they say something that's infuriating. With all due respect to *you*, Commander, if you choose to fight me on this, we will cripple your ship if necessary and take it in tow. Surrender."

Anik paused to consider the situation. She looked to the others, looked to Janice Rand . . . and thought about Captain Sulu.

"Sir," she said evenly, "I will thank you not to utter obscenities."

"Obscenities?" He had no idea what she was talking about.

"Yes, sir. Specifically, the word *surrender*. We don't surrender until the last card is played. But then again, that is a grand tradition of the *Enterprise*, isn't it, *Captain* Harriman." She made it painfully clear that the latter comment was addressed not to the admiral, but to his son.

"Commander Anik," said the admiral in a somewhat

patronizing tone, "you're playing card games with an old pro. I wouldn't if I were you. You can't bluff an old poker man. Surrender. Failure to do so will cause you to be considered a hostile vessel. The consequences will not be pleasant."

And Janice Rand murmured something.

Anik turned to her. "What?"

"I was just saying," Rand said in a low voice, "that there's a more appropriate card game here than poker."

"That being?"

"Well . . . the polite name for it is 'I Doubt You.' The impolite name. . . . Well, I'm sure.' You've heard of it."

And a slow smile spread across Anik's face.

"Yes. I know the game. Risky, though."

"As Captain Kirk once said . . . risk is our business."

"Commander?" came the admiral's voice.

Anik turned to face the screen. As if the admiral weren't even on the screen, she said, "John . . . when I was second year in the Academy, I happened to eavesdrop on a group of fourth-year cadets."

The admiral tried to interrupt, saying, "This is of no relevance, Commander."

But she ignored him, continuing to talk directly to Captain Harriman. "They were talking about hopes and dreams . . . and one of them spoke of wanting to be a starship captain. To command the finest ship in the fleet, with all its proudest traditions. I always remembered him, John, although I never knew who it was . . . until now. I recognize the voice. So tell me . . . do you remember those traditions?"

Annoyed and fed up, the admiral broke in and said, "Last warning: Surrender, or we will fire upon you."

And Anik smiled defiantly. "Bull," she said.

She took a brief moment of pleasure in the admiral's jaw-dropping reaction—and a brief moment of prayer that the entire thing wasn't going to blow up in her face—before turning to Docksey and saying calmly, "Lieutenant . . . lower shields."

Docksey was wide-eyed. "What?"

"You heard me." Without repeating it, she faced Rand and said, "Sever communications. There's nothing more to say."

Rand nodded and touched her comm panel. The picture of the admiral vanished, replaced by the *Enterprise*.

"That took a lot of guts, Commander," said Rand.

"Thank you."

"And it will be an honor working in the prison mines by your side."

Anik nodded slightly. "If we live that long," she said.

Admiral Harriman trembled in outrage. He turned to his son and demanded, "Did you see that? *Did you?*"

Before the captain could respond, Magnus suddenly said, "Captain . . . their shields are down."

Blackjack couldn't believe it. "The *arrogance*. This is exactly what I was talking about, Captain. This outright, unabashed contempt! Well, we're going to make a damned example of them! That's what we're going to do! Helm! Lock phasers on the *Excelsior*."

Chaput hesitated, looking to Captain Harriman for some sort of cue. But he was completely stoic, staring unflinchingly at the unprotected vessel hanging in space before them. "Phasers locked," she said tonelessly.

"Commander, they've locked phasers on us," said Lojur.

Anik, the picture of tranquillity, sat in the command chair, fingers steepled. "Well, well . . . this is getting interesting."

"Shall I raise shields?"

"No," she said.

"Any orders?"

"Yes. Brace yourself."

"Have they raised shields?" demanded the admiral.

"No sir," said Magnus.

There was a long pause, and then the admiral said softly, "The unmitigated gall. They think I don't have the nerve." And then, very loudly, he said, "Helm . . . fire phasers."

Chapter Twenty-nine

IN A HIGH TOWER in the ruined city, Sulu and Demora looked down and watched the hordes coming toward them.

In the mid-distance was the wreckage of the *Galileo*. The vessel had, unbeknownst to Sulu (not that it would have made a lot of difference) taken a partial hit from one of the phaser blasts. Systems damage had played havoc with both the *Galileo*'s power and guidance systems. Consequently Sulu had barely been able to hold the vessel together to make it to the surface. The crash had been rough, although they had at least been able to walk away, or limp away, from the landing, thus making it a good one. Unfortunately, the subspace radio on board the shuttle had been one of the first things to suffer when the systems went down, so they couldn't even call for help.

And things had worsened, for geysering upward from below had been the clone army. Every single one as bestial, as savage as the clone of Demora had been. While floating in the sensory-deprivation liquid of their tanks, they had been helpless. Now, though, they were out . . . they were maniacal . . . and they were looking for someone or something upon which to vent their savagery. And the only things that had suited the bill were Sulu and Demora.

So they had run. They had run as far and as fast as they could, trying to keep one step ahead of the howling hordes. They made it to the city finally, and come to an unfortunate discovery.

The city was built on the edge of a cliff.

Sulu appreciated the fact that, strategically, it was a fairly sharp place to put a city. Attackers couldn't possibly come at you from the rear. Unfortunately it also meant there was nowhere else to go, and as the army of clones, numbering somewhere around five hundred strong, converged, Sulu and his daughter sought refuge.

They had climbed higher, higher, barely speaking a word, conserving their strength. Finally they could go no farther. They huddled in the highest tower, watching the swarm below. The clones rampaged through the city, looking for their victims. Their shrieks were animalistic, bordering on insane.

Demora drew closer to her father, peering down. They appeared to be in something similar to a bell tower, except there was no bell around. It opened on all sides, although there were pillars that provided support for the roof. They were hundreds of feet in the air. If they were lucky, the swarm would never find them. Somehow, though, they weren't feeling lucky.

"Was I . . . like that?" Demora asked, flinching as she heard the shrieking below. Once they'd staked themselves out in the tower, he'd taken the time to fill her in—as quickly as he could—about what had happened.

"It wasn't you, remember?" he said, putting an arm around her.

She looked at him wonderingly. "But you didn't know that."

"No."

"You thought I was dead."

He felt his eyes start to become hot, all the tears he'd been suppressing beginning to flow from him. Yet now they were tears of joy, of relief . . . at least for the moment, however brief it might be. Determinedly, he wiped them away. "Yes . . ." he whispered, "I thought you were dead."

"But you came out here anyway. Risked your career, your life . . . for nothing. For not even a hope."

"I . . . felt you. In my head. I couldn't sleep at night. I felt like you were calling me." He paused. "On the amusement-park planet . . . the equipment there could read your thoughts. The equipment here was related to that. Maybe because of . . . of who we are . . . you were able to reach me somehow." He shook his head. "Either that . . . or something within me just refused to accept it. I had to know. I had to know why you were taken from me."

She could hear them coming closer, and she closed her eyes as if that would eliminate the sound. "And now we're both going to die."

"I was dying without you. Dying with you would be preferable."

She turned to look at him, her eyes brimming with tears. "Oh . . . God," she moaned. "That's . . . that's so sappy." And then she hugged him so tightly that he thought his ribs would break. In a low voice, she said, "Dad . . . this is a bad time to tell you . . . but . . . but it's going to be the only chance I have, I think, and I want everything to be square. . . ."

He lifted her chin and looked into her eyes. "What is it, honey?"

"I really hated you."

He blinked. "I wasn't sure what I was expecting you to say, but somehow that wasn't it."

She forced herself to look away from him, feeling ashamed. "I hated you for what you did for me. For staying on Earth so you could be with me, rather than being in space where you belong. And then, just when I got used to that guilt, you started heading out again. And I should have been happy for you, except all I was was angry at you because I felt abandoned. And when I went to the Academy, part of the reason I went was to please you . . . except in the meantime all the resentment I'd had toward you began to build and build because I was keeping it all bottled inside me . . . and I began hating myself because I was pursuing a career in order to impress you. You have no idea what it's like to feel so many things, and to be ashamed of all of them."

He lowered his head. "I wish I could say that," he said, his voice hoarse.

"What?"

He looked at her. "I . . . I resented you. I did, I admit it. Because I wanted to have it all. I wanted to be there for you, for my child . . . and I felt as if I wanted my life back. And the older you got, and the more you reminded me of your mother, and the more I resented her for doing this to the both of us. I was . . . I was much colder to you than I should have been. I kept you distant, particularly later on when you needed me most. I spoke of honor and principles . . . as if love didn't figure in at all. There's so much more I should have done. Everyone wants to be a perfect parent, and no one has a clue how. And I had less than most."

"You did the best you could have."

"Maybe . . . but I didn't do the best I should have. I wish I could go back . . . take the *Excelsior,* slingshot around the sun, go back in time . . . and talk sense into myself."

"Do you think you'd listen?"

He sighed. "Probably not."

They were silent for a moment, close to each other.

"I'm so sorry," she said softly.

"So am I. More, because I don't have the excuse of youth to fall back on."

Then Demora reached into the pocket of the jacket. "Here," she said. "I yanked this off Taine while we were fighting. I guess . . . maybe you should have it."

It was the jade locket. He took it from her gently, studied it. In the rapidly dwindling light that filtered through the purple sky, the locket still managed to glitter with a light of its own.

"Very old-fashioned," he said.

"Mother could be that way."

He flipped the catch and it opened. There was a tiny picture, just as in the style of centuries ago.

It was of Sulu.

He stared at it. "This is the picture in my service record," he said. "How did your mother get a copy?"

"She was very resourceful," said Demora.

He closed the locket and started to hand it back to her. "You should keep this."

"No, Dad. I want you to have it."

"She was your mother. You should . . ."

And Demora started to laugh. He frowned at her. "What's so funny?" he demanded.

"We're arguing over who's going to keep a locket, totally ignoring the fact that we're probably both going to be dead soon! I mean, aren't there far more meaningful things we can argue about in the short time we have left?"

Sulu stared at her for a long moment . . . and then began to laugh. He had a very odd sort of laugh when he really cut loose. It sounded like an engine trying to rev up . . . a repeated "Uh! Uh! Uh!" On the rare occasions when he allowed himself to laugh like that, Demora would invariably imitate it . . . making him laugh all the more. Which was exactly what happened.

As barely human creatures scavenged the city, looking for something to kill, their intended prey sat hundreds of feet above and laughed.

Chapter Thirty

"BELAY THAT."

Chaput's hand froze over the phaser control as her captain's voice stopped her a moment before she could open fire on the *Excelsior*.

Admiral Harriman turned and looked at his son. "What did you say?"

"Belay that order, Chaput," the captain said again. "Stand down from battle stations."

Blackjack advanced on his son. "What the hell do you think you're doing?"

"Taking back command of my vessel."

"The hell you are." He turned back to Chaput. "I order you to carry out my last order!"

"Don't do it, Chaput," Harriman said. And the tone of his voice was so firm that she tucked her hands under her legs and sat on them. "Admiral, I say again, I am taking back command of my vessel. You are relieved of duty."

Slowly Blackjack Harriman's face purpled. He stepped in close to Harriman. "There are specific regulations under which a subordinate officer can relieve a superior officer. Do you feel that any of them apply to this?"

"Yes, sir."

His voice became deep and dangerous as he said, "Which ones?"

"All of them. And one more." Harriman leaned in close said, "You've really pissed me off. Now get off my bridge."

Blackjack's fists clenched and unclenched. "This is mutiny. This is nothing less than mutiny."

"Call it what you will. I say again, however . . . get off my bridge, or—"

"Or what? Or you'll order security officers to commit mutiny as well as remove me?"

And Harriman shook his head. "No. I'll do it myself."

Blackjack blew his stack. "You little *ingrate!* Do you have any idea the number of times I've interceded for you! The times I've protected you! You owe your command to me! And this is the treatment you feel is due me?" His voice grew louder, more outraged, and the captain simply stood there, arms folded, and took it without flinching.

The admiral turned away and sat in the command chair. Icily, he said, "Even Kirk never did something like this. Not even he treated a superior officer in such a high-handed fashion. You're worse than he ever was."

"We all have to aspire to something, Admiral. Will you leave the bridge quietly?"

The admiral leaned back in the command chair and cracked his knuckles. "Nothing is getting me out of this chair. Now advise your helmswoman to obey my orders. Either that or try to remove me . . . if you think you've got the stones."

"Very well," said Harriman, unperturbed.

The bridge crew held its collective breath.

And Harriman, calmly, touched the comm switch on the helm console and said, "Bridge to transporter room. Lock onto the command chair and beam the occupant, into the brig."

The admiral's jaw dropped and he tried to leap from the command chair, but it was too late. The admiral, vanished in a twinkling of light and hum of molecular displacement.

No one on the bridge could quite believe it. And then, after a moment of dead silence:

"Sir," said Dane finally, "that was utterly inappropriate. In all my years of discipline and background, in all my upbringing . . . I have never seen a display such as that."

"Your point being, Dane?"

"The point being, I thought it was a hell of a display. Because I wasn't sanguine about firing on *Excelsior.*"

"Neither was I. I trust you'll testify to that effect at my court-martial?"

"Absolutely, sir."

"Thank you, Dane. I knew I could count on you. Now . . . Z'on, raise the *Excelsior,* pronto. Let's find out what the hell is going on down there."

Chapter Thirty-one

THEY WERE COMING. Five hundred they numbered . . . beasts with nothng but instinct and a need to destroy. Failed experiments that bore the shells of human beings but the minds of wild animals. Naked and deranged, looking like three men who were dead, or one young woman who was crouched next to her father and shuddering as she looked down upon them. It was like watching ghosts, or one's worst nightmare heading one's way.

She watched the clones of herself rampaging through the streets.

"We're not going to die."

The bottom of the tower shuddered, and they heard triumphant howling from the horde below. Sulu and Demora had bolted the door below, but it had held only a brief time. They heard it crashing in.

Sulu and Demora looked bleakly at each other, Sulu no longer having empty promises of salvation to toss around.

"I don't want to die like that," Demora whispered. "Torn apart by them . . . I don't want to die like that."

He said nothing, but looked at her in a way that had no

despair, no hopelessness . . . but instead pride, even defiance.

"There is a way out, isn't there," she said, knowing the answer.

And knowing that she knew, he simply nodded.

She looked down at the drop. She could see, far below her, the bloodthirsty mob pushing its way in. The tower continued to shudder beneath the pounding of their feet.

"It's not dishonorable, is it?" she asked.

"No."

"Because I know that's important. And I'd want you to be proud of me."

He smiled, keeping back the tears, to be strong for her. "I wouldn't mind having you proud of me, either."

The tower trembled, the shouts getting louder. A few feet away from them was the opening to the stairway that led down. A door was closed over it, but it wouldn't last more than a second.

"Dad . . . I never knew before that you had tests done to make sure I was your daughter. If . . . if they'd come back as negative . . . would you still have taken care of me?" She paused. "Feel free to lie in order to spare my feelings. I promise I won't hold it against you."

"Yes. I would have made you my daughter anyway. And I'd have loved you as much, and I couldn't possibly have been more proud of you than I am right now."

The horde grew closer and closer. Only seconds remained before they would burst out onto the uppermost portion of the tower, and that would be the end.

"Demora," said Sulu, "I am . . . honored . . . to die with you."

"To die would be a great adventure."

Sulu frowned. "I've heard that. Who said that? Ch'en Tu-hsui, wasn't it?"

"No. Peter Pan."

"Oh. Well then," and he rose to his feet, taking her by the hand. "Let's fly."

They stepped to the edge of the tower. The drop yawned beneath them. Beyond them was the horizon, the purple skies seemingly ready to welcome their soon-to-be-freed souls.

"Dad . . . I'm scared."

"So am I."

"Do you believe in life after death?"

"I believe in life before death."

"In that case . . . good job."

"Same to you."

She took a deep breath and said, "I love you, Daddy."

"I love you, Demora." And he did . . . perhaps, for the first time, with all his heart.

They braced themselves, took one last look at each other.

And Demora leaped.

And Sulu didn't.

He did not let go of her hand, however. Instead he clutched on desperately as Demora swung down like a pendulum, slamming into the great stone tower. Sulu held on for all he was worth, still in the tower.

Demora screeched in terror, confusion, anger, dangling with only her father's frantic grip preventing her from plunging to her death. It took a few moments for her father's shouts of *"Look! Look!"* to penetrate, and then— even as she hung there—she twisted her head around to look where he was indicating.

A shuttlecraft was hurtling through the sky, glinting in the purple light, approaching them at high speed. At the pace it was going, it would be there in ten seconds.

Three seconds later, the first of the berserker clones smashed through the door. It was a clone of Taine, followed by several more of exactly the same vintage.

Both hands occupied with preventing Demora from falling, Sulu kicked out frantically. The kick knocked the clone back, sending him crashing into others coming in behind him. They were shrieking, howling, and they converged on Sulu from all sides.

Sulu kicked out again, knocking one off his feet. Another grabbed at Sulu's face and Sulu bit him, sinking his teeth in and drawing blood. But more were coming and Sulu was out of time . . .

And the shuttlecraft was directly beneath them.

Breathing a prayer, Sulu let go. Demora dropped five feet and slammed into the roof of the shuttle. She came near to skidding off, but then she managed to clamber back up. "Dad!" she screamed, *"Dad!"*

They were all over him now. Sulu couldn't pull free of them. His hand was outstretched to Demora, but they seemed separated by a distance of miles.

The door of the shuttlecraft suddenly slid open, and Captain John Harriman was hanging half out of the doorway. He was holding a phaser and, angling it upward, fired. He nailed one of the clones, blasting him backward, and then another, and for a moment Sulu was free.

Sulu tore clear and leaped over the edge of the tower. He thudded onto the roof a few feet from Demora and she reached out, grabbing him by the wrist to hold him in place.

Harriman was shouting into the interior of the cabin, "Gently, Anik! Keep 'er steady! We got 'em! Let's get down and get 'em inside."

The shuttlecraft began to descend gently to the ground, a safe distance from the city. As it went, Demora and Sulu lay flat on their stomachs, clutching each other's hands, gasping, looking at each other and hardly believing what had just happened.

Finally Demora managed to get a sentence out.

"Couldn't have spotted them two seconds earlier, could you."

Chapter Thirty-two

"ARE YOU PLANNING to release me anytime soon, *Captain*," said Admiral Harriman in an icy tone.

John Harriman stood outside the brig, arms folded, leaning against the wall. "That depends. I think I'll debrief you first."

"Debrief me. There is nothing you could say, *Captain,* that could possibly serve as any sort of mitigating circumstance in your upcoming court-martial."

Harriman proceeded to tell him everything. The admiral's eyes became wider and wider the further along Harriman got.

When the captain was finished, there was a long moment of silence.

"So feel free to court-martial me, Father," said Harriman. "Bring everyone on the *Excelsior* up on charges too, if you wish. Of course, full testimony will be offered. As it stands, a rescue mission overseen by one Admiral Harriman, aided and abetted by a captain of some renown who is credited with, among other things, saving the Khitomer conference, not to mention the entire Earth . . . this rescue mission not only recovered a crew woman believed dead—said captain's daughter—but uncovered the illegal use of forbidden alien cloning technology which the Tholian faction was planning to put to use in schemes of conquest. If, on the other hand, you wish the record to show that said admiral was ready to fire on the famed captain's unprotected ship and abandon both captain and daughter, allowing the clone technology to continue unabated . . . well, sir . . . that is your choice to make."

Blackjack frowned. "Think you've got me boxed in, don't you, Captain."

Harriman nodded. "Yes, sir, I do."

"And you expect me to knuckle under."

"No, sir. Merely my fervent hope."

"Hunh." The admiral scratched his chin. "If I go along with this . . . I do not want you to think for one moment I approve of your actions."

"Understood."

"It's for the good of the fleet, you understand. And to make you look good."

"Yes, sir. I very much appreciate that."

Anik and Harriman walked toward the *Enterprise* transporter room. "So he went along with it," she asked.

"Of course he did. My father may be many things, but stupid he is not. Although I tend to think relations will be fairly . . . strained . . . between us for a while. But I can live with that. More importantly, Demora can live with that."

They walked into the transporter room. Anik turned and shook his hand briskly. "Captain . . . it's been an honor."

"The same to you, Commander. I believe Captain Sulu will be along with you shortly; he's just spending a few more moments with Demora."

"He's certainly entitled." She stepped up onto the platform.

"Uhm, Commander . . . one thing," he said.

"Yes?"

"That conversation you eavesdropped on. The one about my talking about honor and tradition and what I wanted from life. I remember having a conversation like that . . . but how in the world did you recognize or even remember my voice from that one fleeting moment ten years ago?"

"Oh, that." Anik laughed. "I made that up."

"What?" He gaped at her. *"What?"*

"I made it up. I never overheard you. I'm not even absolutely sure we went to the Academy at the same time."

"Then how did you know—?!"

She shrugged. "I guessed. Because everyone at some point in their fourth year sits around and talks about what they want out of life. So I figured it was worth a shot." She winked. "See you around, Captain."

Grinning and shaking his head in amazement, Captain John Harriman said, "Energize." Anik of Matern vanished and Harriman walked out of the transporter room, still chuckling.

Hikaru and Demora stood on the observation deck, staring out at the stars.

"You know," Demora said after a while, "most people can sit down and clear the air without having to face an impending death by rampaging clones."

"We're not most people," said Sulu. "For instance . . . why didn't you tell me you were upset about my going with Chekov up to our new assignment at the time it was happening?"

"Well . . . because you'd just saved the Earth by going back in time to get two humpback whales . . ." Her voice trailed off and she sighed. "All right. I see your point."

"Demora." He turned to her. "Have you considered requesting a transfer to the *Excelsior?* I happen to know you'd be favorably received by the captain."

"And I'd be worrying the entire time he'd be treating me with favoritism. Either that or he'd be overprotective of me. It doesn't sound like a good idea."

"It did for a moment," he sighed.

"Dad . . ." She hesitated. *"Did* you lie to me? About . . ."

"About that I would have taken you in even if I hadn't been your father? No. No, I wasn't. Because even if you weren't mine . . . you still would have been hers. And that would have been enough." He smiled. "But I'm still glad nonetheless."

He looked back out at the stars. "And I'm also relieved . . . that you weren't taken from me senselessly. I've spent my life trying to steer my way through the galaxy . . . to understand it. I'd like to think there's some order to it, some reason that things happen. That would give it a sort of elegance. That it is . . . at its core . . . a positive force. After all, Einstein said, 'God may be sophisticated, but He is not malicious.' I've always believed very strongly in the truth of that."

"Einstein. Hmmm," mused Demora.

"What's wrong."

"Well, didn't he also say that it was impossible to exceed the speed of light?"

This stopped Sulu for a moment. Then he shrugged. "Well . . . even Einstein had his off days."

He turned to her once more and hugged her tightly. "I love you, Demora."

"I love you too, Dad. Don't be a stranger."

"I won't. Not anymore."

He released her, reluctantly, and started to head for the door when Demora said, "Oh, and Dad?"

"Yes?"

"I stopped by my quarters earlier . . . and there was mail from you. Just . . . a chatty letter. You don't usually send chatty letters. What prompted that?"

He smiled. "Just thinking of you, sweetheart. Just thinking of you."

"Well it was nice. Keep doing it."

"Same to you, sweetheart. Same to you."

He walked out of the observation deck, leaving Demora to gaze at the stars.

ACCEPTED AROUND THE COUNTRY, AROUND THE WORLD, AND AROUND THE GALAXY!

- No Annual Fee
- Low introductory APR for cash advances and balance transfers
- Free trial membership in The Official STAR TREK Fan Club upon card approval*
- Discounts on selected STAR TREK Merchandise

To apply for the STAR TREK MasterCard today, call

1-800-775-TREK

Transporter Code: SKYD

EX ASTRIS SCIENTIA

FROM THE STARS — KNOWLEDGE

969-9764